Deadbeat Dad

J P Bloch

PEGASUS BOOKS

Pegasus Books
3338 San Marino Ave
San Jose, CA 95127
www.pegasusbooks.net

First Edition: June 2015

Published in North America by Pegasus Books. For information, please contact Pegasus Books c/o Christopher Moebs, 3338 San Marino Ave, San Jose, CA 95127.

This book is a work of fiction. Any resemblance to actual persons, living or dead, events, or locales is entirely coincidental.

Library of Congress Cataloguing-In-Publication Data
Jon P Bloch
Deadbeat Dad/Jon P Bloch– 1st ed
p. cm.
Library of Congress Control Number: 2015944553

ISBN – 978-1-941859-30-8
1. FICTION / Thrillers / Crime. 2. FICTION / Black Humor. 3. SOCIAL SCIENCE / Poverty & Homelessness. 4. FAMILY & RELATIONSHIPS / Dysfunctional Families. 5. HUMOR / General. 6. PSYCHOLOGY / Psychopathology / Schizophrenia.
10 9 8 7 6 5 4 3 2 1

Comments about *Deadbeat Dad* and requests for additional copies, book club rates and author speaking appearances may be addressed to JP Bloch or Pegasus Books c/o Christopher Moebs, 3338 San Marino Ave, San Jose, CA, 95127, or you can send your comments and requests via e-mail to cmoebs@pegasusbooks.net.

Also available as an eBook from Internet retailers and from Pegasus Books

Printed in the United States of America

For Tristan, whose meds need no adjustment.

'And hast thou slain the Jabberwock?
Come to my arms, my beamish boy!
Oh frabjous day! Callooh! Callay!'
He chortled in his joy.

Lewis Carroll,
"Jabberwocky"

Nathan Nightbridge is a genius at getting away with murder. . . or is he? True, people who offend him have a way of turning up dead, but maybe he has bad relationship karma. Nathan beats the court system so many times he develops a cult following. Some see him as an ice-cold sociopath, but perhaps he's just shy.

Nathan's story is told by his deadbeat dad of a father, a double-psychotic homeless man who goes on and off his meds. When Dad is not hounded by the CIA or called back to his home planet, he spies on his son from afar. Dad is the bum in the alleyway that no one notices. He grins from the edges of our bad dreams. And Nathan is his pride and joy.

Dad also may have more than a little something to do with the murders. When he steps forward to meet Nathan, everything gets resolved. . . but not in the way one might expect. Life is as unknowable as death in this dark comedy that celebrates love in all its debauchery.

Deadbeat Dad

JP Bloch

They adjusted my meds. Hooray for me. Before, the anti-depression pink thingies made the mania worse, which likewise made the good ol' paranoid schizophrenia worse. Talk about a basket case. I thought fluctuations in the rings of the planet Saturn sent messages to my dick. I found the name Samuel Succotash to be hilarious. I believed I had my own reality TV series, with the *Laverne and Shirley* theme song given a reggae arrangement for my show.

But now I knew it all to be so much folderol. Everything turned nicey-nice. The sun glistened on my shopping cart as I maneuvered my way through midtown, and the people and cars and noise were all part of the great cosmic oneness. When I ran into a crazy woman I'd met at a homeless shelter, we kissed out of sheer joy, and as she tilted her head back like a movie star, I thought to myself: Isn't life grand? All thanks to these miraculous new purple capsules. I could've change my name to Norman Normal, and no one would've found it ironic.

Still, a shrill, nagging voice inside me wondered how long it would be before the purple things started fucking up something else in my fucked up brain. One way or another, I always ended up back at Square One, mental health-wise. Like many fellow psychos, my love-hate relationship with meds became the dominant pain in the ass of my life.

I would've thrown in the towel years ago if it weren't for my son, Nathan. I never gave up on him, not even when they charged him with multiple counts of first-degree murder. Not that we met face-to-face. I could never let him see me like this. It would've destroyed him. Not to mention the CIA followed me for years, and I didn't want Nathan implicated. Once the government does its number on you, forget about having a life. Still, I like to believe I did a good job of parenting. One advantage to being a shopping cart homeless

person is that nobody notices you, other than to wish you'd
go away. I blended into the busy background, like a mousy-
colored animal blending into the woods. Sometimes I
couldn't see myself, either.

So for years I watched him from a proper distance. I saw
him playing alone in the dirt backyard of the dilapidated flat
in which he grew up. Like a flash of headlights on a window
shade at night, I caught him watching TV while his mother—
my ex-wife Zelda—did her nails. I watched him talking to
himself in bed. Those were the moments he seemed happiest.
I spied on him as he demonstrated his natural intelligence,
while the dummies in class made fun of him. When he ran
away from home at sixteen, I ran with him. I saw him mature
into a handsome young man with a commanding presence.
True, I thought him a bit of an introvert. But this added to
his mystique. He reminded me of someone at a party who
stands alone with his extra dry Martini and never says
anything, and yet is the most interesting person there.

As for me, I became quite adept at hiding and being
furtive, if I must say so myself. Back when I passed for a
respectable member of society, I majored in drama, and the
acting bug never leaves once you have it. Thanks to
dumpsters and Goodwill bins, I became quite adept at
changing my appearance. If the CIA knew how I spent my
time, it would've hired me as a spy instead of tormenting me
with its UFOs and CEOs and Communist Fascists.

Nathan's grandmother Lizzie, who also lived in the
dismal, Charles Dickens flat, hated my guts with the precision
of a sharp shooter. Somehow she knew about me, even
though she never caught me red-handed. "Your father is
watching you, I can feel it," I heard her tell Nathan at age two
or ten or twelve, as if saying she believed in ghosts. Lizzie
may have been a toothless old hag who lived in her bathrobe
and fluffy slippers, but she had a spooky instinct for the truth.

My ex-wife Zelda wished me dead, and spoke but vague
remarks about my existence to Nathan. On his seventh
birthday I overheard him ask her what happened to his

father, and she exhaled her menthol cigarette smoke and said, "Let's just say he missed the boat."

Before long, young Nathan used this explanation to discuss his father's absence to the kids at school. "They had a special boat," Nathan explained. "You only had one chance to catch it, and my dad got there too late. He waved at us from the dock as we sailed away without him."

"Couldn't he just take another boat?" some other kid asked.

"No," Nathan replied. "They only had that one boat this one time."

I wondered if he dreamt about me waving good-bye, like the end of a movie he never even had the chance to see. I dreamt of him often. I'd see him as a toddler—so adorable at that age, a hedonistic despot of a two-year-old. In my dreams we rode on a merry-go-round, or perhaps I tossed him in the sunlit sky and caught him, the air around us as soft as a pillow.

If only other people saw Nathan the way I did. They'd know he could never murder anyone. That someone so innocent should've faced the death penalty shows how deep corruption runs through the system. Everyone knows the federal government is in cahoots with foreign bankers determined to undermine our American way of life.

Nathan had no overt reaction in the police station when they showed him photos of the murder victims. But those smartass detectives didn't realize that Nathan understood what I was unable to understand until I became homeless. Nothing mattered as much as most people thought it did. Everyone ran around all day going through the motions of life, scared to death to face the truth about their own existence. But not Nathan, and not me. Like father, like son.

That's what's so stupid about the murder charges. Nathan knew the victims already were dead, soulless people. He inherited his father's hypersensitivity to the human condition. Why would he tie up a family of three with Boy

Scout knots, set their house on fire, and burn the bodies to a crisp? I get the creeps just thinking about it.

In fact, I think I need an extra purple capsule.

2

I met Nathan's mother, Zelda, as a drama major at Yale. As a rich kid and fourth generation Yalie, I wasn't what you'd call a serious person. My family hoped my infatuation with the theater would prove a passing phase, but at least I kept up the tradition as a New Haven man—Alexander Nightbridge IV, to be exact. The daughter of an impoverished widow, Zelda had a full scholarship and seemed destined for bigger and better. Indeed, she snatched lead roles right away, like a hamster stuffing its cheeks with sunflower seeds, and local drama critics went gaga over her Thespian prowess.

Then, junior year, she starred as Maggie in *Cat on a Hot Tin Roof*, and as understudy, I had to fill in for the actor cast as Big Daddy. We clicked on stage, and by the next morning I knocked her up. She had some other steady guy up until that time, but millions of meds and many friendly rounds of electroconvulsive therapy deleted his name—or even his face—from my long-term memory. It may have been, "Something Something Brown," but it's also possible I inserted the name "Brown" into my vacant brain because I thought of somebody else.

Abortion crossed Zelda's mind, but she decided instead that I should marry her. Did my being a millionaire figure into her decision? Do goldfish poop in their bowls? Her master plan had her giving birth to our child, passing it off to a nanny, and going on to be a great actress while also being stinking-to-high-heaven rich.

"That way," she explained without apology, "I'll only accept parts worthy of my instrument, instead of wasting it on some commercial piece of crap."

Like many theater people, she referred to her acting talent as her instrument. My family raised me to loathe such pomposity.

However, as Fate would have it, she'd have considered herself lucky to get offered any piece of crap whatsoever. We got married all right, but just before she had the baby, my dad, Alexander Nightbridge III, got busted for a Ponzi scheme of epic headline proportions. At the time, it seemed in poor taste to present to the world Alexander Nightbridge V, so we named the baby Nathaniel, after some stinkpot relative from 100 years ago. But our son would always be called Nathan.

So—Bummer Number One for Zelda—she found herself married with child, but her husband had no money. How do ya like that? Bummer Number Two came about the same time, when I went off my rocker.

I knew Ponzi schemes were supposed to be bad, but the word "Ponzi" kept making me think of Fonzie from *Happy Days*. Though I didn't say anything, I had my first glimpse into a separate part of me that made no sense, and which I couldn't control. The press followed me everywhere, and at first I refused to give a statement. But one time a TV reporter asked, "What would you say to the penniless victims of your father's Ponzi scheme?"

"I like Fonzie," I replied. "The Fonz. James Bond. I watch reruns sometimes. Sometimes I just run. Why re- when you can run? Why pee when you can pun?"

The family lawyer made a statement about how I suffered a great deal of stress, and everyone made certain I never left the house alone again. I withdrew from Yale, which my mother didn't mind at all. When she heard there might be something wrong with me—as in, I turned nuttier than a fruitcake—she said, "I'm not surprised in the least. All those left wing plays warped his mind."

He died of a heart attack while awaiting trial in jail—my father, that is, not Fonzie. Mom never permitted anyone to mention Dad again. Everything had to be auctioned off to pay back the many people my father screwed over. In my more lucid moments, I felt sad for these people, but a shrink told me not to worry about them, since I couldn't help them anyway. Shrinks are full of shit, you can see the shit plopping out of their mouths. But now and then they say something worth listening to.

Because of my father, no one wanted to hire me as anything, but an insurance company gave me a chance as a salesman. Instead of selling annuities, in secret I bought endless containers of take-out Chinese to get the fortunes out of the fortune cookies. Then I photocopied each fortune and filed it alphabetically in a strong box I kept hidden in the floorboards of the modest apartment I shared with my wife and son. After maybe three months of this, Zelda finked me out to the mental health Nazis. They straightjacketed me and shipped me off to the funny farm faster than you could say lobotomy.

My parting words to Zelda were: "You could at least throw some confetti."

I spent about twenty grand on the fortune cookies, wiping out what remained of our savings. Which was pretty funny if you thought about it in a certain way. But Zelda became a rigid person. You might've thought that as an actress she could see the romance in my grand gesture, but instead she gave me a black eye.

If truth be told, I preferred the nut house to having to hear yet another time how I drove Zelda and baby Nathan to the poorhouse. I mean, enough already. It's not like I begged the universe to be diagnosed doubly psychotic. Besides, something about my illness made me climb the walls when people repeated themselves, and Zelda's accusations were relentless. In the loony bin, some dude kept saying over and over, "Power control, power control, power control," and it drove me crazy, if you'll pardon the expression. But, ever resourceful, I shoved him down a flight of stairs, which selfless, heroic deed got me demoted to the so-called violent ward. I say so-called because everyone stayed so doped up, we acted about as violent as Teletubbies.

Anyway, Zelda decided the tragic denial of her ticket to upper-class frigid bitchdom reached the level of favorable comparison to Joan of Arc. Looking back, I bet she couldn't wait to kidnap her first illegal immigrant into slavery. Not that she came right out and said this type of thing, but I've always been a shrewd judge of character. I knew what everyone thought all the time. Zelda stood there smoking her Virginia Slims menthol, our eyes met, and nothing needed to be said.

Zelda had to be the most beautiful girl I ever saw. Before we parted ways, I just stared at her, which for some reason creeped her out, like a little girl with a child molester. But I could never comprehend that such a looker married me, even if only for the money I didn't have. I should write a poem about Zelda. I'll call it, "Zelda the Beautiful." It will be based on "America the Beautiful," which song, by the way, I am not alone in thinking should be our National Anthem. My poem will make me billions of dollars. I'll move to Brussels or maybe Boston or Beirut.

Well, once my mind went bye-bye, so did wifey, who, with Nathan in tow, moved back to the dismal flat she grew up in with her harpy of a mother. As part of the divorce, they permitted me one supervised visit per month with my son, provided I stayed out of the hospital and took my meds. But my mental wellness became a dubious prospect at best. I struggled between being so drugged out that I considered drooling in bed to be a major life achievement, and lowering my meds so that I could walk and talk while risking manic depression and/or paranoid schizophrenic delusions. I got a small disability check each month, plus food stamps and Medicaid. Or at least I did, until I wasn't able to eat and pay the rent at the same time, which, for the person on disability, is about as easy as juggling while riding a unicycle. Without an address, I couldn't collect any benefits—so guess what—I became homeless, la-de-da. But thanks to a free clinic, I still got my meds when in the mood to take them.

As for my mother, she kicked the bucket while I vegetated in the violent ward, so I couldn't attend her epic funeral. She spent what money she had on her last rites—I imagine there's a mirror on the ceiling of her coffin so she can look at herself—and left me but a pair of lamps that were the last vestiges of our fortune. Zelda hocked the lamps by the time I returned to civilization. I still remember them, though. They were hand blown crystal, and when lit they shone like mother of pearl.

I'm sure Zelda never stopped blaming me for her having to work as a waitress in some shitty greasy spoon in order to support our kid. But she dropped out of college to have the baby. After a brief period of going on auditions and trying to get an Equity card, she gave up. Her mother had been her greatest fan, but she lost sympathy when Zelda proved stupid enough to get pregnant by a virtual stranger. Lizzie decreed that her daughter should not go on frivolous auditions with a child to feed. So, thinking it temporary, Zelda got a job waiting tables at some snooty restaurant. But the restaurant folded—as did many in the economic downswing—and as a lousy waitress she got stuck at a local dive. She spent her free time trying to set a new Guinness World Record for alcohol consumption. When Zelda ran into someone she knew from Yale, she insisted she had never seen them before.

Sometimes, I followed her to and from work, though of course she never saw me. Waiting tables aged Zelda. By age thirty, she looked fifty, and her once mellifluous speaking voice grew coarse and mean. Yet at night, she cried and cried into her pillow, and watching her sometimes made me cry, too. There we were, two lone wolves howling at the moon.

Strange to say, I barely aged at all. Over the years, whenever I passed by a mirror, I swore I could still pass for twenty-something. Beyond a doubt, one's appearance is connected to one's attitude. This has been proven on TV. I always maintained a fresh, youthful outlook, and it showed.

3

Try though the government does to conceal the truth from its people, planet Earth is abundant in alien life forms. I should know, for I am one of them. I cannot tell you the name of the planet I come from—I'd never hear the end of it from my higher-ups—but it is similar to your Earth. The main difference is that we have five seasons instead of four. During the fifth season, Shmidliadidlia, there are millions of lights exploding into the atmosphere, showers of blinding color—

Oh, geez, sorry, I meant to talk about my son, Nathan, the so-called murderer. Well, he grew to be a gifted child who insisted on playing in solitude. By first grade, he told the school nurse he felt sick, so he could go home and daydream far greater ideas than he got from the classroom. Every time he did this, Zelda called him a louse of a liar like his father, but Nathan wasn't easy to scare. Even as a kid, he had. . . what would you call it? Strength? Intensity? He had some kind of somethingness that drove people crazy over how little mind he paid them, even, or especially, when they courted his attention. And yet I knew he craved the company of others. What few toys he had—stray marbles, broken Legos—were always turned into human characters with names, best friends, and adventures.

My son's nemesis proved to be the most popular kid at his grade school, a full-of-himself fuck named Bosco Sinclair. Bosco—an assy name for an asshole kid. Whatever happened to normal names? Anyway, as life is nothing if not a series of ironic twists and turns, Bosco played a major role in Nathan's story, though one wouldn't have suspected it from the way things began.

Bosco's show-off father, Crazy Seymour Sinclair, owned a big car dealership, which produced repugnant TV ads that ran like every other minute. Crazy Seymour also cut ribbons at shopping plazas or showed up at car washes for charities, and doubtless thought of himself—God help us all—as a celebrity. Fortunately, as a homeless person I had no TV, so I only had to deal with Crazy Seymour on billboards and the occasional broadcasting TV in a store window.

The apple did not fall far from the tree. It never does, does it? The super-popular young Bosco worked as hard as his father at being ingratiating to everyone. Everyone, that is, except Nathan, whom he made fun of nonstop. Obviously, Bosco saw Nathan as competition, because while Bosco never stopped trying to please everyone, Nathan never even started to do so, making Nathan seem weird. Weird meaning that he understood something Bosco didn't.

"Hey, Nathan," Bosco said to him every morning, knocking my son on the head. "How much did your crazy mother drink last night?"

You see, Zelda became something of a local legend for liking her liquor. Unless she merely fell into a festive mood when, for example, she ran bare-breasted down the street, screaming that she wanted someone to fuck her.

Nathan kept walking, as if Bosco hadn't said a thing. This only made Bosco angrier; he had no idea how to handle being ignored.

"I bet that's why you have no father," he continued. "Zelda the Drunk made him puke. Do you have to clean up her puke? Or do you like to eat it?"

Once when they were in the fourth grade, I worked a few days at the school, and I put four magnificent specimens of stinky dead mice in Bosco's desk. The other kids were grossed out. Only Nathan did not react and just sat there reading his book.

Still, Bosco haunted him at every turn. The grade school had this stupid thing called the Good Citizenship Brigade, to which the poor kids had to bring some fascist cop to school once a year to talk about how thou shalt not drink or stink or however it goes. In fifth grade, Nathan got selected by the teacher to be a member of the nerdy brigade. Why, remains a mystery, other than maybe the teacher thought it would make Nathan more outgoing. He got selected again the following year. As the member with seniority, he offered to be the group captain, but this smarmy girl nominated superstar Bosco instead, even though he'd never been on the brigade before. Bosco won the election. As if rubbing dog shit on the wound, he grinned and said, "Can you believe it? Nathan wanted to be the leader." Everyone laughed, and the teacher serving as advisor did nothing to stop them.

Nathan declared the Good Citizenship Brigade a joke and made a big speech about how it couldn't compare with real cops who used real guns—possibly an unfair comparison. When he deemed the yearly lecture from the cop to be "childish," the same dumb girl protested, "I think it's fun."

Twelve-year-old Nathan gave her the finger and replied, "No one will ever fuck you."

The girl cried, and Nathan got sent to the principal's office. The fat-ass principal lectured him on how girls were very sensitive, and he must stop being a bully. Needless to say, Bosco never once received a similar lecture.

I remember, though, on the last day of school an assembly in which all students who participated in extracurricular activities were announced. And my son refused to stand up as his name got called for serving on the brigade.

I cried out of sheer pride.

On that same last day of school, Nathan got in trouble again, for a supposed attempt to strangle the brigade girl. I saw the whole thing, and as Nathan said to the police officers who were called in, he shook her by the shoulders to make her stop teasing him.

"You're so weird, Nathan," the girl hissed at him, recovered from her near-death experience.

Zelda got pissed when she found out. "Are you some crazy person?" she asked him, in that belittling voice I knew all too well. "It's like if you kill someone, everyone's going to think you're wacko. You'll end up in a nut house, with rat shit all over the floor."

"I didn't do anything, Mother." Zelda always insisted that Nathan call her nothing more casual than "Mother."

"Ha!" Zelda shrieked. "You think you're a good liar, but you're not. You smile and twist your hair and say, 'Oh Mother, I didn't do anything.'"

She did a cruel, exaggerated imitation of him. "You know, I think I'll call Mr. Brown. He'll know what to do with you."

At periods throughout Nathan's childhood, Zelda threatened to give Nathan away to someone she called Mr. Brown. She never much described Mr. Brown, but she didn't have to. The creepy grin on her face spoke volumes as to the relentless yet mysterious cruelty that awaited Nathan should he be sent off to this Mr. Brown person.

Zelda didn't mention Mr. Brown often; she treated him like a misbegotten ace up her sleeve for special occasions. But when she did, Nathan cried. Come to think of it, these were about the only times I ever saw him cry. Zelda never cried at all in front of Nathan. A lot of parents never cry in front of their kids. Heaven forbid kids should think their parents are human beings.

She took out her phone and typed in some meaningless series of numbers. "Hello, I want to talk to Mr. Brown." Her yellowed teeth were only a slight distraction from her perfect smile.

Nathan fell to his knees, pleading with her.

"Please, Mother, don't send me to Mr. Brown." He looked most like me when he got scared.

She ended the fake phone call. "So, Mr. Hot Stuff, you're not so hot after all, are you?"

Then she laughed and laughed.

4

Life with Zelda became a living nightmare, yet she acted like she won an Oscar. Not that she pretended to Nathan she starred in a movie, when in reality she waited tables at the sleazo diner. But she thought he wouldn't notice her foul-mouthed bad moods, that he'd be impressed if she told him how in college she played lead in some hoity-toity play. Nathan had to pull off quite a balancing act in her company. Would anyone like to fend off a fire-breathing dragon while tending to her feelings, as if she were a fragile piece of crystal? When reciting her litany of martyrdom over Nathan's existence, I'm sure that Zelda never realized the fortitude that went into having even the shortest of conversations with her. She took it for granted that people existed to eradicate the pain of her own life. I wouldn't say she frightened Nathan. But he couldn't understand the cruelty of Fate, which required him to have to deal with her when other people didn't—let alone be the person who dealt with her more than anyone else. It damn near broke him. It also insulted his keen intelligence. It was amazing the kid had any balls at all.

"Shut the fuck up," she'd tell her eight- or eleven-year-old son, who perhaps made a bit of noise closing the door. "They're doing *Streetcar* on TV. I played Blanche. And I did it a hell of a lot better than this cunt bitch. Lord knows who she fucked to get the part."

She would pour herself more scotch and light another cigarette. "No, no, no, you no-talent whore. You need to put the emphasis on 'strangers,' not 'kindness.' When I played Blanche, I had a fever of 101, but it added to my performance, since she's in a fever anyway. A real actor knows how to use everything as a tool. I got I-don't-know-how-many curtain calls. Flowers everywhere. So many smiles, so many tears of joy."

She'd pour herself yet another drink. "But, of course, other things happened. Like your father. He might as well have cut me into little pieces and eaten them with a sprig of parsley on the side. Always remember—you hate him."

"It must've been nice, getting all those flowers," Nathan would say.

"Are you a retard? Jesus, I'm talking about art, art, art, and all you can say is that flowers are nice. Go away. Go do something."

"Okay, Mother." He would turn to leave.

"Where the hell are you going? Rub my neck for me. It's stiff after work." She always referred to her job as work, as if it would be un-genteel to call it anything more specific.

"Okay, Mother." He'd stand in back of her and rub her neck.

"My neck, my neck," she'd scream. "What are you doing, touching my hair? Are you some fag hairdresser?"

"Sorry," he'd murmur, and live another day to tell about it.

I never believed for a second that Nathan murdered Zelda. How could a thirteen-year-old stage such a realistic crime scene? It looked like a break-in gone wrong, and that should've been the end of the story. But Zelda's multiple stab wounds—seventy, as I recall—made all these self-appointed experts claim that it was a crime of passion. Everyone's heard the old wives' tale about how excessive attacks signal a personal relationship between killer and victim. But the thieves could've done it on purpose to throw the cops off track. Or maybe they were high on pot or some other junk. For that matter, Lizzie had a sucky relationship with Zelda, too, yet they never considered her a suspect. Whatever. I always thought it more cosmic euthanasia than anything else. Zelda had such an ugly life that God put her out of her misery. Not to mention the rest of us.

Zelda's absurd memorial service transpired outdoors in a park frequented by homeless people, so I had no trouble blending into the background. I assumed no one would show up except her mother and son, if even them. Hell, even the corpse failed to put in an appearance. But there were the other waitresses from the diner, and the cook and busboy from the diner, and the owner of the diner, and customers from the diner, and a hundred or so people from Yale. This baffled me until I remembered that shitty drunks often came across as highly charismatic from a safe distance. Still, the service had as much in common with realism as *The Muppets Take Manhattan*. From the way people talked, you'd have thought we just witnessed the passing of Mother Teresa. I got so pissed off, I almost came forward and blew my anonymity.

The diner people said things like, "When Zelda waited on a table, she lit up the room." It made me think of light bulbs. One of the Yalies said, "Zelda went out with a bang, the same way she lived."

What the fuck did that even mean?

Everyone kept urging Lizzie to say something. She acquitted herself with the rhetorical statement, "What is there to say? My daughter is dead."

I heard some dipshit whisper, "She's holding up so well."

Taking advantage of a pause in speakers, Nathan—not scheduled to say anything—stepped forward. He carried a boom box and turned it on as he set it on the ground beside the flowers. The boom box played, "Ding-Dong! The Witch is Dead," from *The Wizard of Oz*. Some bitch in a stupid flowery hat came up to him and slapped his face.

"Turn that damn thing off, and stop laughing," she commanded. "This is for your *mother*."

But I understood how Nathan felt. I found it impossible to miss Zelda. Not for a single moment of existence would anyone who knew her think, "Gee, if only Zelda were here."

Actually, I take that back. It's probable Nathan wished Zelda would spring back to life when some plainclothes cops came over to arrest him for her murder. The merry song kept playing as they walked him away in handcuffs. Several people fumbled with the boom box buttons before the thing shut off.

5

At age thirteen, my son got tried as an adult for second-degree murder. Had he been Jewish, the trial might've been viewed as a kind of Bar Mitzvah—at thirteen he faced the first, but by no means the last, of bogus murder charges that would be filed against him. For Nathan, murder trials would be like potato chips; who can stop after just one? The state's case seemed thinner than a Swedish cracker: Nathan tested as antisocial, according to his school shrink. Again, the multiple stab wounds came up, only they never found the knife.

Not surprisingly, the press wasted no time making the public aware of Nathan's connection to Alexander Nightbridge III, Ponzi scheme felon par excellence. This did much to sway public opinion against Nathan, even though the two crimes had nothing to do with each other. As for *moi*—Alexander Nightbridge IV—the press announced my status as legally dead and a probable suicide after slipping into hopeless insanity. Another point that failed to skew in Nathan's favor.

A neighbor who heard yelling was the closest thing to resemble evidence; something about how Mr. Brown arrived, though the drunk-as-a-skunk neighbor couldn't tell if the voice belonged to a grown woman or an adolescent boy. I thought it obvious that the corrupt detectives persuaded the stupid neighbor as to what he heard. To create a sympathetic portrait of her grandson, Lizzie no doubt told the cops that Zelda pulled that Mr. Brown shit on her son when she had nothing better to do. Then the cops misused the information to give Nathan a motive. One so-called newspaper even had a headline that screamed, "Mr. Brown Made Him Do It!" They should have realized that Nathan's terror of Mr. Brown paralyzed him. He never could've responded with aggression upon hearing the name. And since Zelda got stabbed, why would she say it? Besides, Zelda had a high voice and

Nathan's voice already changed to a baritone, like mine. In both a physical as well as mental sense, he matured quickly. There would've been no confusion as to whose voice was heard mentioning Mr. Brown, assuming of course that either of them had spoken. Go to the dictionary and look up, "third party," since the facts are clear that's who killed Zelda.

Over the strenuous objections of the prosecution, Nathan got released into Lizzie's custody. Since a court-appointed social worker kept her eye on them, Lizzie had to send Nathan to school. The kids ignored him. At least it meant no more snubbing or jeering; most people don't tease someone that they think is going to stab them to death.

The one predictable exception, Bosco Sinclair, pointed at Nathan and said things like, "Ha-ha, you killed your mother," or "Ha-ha, your family is a bunch of crooks."

About three months later came the trial. Nathan tended to be one to hide his light behind a bushel, so it came as a surprise when he chose to take the stand. I imagine he did this against the advice of his attractive and likeable public defender, but she didn't make it seem that way.

"Nathan, where were you while your mother got stabbed to death?"

"Out," he explained, for the benefit of the courtroom. "I often stay out all night. Just walking and thinking. My mother doesn't care—I mean, she didn't care."

"Would you call your relationship with your mother a close one?"

"Yes, ma'am," was his polite answer. "But she drank a lot. You see, my mother wanted to be . . . she wanted things she couldn't have, and when she drank, she blamed her failure on me."

"On you?"

He looked down and played with his fingers. "You know, my being born and all. She had to raise me as a single mother. She had a hard time. My father disappeared so I never knew him."

"Well, it sounds like you may have been angry with your mother, especially if she took out her frustrations on you. Maybe you couldn't take it anymore and stabbed her. Then you had to make it look like a break-in."

"No, ma'am. I never could've done that. Not my own mother."

"Then why play 'The Witch is Dead' at her funeral?"

"It's 'Ding-Dong! The Witch Is Dead.' Mother used to sing it as she danced around the room. You know. Drinking."

"Why did you laugh?"

"Nice memories make me happy."

"Did your mother ever talk about sending you away to someone named Mr. Brown?"

Nathan smiled with melancholy. "An old joke between Mother and me. She'd say she'd send me to Mr. Brown and then I'd say I'd send *her* to Mr. Brown. Then we'd laugh and hug."

"And you had nothing whatsoever to do with her death?"

He managed to look the attorney in the eye while also looking every member of the jury in the eye. "I had nothing to do with her death."

"Your witness."

The wimpy prosecutor buttoned his jacket as he stood up, just like they do in the movies. "How are you today, Nathan?"

He asked this to throw Nathan off-kilter.

"I'm nervous, sir. I'm frightened."

"Nervous and frightened. Why do you say that?"

"I'm under oath, sir." A titter passed over the courtroom. The gray-haired woman judge banged her gavel to bring the court to order.

"If you've done nothing wrong," continued the dopey DA, "why are you frightened? And maybe you're nervous because you have a guilty conscience?"

"Objection, your honor." The courageous public defender stood up.

"Objection sustained," replied her honor. "Jury will disregard the question. Counselor, let's not waste the court's time on magic tricks."

After apologizing to the court, the DA said, "I'm curious, Nathan. You seem like an intelligent young man. I imagine you watch TV shows, plus you go to school, am I right?"

"Yes, sir."

"And based on what you've observed, would you characterize the household you and your mother shared with your grandmother to be affluent? In other words, rich?"

Nathan flashed a sad smile at his grandmother, who returned the gesture. "If you mean rich in love, yes."

The DA harrumphed into his hand. "I mean money. Did your household have any expensive objects to steal? Lots of cash sitting around?"

Nathan smiled again at Lizzie. "We're poor, but we're proud."

"I'm confused. Why would someone break into a house that had nothing worth taking?"

"Objection, your honor. Calls for expert testimony as to state of mind of the intruder."

"Sustained. Nice try, counselor. Jury will disregard."

The pathetic prosecutor pounded his fist on the wooden railing of the witness box and stared at Nathan like a shark.

"Isn't it true," he shouted, "that you hated your mother, murdered her, and then staged a break-in?"

"Objection, your honor. Already asked and answered."

The judge looked down on the prosecutor. "That is correct, and you know it, counselor. Objection sustained. Jury will disregard."

"Nothing further," said the DA, with a sardonic roll of his eyes, as if we all knew Nathan to be guilty as all get out.

Before stepping down, Nathan turned to the judge. "Your honor, may I please say something?" Receiving permission, Nathan cleared his throat and said, "I loved my mommy. And she loved me. Every day, I miss her so much."

I thought it ironic that now of all times Nathan finally got to call Zelda "mommy" after years of always having to call her "mother."

Despite common wisdom about not taking the stand at your murder trial, Nathan cleaned up well in a suit and tie and came across as a polite young man. It took the jury a little over an hour to return a verdict of not guilty. He mouthed the words, "Thank you," to the jurors, who beamed at him with kindness. He shook hands with his attorney, and, Nathan being Nathan, also offered his hand to the prosecutor, as if it were a matter between gentlemen. After registering incredulity, the man shook Nathan's hand. Not enough has been said about Nathan's ability to get people to do things you wouldn't expect them to do. When he felt like it, Nathan could disarm anyone.

Then he walked toward Lizzie, hugged her and said, "What's for lunch?" Several people chortled.

Outside the courthouse, I noticed a few people with signs saying things like, "Right on, Nathan," and "Power to the People." However, they were far outnumbered by the anti-Nathan contingent, which proclaimed he should rot in hell for disrespecting his mother. Nathan did not appear to acknowledge either group, as he and Lizzie slipped into the defense attorney's car.

Once he got acquitted, the kids at school picked up where they left off before the trial. It became safe to make fun of him again. Bosco continued to rule supreme and said things like, "Where's the knife, douche-bag?" Books and papers were thrown at Nathan, he got slammed against the wall and had to face those ice-cold, squinty-eyed stares that bullies like Bosco excelled at giving.

Nathan showed no reaction to any of it. Instead, he'd be off on a cloud, talking to himself, and whatever he said made him smile.

The one bright spot during this time came on Christmas Eve, for Nathan and I had a brief, accidental meeting of sorts. We bumped into each other on the street, and Nathan said, "Excuse me."

A Salvation Army choir sang, "It Came upon the Midnight Clear." The falling snow looked so pretty in the glow of the streetlamps.

About a month after the trial, Nathan's grandmother, Lizzie, did something that grabbed his full attention. He sat at the kitchen table, eating a typical Lizzie-made dinner of nuked hot dogs with supermarket brand macaroni salad.

"I'm kicking you out," she said. "I'm too old for your phony baloney."

Nathan set down his frankfurter. "What do you mean, kicking me out? Is this a joke?"

She took a swig of her beer. "Kid, what am I supposed to do with a nutso teenager? I took enough crap raising your mother. I'm not going through that again."

"I'm only thirteen," he protested. "You're my legal guardian. They'll put you in jail. What am I supposed to—"

Lizzie laughed. "Me, in jail? Fat chance. Relax, kiddo. I'm not feeding you to the pit bulls. My sister-in-law, your Great-aunt Sophie, has a niece named Elena. You'll be living with your Aunt Elena and Uncle Thor. You met her once. You'll be happy. They have a son who's a few years older than you. I can't think of his name."

"But why would they—"

"You get Social Security every month because your mother died and your so-called father is supposed be dead, though I don't believe it for a minute. Anyway, I worked it out with Elena. We'll split each check down the middle. It's a win-win for everyone."

"Isn't that money supposed to be for me?"

"You ask too many goddamn questions. You better be quiet and mind your place with Aunt Elena, or who knows where you'll end up."

"Maybe I should turn invisible."

"That's a good idea," Lizzie replied, not getting the sarcasm. "You used to be so quiet when you played by yourself. You were a good boy—once."

Nathan started to say something else, but Lizzie pointed her finger, and it shut him up. "Don't push your luck. You know what I'm talking about."

6

Nathan's trial made headlines, but when his guardianship switched to hippie-dippie Thor and Elena Rainbow, the matter drew far less publicity. This worked well for Lizzie and the Rainbows, given their Social Security scam. As I think of it, that sounds like the name of a lounge act: *Lizzie and the Rainbows*. I did not faint from shock when I learned that Thor and Elena invented their pukey names. They used to be Sherman and Eunice Kline.

Still, Lizzie pretended to be sadder than an empty beer can to have Nathan taken away from her. Not because she'd miss him but because she didn't want people thinking she didn't love her grandson. Although, given the trashy welfare neighborhood she lived in, I didn't see why she'd care what the neighbors thought, if indeed they thought about it at all. It's weird, but you live for like seventy-plus years and people treat you as if you're a housefly they keep trying to swat. Still, she put on a brave face to the world.

"I'm an old lady," she told anyone who'd listen, usually some strung-out whore. "How can I give such a young boy what he needs?"

When on occasion asked if she thought Nathan murdered Zelda, she answered, "No, but who cares? It's over and the hell with it."

Thor, an aging, glorified bum who wore his long hair in a braid down his back, pretended to be Mr. Tranquility, laid-back dude of the universe.

"You have to go with the flow," Thor explained to a group of reporters. "There are no accidents in the universe. Eagle is a gift from the cosmos."

He rechristened Nathan "Eagle," which reminded me of Boy Scouts. I'll have you know I made it to Eagle Scout. A family tradition. But speaking of gifts, per the deal with Lizzie, Nathan (I could never bring myself to call him Eagle) by his mere existence made a significant contribution to Thor's bank account .

"I'm excited to have a brother and a new best friend," sixteen-year-old Wolf Rainbow chimed in, putting his arm around my son.

"God is love, and I am God's vessel," proclaimed a modest Elena Rainbow. "Now we have more love to spread around."

Though as I discovered, as indeed did Nathan as well, love is a relative concept. Something got spread around all right, but I wouldn't call it love.

"Just look at you, Eagle," Elena continued. "You remind me of a neighbor's cat. They had it declawed and never allowed it to explore. It lived under the bed, afraid of its own shadow. But all that's in your past. Now—why, there's no telling what heights you might reach."

"Maybe I'll be tried for murder again," Nathan replied, to which casual remark Elena lacked a response. The press misunderstood Nathan's dry wit and used this quote in their hysterical headlines.

I will say this for the Rainbows: they gave Nathan his first exposure to spirituality, if you wanted to call it that. His birth mother and grandmother each had their reasons for not believing a whole hell of a lot in cosmic goodness. At nine, he asked Lizzie and Zelda if God existed, and they both burst out laughing. As for myself, I grew up as the generic, blasé Episcopalian one would expect of a Yalie. My only contact with churches now consisted of soup lines, but I did consider myself a spiritual person, if not a religious one. Like many people in today's world, I found my own type of Higher Power that worked for me. But I had the decency to keep it to myself.

The Rainbows embraced a hodgepodge of New Age beliefs: meditation, yoga, astrology, numerology, runes, tarot cards, the I Ching, the Bling-Bling, and the Beep-bob-a-lula. They were the sort of obnoxious people who ran around saying God is everywhere in everything, God is inside everyone, we are all God, and all that garbage. If Zelda and Lizzie believed everything stank, the Rainbows believed everything radiated beauty, which, if you think about it, is even worse. It's more delusional.

Besides, who wouldn't find everything beautiful if they had a Nazi-like determination to surround themselves with nothing but so-called beautiful things? The local paper did this stupid photo spread about how the Rainbows lived in a storybook cottage in the woodsy outskirts of town. Elena tended a smarmy flower garden and sold bouquets by the roadside on Saturdays. The customers were few and far between, but nothing could diminish her big, fake smile, as if to indicate she had all the patience in the world. Maybe underneath it all there lurked a frustrated, would-be Miss America. Elena also claimed to have supernatural powers that brainless twits paid money to witness. She called these payments love offerings, and at the end of the day, when she licked her thumb to count the money in her humble basket, love indeed filled the air.

Supposedly, Elena could take you into your past lives. She also had a guided meditation you could purchase on CD that told you about Atlantis—or what an idiot you were, take your pick. According to the self-appointed expert, the fruit in Atlantis resembled tangelos, and the structures were all octagonal. I had this image of an Atlantian getting out of his octagonal bed in the morning and declaring, "Guess I'll go pick me a tangelo."

Thor worked as little as possible as a landscaper. His cut of the monthly Social Security checks stolen from Nathan made it all the more easy for him to achieve his goal. When he did "work," it meant ordering Nathan to do everything, while Wolf got to supervise. And supervision meant sabotaging the work Nathan did, so he'd get in trouble. Though Thor differed from my father, they shared in common a gruff, distant exterior, as if they resented being interrupted from hibernation, their normal state of being.

Thor smoked so much pot that I don't think anyone ever saw him not stoned.

I worried for Nathan and it frustrated me that I couldn't step forward to help. Thus far, his sole male role model lived to do nothing. Call me old-fashioned, but I've always been appalled when men refuse to be productive members of society. Grow a pair, for crying out loud. Even worse, Nathan's images of motherhood consisted of Zelda and Elena, opposite extremes on the crazy continuum. I wondered if he'd be capable of sustaining a normal, healthy relationship.

The inside of the Rainbow cottage featured worn tapestries and whimsical paintings of wizards and elves and unicorns and other such fanciful things. It made you want to puke. They had three fat, lazy cats named River, Lake, and Pond, and a pleasant, dumb Irish setter named Ecstasy. Speaking of drugs, they limited themselves to pot, which they grew in a hidden field beyond the boundaries of their property. Wolf smoked dope all his life with his parents, though Nathan, I am proud to say, never indulged. For people like the Rainbows, mellowness equaled enlightenment, but mellow was not a natural trait for Nathan. Life taught him to keep his wits about him, and so he did. Nathan had far too much vital intelligence to turn himself into a human vegetable with bloodshot eyes. Besides, his inner landscape didn't consist of babbling brooks and swaying trees, but dirty sidewalks and broken glass.

In other words, the Rainbows never saw a ghetto, they never went hungry, they never had to step over a drunk on the sidewalk, they never saw the snow turn black with soot or heard an ambulance rushing a gunshot child to the hospital. Their idea of social problems consisted of things like corn syrup in fruit juice. Things that most people were far too busy to even have heard of. So yeah, everything was beautiful. Big deal. Anger, sorrow, frustration, impatience, and the like were what they called false emotions. If you transcended into a true state of enlightened bliss, you'd be shit-faced happy

24/7. When something lousy happened, they didn't care as much about solving the problem as they did about maintaining their Higher Consciousness. And this, regardless of the circumstances, always turned out to be one hundred percent the fault of the other party. Which, in practical terms, meant Nathan—or Eagle, as they would've said.

Nathan and Wolf were supposedly homeschooled, which consisted of sitting around in the woods and smoking grass. Nice work if you can get it. In my mind, the lessons I overheard blend into one giant pile of Silly Putty, so let this one recollection stand for them all.

"It's like, you know, everything is connected," a bleary-eyed Thor said, as the family sat outside in a circle, passing around a joint. "That squirrel over there. It's connected to the tree it's climbing. And the tree is. . . the tree is. . . what am I talking about again?"

"Like how everything's connected, honey pot." Elena wheezed as she inhaled a strong hit of dope.

"Oh, right. See, without the tree, there'd be no squirrel. And without the squirrel, there'd be no tree." He took his turn with the joint and passed it to his son. As he took a hit, Wolf grunted in complaint for having to reach across Nathan to give the joint back to his mother.

Nathan considered the argument. "Why wouldn't there be a tree? If the squirrel died, the tree would still be there."

Never at ease with being corrected, Thor quirked an eyebrow in challenge. "You might think it's still there, but how do you know it is?"

"Yeah," Wolf agreed, with the fervor of a jealous and favored sibling. "How would you know?"

A nervous Nathan shrugged. "I could see it. I could touch it."

Well, you'd have thought my son just said that coconuts grew on the North Pole.

"What you have to learn," Thor said, "is that everything is a hallucination. We create our own reality. Nothing matters.

That's the Zen of life—the dance of life. The secret to happiness that's staring you in the face if only you'd let it in."

"You have to let go," Elena added. "Like. . . well, like the squirrel. That's enlightenment. That's the essence. Can't you feel it? Thor does. I do. So does Wolf." She and Thor smiled at Nathan, though Wolf directed a snide look at him, as if Nathan did not deserve to exist for not being a squirrel.

They all stared at Nathan, waiting for him to say something.

"I'm sorry," he said.

"You dumb fuck." Thor, Mr. Mellow, threw the homeschooling book at my son. It missed him, so Thor forced himself to stand up, retrieve the book, and whack Nathan on the side of the face with it.

"It's not about being sorry. It's about feeling the universe pulsating through every vein of your body. It's about looking around and seeing nothing but love, and knowing that you're nothing but love."

"Love is everything," Elena concurred.

"Right on," seconded Wolf. As he spat on the ground, it seemed like he spat on Nathan.

"I achieved such a blissful place," Elena complained. "But Eagle spoiled it."

"Me, too," Wolf shared.

"When are you going to stop acting so goddamn nervous?" Thor asked. "Your downer vibes spoil everything we've created here."

"I'm sorry," Nathan said.

"Jesus, here we go again." Thor ran out of what little patience he had. He shook Nathan by the shoulders, grabbing him so hard that his thumbs must've left bruises.

"Change, damn it. Why can't you change?"

Nathan showed no reaction, which only frustrated Thor all the more. He grabbed his baggie of pot and said he had to go for a walk in the woods to regain his serenity. His son went with him. Elena said she wanted to take a nap but would at the same time be joining her husband and son on their walk because, as she put it, "You don't have to be there to be there." Thor told Nathan to spread a giant bag of leaf mulch in Elena's garden.

Thus did three years go by. Now and then, Nathan expressed a desire to talk to Lizzie, but Elena and Thor screamed that Lizzie didn't care about him, only they did. Wolf more or less picked up where Bosco Sinclair left off, slapping Nathan around and setting him up for trouble. While Zelda thought cockroaches were diamonds, Elena resembled Attila the Hun when it came to kitchen rules. She screamed at Nathan for not ringing out the kitchen sponge the proper way or leaving crumbs on the table, when in fact Wolf had done it or not done it, as the case might've been. One time, Wolf knocked Nathan out with a rock, and Elena lectured Nathan on how he had to stop making Wolf upset. She spat cuss words, for tending to Nathan's head injury took precious time away from her garden. When one of the cats died rather prematurely—River, I think—Elena said Nathan carried death vibes wherever he went. The other cats were aloof in the manner of cats, and since Ecstasy the Irish Setter belonged to Wolf, he forbade Nathan to pet the creature without permission. Naturally, Nathan had too much pride to ask. Thor kept yelling at Nathan to not be so high strung.

One time when he was sixteen, Nathan walked in on Elena when she was giving a supposed psychic reading to some dumb-shit girl who didn't know her ass from her elbow. My son had caught the girl fucking Thor, though Nathan knew it best not to say anything. Elena forbade Nathan to be anywhere near when she leapt across time and space, but in the presence of a third party she didn't yell at him. Instead, she smiled and said in a whisper, "Eagle, come join us."

Reluctantly, he said, "Sure."

Even just that one word didn't sound enlightened enough, and Elena winced for his mundane presence.

The two women sat cross-legged on a worn oriental red carpet that had seen better days.

"You were in Egypt," Elena said. "You were the Pharaoh's favored daughter. And then in Greece, you were a priestess at the temple of Aphrodite."

In other words, a whore, but "priestess at the temple of Aphrodite" sounded better.

The girl appeared relieved. "No wonder I've always felt such a connection to ancient times. It's like I got reincarnated into the wrong era. That's why I can't find true love."

Even the most downtrodden among us reach a point where they can't swallow another drop of bullshit. For better or for worse, Nathan reached this point at that precise moment.

"Then, in your next life, you worked at a doughnut factory in Sheboygan," he interjected.

Elena's face flustered to a darker shade of red than the carpet. "Why must you always ruin everything?" she shouted. "Get the hell out of here."

Nathan stood up, with his hands in his pockets. "No. I want to stay and soak up your cosmic vibrations."

Elena stood up, too. "There are no cosmic vibrations when you're around. You only know how to kill everything beautiful with your negative energy."

"Nothing is beautiful," Nathan said. "Everything is ugly."

Well, that did it. Elena started punching his arms, screaming at him with each blow. "Doesn't all I've done for you mean anything? People pay to spend time with me. I am Nefertiti reincarnated. I know it. I feel it. Why can't you treat me with respect?"

Nathan kept his hands in his pockets. "No, I'm not grateful that you steal my government checks, Nefertiti."

She pummeled his chest. "I gave up my life to take care of you. Why can't you love me?"

The former resident of Egypt and Greece said, "Stop hurting your mother."

Just then Thor and Wolf came into the room. Elena burst into tears as she ran to them for comfort.

"I can't stand it," she whimpered. "He drags me down to his level."

The girl left the house, leaving a love offering of twenty bucks in Elena's basket by the door. Nathan started to leave, too, but Wolf tackled him to the floor. He punched Nathan in the face, one side and then the other, screaming, "No one makes my mom cry and gets away with it."

"Okay, Wolf, that's enough," Thor said, which surprised me. As Nathan left the house, Elena screamed at him, while Thor restrained her with his arms locked in hers.

"Go ahead," she shrieked. "Walk away from all the love and beauty I've given you. You'll always be nothing but a pile of shit. You'll always be—"

Nathan shut the door and ran into the woods. Finding a quiet spot, he lay down on the leaves and sticks and looked upward at the treetops against the sky.

Two days later, the police removed the three dead bodies of the Rainbows from their burnt-down house. Or at least what remained of them after the fire. The dog and two remaining cats were unharmed and taken to an animal shelter.

Nathan ran away. Though innocent as ever, he knew it would be only a matter of time before the cops suspected him. He left with nothing at all. This is both the best and worst way to leave one place for another. To keep from being recognized, he could do nothing but flip up his shirt collar, pull his baseball cap down as far as it would go, and turn his head toward the shadows. And to get the hell out of town, he had to walk for miles and miles down a twisting shoulder of road covered with dead leaves. Finally, he reached the city, where he could get lost among the many people. There, a new life awaited him, and by the time he met up with it, he looked scruffy as a street person.

He ran away from everything. I never felt so close to him.

A woman came up to him with a pamphlet and said, "Would you like to learn about salvation through the Lord?"

"No thanks," Nathan answered, and he kept on walking.

7

Nathan had to find shelter. And somehow, he knew how to get it.

A rundown bus depot simmered in the heart of downtown. Drug dealers, whores, homeless drunks, scared runaway kids. . . it reminded me of one of those plastic rectangular things filled with stuffed animals, and you guide the tongs to pick up the one you want. Nathan stood inside the depot with one leg bent against the wall, I assumed in anticipation for someone or something. . . for whatever life had to dish out next. A couple of dangerous-looking dope pushers looked him over, then kept on walking. A dirty old man with yellow-green teeth winked at him, and Nathan turned his head the other way. A bum asked him for a quarter, which he didn't have, and a whore offered him a good time, which he claimed not to want.

He glanced through a morning newspaper someone left on a bench. I could tell he sighed with relief for the murders not being in the news. As I learned later on, the cops kept their investigation as low-key as possible, hoping that this time they could build an ironclad case before filing formal charges against him.

A good half hour later, who should walk by but Nathan's former nemesis, Bosco Sinclair. He grew into a bear of a young man, with fancy tats on his arms and neck that he showed off with a sleeveless T-shirt. Bosco looked a far cry from Most Popular, Most Likely, Most Everything. He became an in-your-face badass who left home after several years of skipping school and getting busted for pot and shoplifting. Seems the high school sophisticates figured out that Crazy Seymour Sinclair sucked donkey dong, and they took out their repulsion on his son. Yesterday's source of popularity became today's source of ostracism. Such is the fickle way of youth. Bosco's only respite came from the so-called bad kids, with whom he wasted no time fitting in. After all, he excelled at fitting in. One thing led to another, and presto, America had one more homeless youth.

He stopped walking and looked Nathan over.

As their eyes met, Bosco said, "Nathan? What the fuck are you doing here?"

"I ran away," Nathan replied.

"No shit?" Bosco grinned from ear to ear.

"No shit."

Bosco roared with laughter and gave Nathan a bear hug. "Cool, man. I can dig it." Then he added, "I'm really sorry, dude, for how I treated you. I feel like a total scumbag."

"No one's ever apologized to me before. That means a lot."

Nathan had no use for pride or fear, and he hugged Bosco back. The two guys understood each other at once. For not the last time, I admired Nathan's grit. Somehow, out of all the craziness, he became a man. A class act, he could forgive and move on.

"How long have you been on your own?" Nathan asked.

"About a year, but I'm not anymore. I stay with Mr. Rogers. He takes care of us kids. We take turns going to the depot to find. . . well, someone like you, to join us. Small world, huh?"

Nathan sat down on the nearest bench. "Mr. Rogers? You mean the creepy guy who used to have a kiddie show?"

"He's not that Mr. Rogers. But that's what we call him. He never tells us his first name." Bosco laughed and sat down next to him.

"What's the catch?"

"Hey, it's not what you think. No drug dealing, no sex, no monkey business. He's just this rich dude who takes in homeless kids. I've been there six months. There's like ten of us."

"So what do you do all day?"

Bosco lit a Marlboro. "We chill. We read or listen to music or watch TV. We take turns cooking and cleaning."

"And he does this because. . .?"

"Because he's cool, man. He used to be a runaway himself. He says we need to heal. When he thinks you're ready, he gives you some scratch and you move on."

Nathan moved away from the cigarette smoke. "What do you have to heal from?"

"You mean me, or everyone?"

"Either or both."

"I got tired of my old man beating me," Bosco replied. "I'm a big guy, but I couldn't hit him back. He's still my dad."

"You used to brag about your father being on TV and all."

"He beat me plenty back then. That's why I talked so big, and why I used to. . . you know, like if you had it worse than me, I felt better."

"I can dig it," Nathan said. The two young men touched fists.

"The other kids," Bosco continued, "Are a mixed bag. A few girls molested by their fucking father or some other asshole. Kids who ran away from mean drunks. A couple of gay kids thrown out of the house. One of them said his dad came after him with a shotgun."

Nathan looked skeptical. "But what about cops or social workers?"

"Mr. Rogers has them wrapped around his finger. Like I said, the dude has money, plus I think he knows some shit about the mayor or something. But he never talks about that stuff."

"He sounds cool," Nathan said.

"So what made you say bye-bye to that new family they gave you?"

"I. . . I'm not ready to talk about it."

"I can dig it. Is your grandmother still alive?"

"I guess so. I'm not interested."

He never agreed to go with Bosco, he just started following him to an alley a couple of blocks from the bus depot. They walked through an obstacle course of banged-up dumpsters, smelly trash, and oil puddles. A stray cat nibbled on a mouse. A homeless man slept beside an abandoned loading zone. I recognized him as my friend, Charlie, but of course I didn't come forward to say hello.

The twosome came to an industrial building in the alleyway that, at least from the outside, had seen better days. Nathan followed Bosco to the back of the building. A few stairs led to a door part way below ground level, with squat windows suitable for sneaking looks from the outside. Just before he opened the door, Bosco touched Nathan's shoulder.

"You turned out all right, dude, no thanks to me. And don't worry. Mr. Rogers doesn't force you to go down on him or anything."

"Did you ever . . . you know, do stuff like that?"

Bosco shrugged. "When you're hungry you do all sorts of things. I know I'm straight, so I don't have to prove anything. Everyone's both male and female, anyway. Though some people more than others."

I could tell the cryptic answer confused Nathan. After hating Bosco's guts all this time, I found myself feeling sorry for the young man and kind of liking him. He had this teddy bear quality. Bosco. I decided the cuddly name suited him.

"Be cool, but not too cool," Bosco advised, as they entered the building, a large industrial space that could've been made into a fancy loft. The brick walls had been spray-painted with colorful graffiti many times over and for that matter, so had the wood floors. There were hospital-like rows of cots and sleeping bags at one end, with an old-looking stove, refrigerator, and industrial sink more to the middle. Shipping crates were arranged as shelves for cheap, basic foods like rolled oats and dried beans. I spotted what I assumed to be a bathroom, and another room that I took to be Mr. Rogers' living space or office. A sign hung on the door that read, "Go away, leave me alone." Presumably on the reverse side, the sign offered a more welcoming message.

Though rich, this Mr. Rogers person spent next to nothing when creating his bare bones living space for runaway teens. I wondered if maybe he didn't want them to get too comfortable. Or maybe Bosco had a stilted impression of him.

A tough-looking young woman with short hair who sported a studded black leather jacket greeted them at the door. "Hey, Bosco, I see a stray dog followed you home."

Bosco winked at Nathan. "An old friend from grade school, if you can believe it."

"Sweet," she commented, smiling at Nathan. "Biv," she added, extending her hand.

"Excuse me?" Nathan shook her hand.

"Biv. My name is Biv."

"Bev?"

"No, Biv. My name used to be Beverly, and all I want to do is live. So now I'm Biv."

"Uh, okay. Hi, Biv. I'm Nathan."

But Biv lost interest in Nathan and walked past him to give Bosco a big fat kiss.

Another girl approached who looked like Biv but had longer hair. She, too, gave Bosco a jumbo-sized kiss. She nodded at Nathan.

"Montana," she said.

"Um, what about it?" Nathan asked.

"That's my name. And yes, it's my real name. And you are. . .?"

"Uh, Nathan."

"Uhnathan? Is that like a foreign name? I sort of like it. So, Uhnathan, how's tricks?"

Biv spoke before Nathan could. "His name is Nathan, you brainless wonder. He just says um and uh a lot."

"Guess he's not used to being around people," Montana decided.

"Or at least not nice people," Biv surmised.

"You're right about that," Nathan said.

"Do you use?" asked Montana.

Again Biv answered on Nathan's behalf. "Can't you tell? He's cleaner than Mr. Clean. He's so clean you could eat off his ass."

"That's good," Montana said with approval. "Mr. Rogers kicks out users. Even booze is a no-no. Even cigarettes."

"Well sort of," Biv qualified. "You can go outside to smoke. And we're not chained to the wall. So in that big ol' ball of a world out there, we've been known to take a sip or two of wine. Or a puff from a joint."

"Or puke your guts out onto my lap after snorting too much coke on top of fifteen tequila shots," Montana added.

"Would you stop bringing that up?" Biv complained. "I apologized about a zillion times."

"Well, look what the wind blew in," spoke a man's voice from a slight distance.

The foursome turned to find the body that the voice belonged to—the hallowed Mr. Rogers.

I remembered, as a little kid, having nightmares about a kidnapper, and I swear he had the same face as Mr. Rogers. He didn't look at people. He leered at them. When he smiled, his mouth became a near-perfect triangle that matched his pointy chin. He wore a black hat, the kind that businessmen used to wear—I assumed to hide a bald spot—and a black vest over a black T-shirt. His black clothes made his ghost-white skin seem even whiter. His arms were so scrawny, the lower halves were thicker than the forearms. I guessed him to be about forty.

"This is Nathan," Bosco shared, as if having found a treasure chest.

"Welcome, Nathan, to our humble abode." Mr. Rogers extended his hand, and Nathan shook it. Me, I'd rather have shaken hands with a spider.

"Does he know the rules?" Mr. Rogers asked Biv.

"He knows the zero tolerance drug policy," Biv answered, like a kid telling a parent that she went to a friend's house to do homework when in reality she got laid.

Mr. Rogers sighed. "I can see that as usual, I have to do everything. Listen up, Nathan. All food brought to the premises is used for group meals, which happen at noon, five and midnight. There's a pile of clothes next to the sleeping bags. Feel free to help yourself. Once you pick your sleeping space, stick to it. Nothing's a bigger waste of time than fights over where to sleep. If you're into anything illegal, do it someplace else. Never under any circumstances disturb me when I have my 'go away' sign on my door. I don't care if you're dying. I don't care if the building's on fire. And remember, you don't owe me anything but to follow the rules. Don't daddy-figure me, and don't get a crush on me. It's such a hassle. That's about it. Did I leave anything out?"

"What about sex?" Montana added in support.

Mr. Rogers slapped his forehead, as if to indicate he couldn't believe his own absentmindedness; his fingers were long and bony, like talons.

"Right, how could I forget? No one, including me, especially me, forces anyone else to have sex. And no sex for money or drugs. You know-it-all kids need to learn the value of making an honest buck. There's a fishbowl full of condoms in the can. Beyond that, your business is your business." He looked at Nathan impatiently, as if it taxed him beyond endurance to have to interact with people. "Any questions?"

Nathan thought for a moment. "Who owns this building?"

Nathan's direct and unusual question caught Mr. Rogers off guard, yet he tried not to let it show. Though new to the urban scene, Nathan had more inherent street smarts than kids who spent much more time there. This Mr. Rogers weirdo had some sort of hidden agenda, though I couldn't figure it out yet.

"So. . . a good head for business. I like that. Maybe someday you'll be my broker. I own the building, you know-nothing little shit. I inherited it."

"I never knew that," Montana said.

"Well, you should've, because I remember telling you," interjected Biv.

"You never told me," Montana insisted. "I'd remember something like that."

Biv begged to differ. "I know I told you because I remember it exactly. We were hanging in the park, and I said—and these were my exact words—'Thank God Mr. Rogers inherited the building. We'll never have to squat.' You said, 'I didn't know he owned it.' And I said, 'Well, now you know.' Then we argued with some fucked-out whore."

Montana shook her head in defiance. "Never happened. I don't know why you make these things up. The sad part is, I think you really believe they happen."

"Aren't they adorable?" Mr. Rogers licked his upper lip with his pointy pink tongue. "Like an old married couple."

"Biv and I are just friends," Montana corrected.

"Oh yes, such wonderful friends," Biv added, in a sardonic tone.

The sudden presence of five more teenagers interrupted the silly argument. A girl and a boy were sort of making out.

"How'd it go?" Mr. Rogers asked, as if speaking in code.

"Mission accomplished," the kissing boy replied.

Mr. Rogers gestured at my son. "This is Nathan, everyone. He's one of those smart-ass cynical types who thinks he knows everything, but he's okay."

They welcomed him with pats on the back and hugs. Following a meal of plain beans and rice, the entire group of eleven kids plus Mr. Rogers gathered in a circle on the floor.

"Who wants to share tonight?" Mr. Rogers asked, inflated with self-importance.

"Me." Montana raised her hand like an ass-kissing student in a class.

From the eye rolling and whispers of contempt that followed, I got the impression that the group had tired of hearing from Montana, though she didn't seem to notice.

"Very, well. What would you like to say, Montana?"

"Well, for those who may not know the story"—she smiled at Nathan—"I thought I'd share how I wound up here."

A disgruntled Biv said, "Nathan, her asshole preacher stepfather had sex with her. Afterward, he'd have her get on her knees and ask God for forgiveness."

Montana interjected. "Let me tell it, you're leaving out the good parts. It's my story."

"All right, fine," said Biv, with an air of resignation.

"Okay, then." Montana cleared her throat. "My stepfather had sex with me since my tenth birthday. Afterward, I had to get on my knees and ask God for forgiveness. A preacher. So-called."

"I just said that," Biv complained.

"Yeah, but it needs to come from me. So anyway, Nathan, at fourteen, I ran away. I met this pimp named Arnold."

Biv sort of giggled or sighed. "Arnold the Pimp. Sounds really scary, doesn't it?"

"Arnold is six foot six and strong as shit," Montana offered in defense. "He has guns and a bad temper, especially after taking a toot."

"Did you just say, 'after taking a shit'?" Biv asked with mock seriousness.

"I'll ignore your childish behavior," Montana decided. "When we had sex, he'd pull my hair and shove me and slap me around. I didn't think I deserved any better. Then I'd have to fuck or blow any guy who offered. At first, Arnold gave me a cut of the money, but after a while, he paid me in crack. I got so wasted. I thought I'd be dead before I turned sixteen."

Nathan felt obliged to ask, "What saved you?"

"Biv," Montana replied solemnly. "She may joke around, but she knows that bringing me here to Mr. Rogers is what got me off crack. Just knowing that people cared about me. I owe him my life. I owe Biv my life."

"Are you done now?" Biv asked.

"Not quite," Montana said through clenched teeth. "I'm studying for my GED. Then I want to go to college and become a nurse."

"Free access to pharmaceuticals," Biv added.

"That's not the point," Montana insisted. "I'm not going to ruin my life as a prostitute. I have too much self-respect."

Behind Montana's back, Biv made her fingers into a hand puppet, as if to say blah-blah-blah.

"Thank you, Montana," Mr. Rogers said. "We can always count on you to share with newcomers."

"Thank you, Mr. Rogers," Montana enthused. "Now I think we'd all like to hear from Nathan."

Everyone looked at my son, who looked down at the floor.

"C'mon, man, go for it," Bosco encouraged.

"Yeah, c'mon, Nathan," said someone else.

"I don't think I can," Nathan said. "It's too painful."

"Let's see if we can help," offered Mr. Rogers. "Who did you grow up with?"

Nathan moved his finger on the floor, as if drawing an invisible picture. "First I lived with my mother and grandmother. Then someone killed my mother."

"Hey, I know who you are," said one of the kids, "You were on trial, right?"

Nathan kept looking down at the floor. "Yeah, that's me. But I didn't do it."

All the kids registered approbation for being in the company of a former murder suspect. One of them called out, "Nathan rocks."

"What about your father?" Mr. Rogers asked.

"I never even knew his name until the trial."

This threw me for a loop, until I realized he didn't want to badmouth me.

"Then I lived with these other people," Nathan continued. "The parents. . . I don't even think I can say it."

Biv took hold of Nathan's hand. "Try. Remember, you're among kindred souls."

He gulped down hard. "They—I mean my new mother and father—they were in love with me or something. They worshipped me. They made me have sex with them. I had to. . ." Nathan stopped himself, as if unable to say more. "Do I really have to go on?"

Mr. Rogers looked at him like a salivating tiger. This prick perv got off on stories of child molestation. "That's enough for now. Thank you so much for letting us get to know you better. You're very brave."

"He sure is." Bosco gave his new friend the thumbs-up.

As far as I could tell, Nathan sought to insure he qualified to stay in the household for at least a while. True, I didn't spy on him 24/7, but I doubted that Thor and Elena Rainbow would've fooled around with him in that way. Among other things, they hated him too much.

Yet I uncovered a larger pattern to Nathan's life. His natural intensity compelled him to go all the way with whatever he did. As Zelda's whipping boy, he let her whip away. Same thing with the Rainbows. So now, he had to be the crème de la crème of abused teens. Okay, so he lied, but for all anyone knew so had Montana, or any of the kids who wanted to be the center of someone's attention.

I caught up with my friend Charlie at a shelter and asked him why kids needed so much attention, when it didn't make any difference once they got older. My family would've had a fit if they knew I spoke to Charlie, a Harvard man through and through, but he knew a lot.

"Kids think other people can do things for them," Charlie replied. "Then they mature, and they realize no one can do anything for them at all. I went to my father's funeral and walked right up to the open casket and started choking his corpse. What difference did it make? But everyone got on my case, and I ended the night in jail. It made no difference. Jail is everywhere. The universe is a prison."

"Huh, I never thought of that before," I had to admit. "'The universe is a prison.'"

"It's pretty hard to escape it," Charlie reflected. "But kids don't know that. So they fuck everything up."

8

For Nathan, the next few months were like one of those movie montages of people doing happy things together: Nathan pitching in with peeling potatoes for the group dinner; Nathan hugging someone in the evening circle; Nathan and Bosco playing Frisbee in the park; Nathan watching as Bosco, Biv, and Montana rocked out to a song on the radio; Nathan blowing out the candles of his seventeenth birthday cake, while everyone applauded. Several young residents asked him for his autograph, which he declined to provide out of modesty. There were a few kids who came and went, but Nathan, Bosco, and the two girls formed a loyal foursome. Yet as far as I could tell, everything remained platonic with Nathan, and I grew more than a little impatient. When would Nathan lose his fucking virginity? Or should I say his unfucking virginity?

Still, his aversion to drugs and booze pleased me. The other three sometimes smoked pot and drank, but Nathan always passed. I guess Nathan had what you'd call an old soul. He didn't have to experience the same rites of passage that other people did.

What he did need, and what he got, was some sense of belongingness with other people. He found affinity with his fellow fucked-up runaway teens. Bosco Sinclair went from being the person who tried hardest to keep Nathan from fitting in to the person who tried hardest to make him feel like he had a family.

Of course, not everything about his environment met with my approval. Mr. Rogers gave me the willies whenever I saw him, and for some reason I found him even creepier when he spoke. This might have been because the superficial benign words were so unconvincing. It pleased me that Nathan kept a subtle distance from him.

Nathan's childhood served him well. He mastered how to isolate himself while still being in the presence of other people, a good skill to master as you maneuver your way through life. Inside him was an inner core that no one could touch, and take it from one who knows, that's a smart way to live.

In the meantime, Bosco Sinclair, of all people, seemed to be getting closer to the real Nathan than anyone else ever had. They were chummy late at night, when they'd go outside and sit by the doorway to take in the urban darkness.

"I wonder why people hate their kids," Bosco said one night, smoking his Marlboro. "What happens after all those happy baby pictures to change them so much?"

Nathan replied, "They already hate them. They just don't know it yet."

"I guess you're right. My dad hated me from the moment of my birth."

"Did he ever do stuff with you? Like, go fishing?"

"Nah. He worked all the time. He worked and he yelled and he beat me."

"You know, it's weird. Listening to you, dude, I wonder sometimes if maybe I lucked out, not having any dad at all."

"Except when you moved in with those crazy people," Bosco said. "Sounds like you had a real dad-and-a-half."

"Yeah, it got. . . really awful. Getting kicked out of the house had to be the best thing that ever happened to me."

"Why do you suppose they never went looking for you?"

"Because they're scared. They know I could put them in jail."

"Hey, dude, are you crying?"

"No," Nathan assured him, rubbing his eye like something got caught in it. "I just couldn't swallow for a moment."

"Well, one thing's for sure. No one will ever come looking for me. My dad probably told people I died, rather than admit the truth. It would hurt his business."

Nathan looked up at the moon. "Do you think you'll ever have kids?"

Bosco gave Nathan a friendly punch to the arm. "Hell, no. I may be fucked up, but I ain't crazy. I'd be scared, you know? Scared I'd do the same things to my own kid. Didn't somebody famous say, 'You can't give what you never had?'"

Nathan laughed. "It sounds like something someone famous would say. Clever."

"That's another thing," Bosco said. "Education. I hated school, but now I want to know stuff. I'm missing out. What'll I ever do with my life?"

"There's plenty of time to get your act together," Nathan assured him. "You're smart, and that's what counts most."

"If you could be anyone in the world, who would you be?"

Without hesitation, Nathan answered, "God."

"Dude, are you serious?"

Nathan shrugged. "Of course."

"What would you do if you were God?"

"I'd give a lot of people the big cosmic whammy. People who deserve to suffer would suffer."

"Would you do anything nice?"

Nathan considered. "Nothing I can think of offhand. What about you?"

Bosco put his hands behind his head. "Nothing that special, I guess. Maybe I'd like to drive a truck. Be on the open road. And then come home to my wife."

"So you want to get married?"

"Sure. I just don't think I should ever have kids. A goldfish, maybe. But not kids."

"Maybe you'll have some anyway. As God, I'll make sure that you do. And you'd be a good father, Bosco. You'd know so much about what not to do."

"What about you? I guess if you're God you don't get married, unless you count nuns. They get married to God, right?"

Before Nathan could respond, the voice of Mr. Rogers called out from his private window: "Nathan, I'd like to talk to you, please."

Mr. Rogers literally lived like a night owl, and the lights in his private quarters stayed on until morning. Small wonder the first group meal of the day began at noon or even later.

This marked the first occasion I looked inside the private world of Mr. Rogers because Nathan had never before been called to step inside of it. And Mr. Rogers never before left the window open by mistake. In dramatic contrast to the rest of the loft, Mr. Rogers spared no expense on himself. The room looked like a designer showcase, and everything in it said money. He had a high-end bedroom set, a solid mahogany desk, a state-of-the-art computer, and a crystal chandelier. Mr. Rogers sat at his desk to occupy the position of power. The powerless Nathan had to make do with sitting on the floor.

Mr. Rogers got right to the point. "Nathan, I see something in you I like very much. I feel I can depend on you more than any kid who's ever stayed here, and I've been doing this for almost twenty years."

"Gee, thanks, Mr. Rogers." Nathan moved his lips into what passed for a smile.

"I know I can trust you to share nothing of what I'm about to say with anyone."

"Uh, sure."

Mr. Rogers clasped his bony fingers together, as if about to eat a dead child. "The truth is, there's more to this household than taking in stray children. That's just a cover, you see."

"Oh, okay." It was obvious Nathan already knew Mr. Rogers had a secret plan.

"That's what I like to see," Mr. Rogers said. "Nothing fazes you. I've never seen anything like it."

"Thanks."

"The truth is, we move drugs. Smack and crack. Thousands a week come pouring in. Those kids you hang with—Bosco and the silly girls. They can't know anything about this. You see, two kinds of kids stay here. The dumb ones who think I do this out of the goodness of my heart. They provide the cover. And then there's the occasional smart ones, like you."

"But the cops know you take in these stray kids," Nathan said. "Why wouldn't they suspect—"

"Ever hear of being careful? Or smart?"

"What if I don't want to deal?"

Mr. Rogers laughed. "It's a bit too late for that. Now that you know, you haven't much choice. Either you become a dealer, in which case you wouldn't want to tell anyone, or I tell the cop detective who called me a while back and say that I found someone who matches your description. Namely, you. A little something about that family you lived with. You're one of those snobby brainiacs, Nathan, but you're still just a snot-nosed kid. Whatever you did, didn't you think they'd try to find you? Though I give you props for your cover story, assuming it is a cover story. Did you really have to put out for them? Who did what? Tell me, I like to hear about these things. I care so much about my kids."

After a moment of silence, Nathan asked, "What are other kids selling for you?"

"That's the beauty of it. None of you know. So the secret becomes that much more of a secret. Secrets are such beautiful things, don't you agree? They require such delicacy. The deepest person is the one with the most secrets. As I'm sure you already know."

Nathan ignored Mr. Rogers' remarks. "Just to make sure. Bosco, Biv, and Montana—"

Mr. Rogers always had limited patience. "Yes, yes, and yes. I already told you they're idiots. I have no idea why you waste your time with them."

Nathan sighed. "Okay, what do I have to do?"

"You truly are a pragmatic young man. We've got bricks of Baby T coming in. And hundreds of vials of BF. It'll go chronic. All you have to do is make some drop-offs, and they're all right here in the city. You also get cash only—and I mean cash only—at every site. If someone says they won't have money until tomorrow or a week after next Halloween, give them nothing and let me know. Tell them you're going to let me know."

"Will any of them get violent with me?"

"They're stupid, but not that stupid. And what do you take me for? You think I'd risk the safety of one of my kids?"

"No, I guess you wouldn't. The cops would be all over you."

"For your information, Mr. Smarty-pants, I have long since made certain we have nothing to worry about from the cops. In fact, if you get any noble ideas of going to them, all you'll do is throw your life down the drain. Unless your idea of a life well spent is a life sentence without parole. If you're lucky."

"When will I have to do this?"

"Soon. I'll let you know."

"'Soon' as in a couple of days? A week?"

"Soon. Now get the hell out of here and leave me alone."

Nathan went to his cot to go to sleep. Bosco already lay in his, looking up at the ceiling.

He whispered to Nathan: "What did he want?"

"We talked, that's all," Nathan whispered back.

"I've never been in his private room. What's it like?'

"It's okay. Nicer than the rest of this dump."

Bosco laughed. "I'm surprised. Mr. Rogers is always so generous with us."

"Yes, he's very generous."

A few minutes later, Bosco fell asleep, and it became Nathan's turn to stare up at the ceiling. I had no way of knowing what he thought about, but I could've made an educated guess.

9

As if testing Nathan or maybe to mind-fuck him, the following afternoon Mr. Rogers made a point of sending Nathan, Bosco, Biv, and Montana on what seemed a harmless but long errand on the other side of town. They were to pick up a package that an old friend had for Mr. Rogers—an antique bust of Napoleon that the old friend didn't want anymore. The doorman in the lobby of the building had the package. I saw no reason for four people to be running this errand, but none of the kids questioned Mr. Rogers' decisions. Besides, the four of them liked hanging out together. I knew that Nathan would be tested on whether or not he spilled the beans about the drug traffic or opened the package, thinking it had drugs inside.

But there were other possibilities that narcissistic Mr. Rogers did not consider.

The trip across town started in an innocent fashion—a moody, overcast day, neither hot nor cold. The kids decided to walk the two hours each way. Teenagers have so much energy. Mr. Rogers always gave kids a few bucks to spend when he sent them on errands, so they bought themselves candy bars. Biv and Montana got into a heated argument over which tasted better, Almond Joy or Mounds. Their loud voices competed with the constant roar of traffic.

Biv said, "Mounds is a rip-off. You think something more is going to be there, but nothing is. There aren't any nuts."

"You never can get enough nuts in your mouth, can you?" Montana asked.

"Look who's talking," said Biv. "This must be a first for you, walking down the street without giving anyone a blowjob."

"You're just jealous. Mounds has rich dark chocolate, not that wimpy milk chocolate in Almond Joy."

"Yeah, like I'm really jealous of you over dark chocolate."

"That's not what I meant, and you know it."

"Okay, guys." Biv said to Nathan and Bosco. "You settle the score. Which is better, dipshit Mounds, or delicious Almond Joy?"

"I like them both," said Bosco.

"I don't like either one," Nathan said.

The kids weren't paying attention to traffic and almost got hit by a taxi, which screeched its brakes. Montana went up to the driver and said, "Sir, don't you think Mounds is better than Almond Joy?"

With a deep sigh, Biv grabbed Montana by the neck of her T-shirt and led her back across the street.

"You didn't give him a chance to answer," Montana complained. "That's because you knew you'd lose."

"Fine. Mounds is better, you win."

"What do you mean, I win? You're just giving up. That doesn't count."

Bosco laughed, but Nathan said, "I've got an idea. Let's never talk about this again."

They picked up the package from the doorman, admired the expensive lobby for a minute or two, and then headed back into the congested city streets to walk back to the loft. Bosco and Biv each offered to carry the rectangular box, but Nathan insisted on doing it.

"I've been thinking," Nathan said, pretty much out of nowhere. "What if we don't go back to Mr. Rogers?"

"You're joking, right?" Biv asked, dodging a car stopped at a red light.

"Yes and no," Nathan replied. "Of course we can go back. I'm just saying—what if we didn't?"

"Oh, I get it," Montana said. "We'd be totally up shit creek without Mr. Rogers. And you're just reminding us of how much we owe him."

"Not exactly," Nathan replied. "Sooner or later we have to leave, right? So why not do it now?"

"We're still underage is why," Montana said. "We can end up in fucking foster homes. Or going back where we came from. No thanks, I'll pass."

"But who says we have to get caught?"

Bosco said, "Look, Nathan, buddy—you're right, I never got caught. I lived on my own for over a year. But I didn't eat much, and every time I saw a cop car it scared the shit out of me. I had to—look, it's no fun living like that."

They ran across a street before the light turned red. Nathan spied a large, fancy department store and said, "I'll be right back." Like he had to take a leak or something.

Riding the escalators to the all-but-impossible-to-find men's room, Nathan entered it. A minute or two later, he came back out, minus the box.

Back outside, he rejoined the others. Biv and Montana were singing some dopey rock song about how people don't need to talk when they're in love, because they already know what's in each other's hearts. Tell me another one.

"Listen, everybody. We have to get out of here. I opened the box and—"

"You peeked at Mr. Rogers's personal possession?" Montana said. "Nathan, I'm surprised at you."

"Chill, Montana," said Biv. "Let him finish."

"What's inside?" Bosco asked, sounding concerned. He knew Nathan never overreacted.

"A bust of Napoleon, all right. But inside it a plastic bag filled with white powder and another bag with these shiny chunks. I left the box in a stall in the men's room."

"Maybe it's flour and rock candy," Montana offered.

"Let's ignore her," said Biv. "Are you saying we carried smack and crack?"

Nathan said, "Look, I'm going to have to trust you guys," and proceeded to tell of his recent encounter with Mr. Rogers, leaving out of course anything to do with the Rainbows. "He's testing me," Nathan concluded. "To see if I'd peek, and if so, what I'd do."

"I don't believe you," Montana said. "Mr. Rogers is good and kind. He likes us. Why should we take your word for it?"

"She has a point," Biv admitted. "It's not that I don't believe you, Nathan, but it would be better if we could see for ourselves."

Nathan looked at Bosco and said, "You, too?"

His friend nodded in affirmation.

"Okay, fine. I'll go back and get it. Hopefully, it's still there." He commented in a pissed-off way, which invited the others to tell him not to bother, only it didn't work.

I could tell Nathan's heart raced as he climbed the escalators, skipping steps, to get back to the men's room. Yet he seemed careful not to go fast enough to draw attention to himself.

He entered the men's room. Once again, he emerged, this time with the box. On his way out of the store, he made a point of stopping to look at a male mannequin in a fancy suit, just like a customer would. A security guard stared at him.

Back outside, he led his friends to the nearest alleyway and opened the bottom of the bust, taking out the two suspicious bags.

Bosco opened the bag of white powder, stuck in his finger, and licked it. "Yeah, that's H, all right. I've snorted it a few times. Damn, to think I trusted that fucker."

"I'd know the sight of apple jacks if I went blind," Montana said.

"'Apple jacks?'" Biv repeated back. "Who the hell calls crack apple jacks anymore? Where did you grow up, on like a farm or something?"

"What are we going to do?" Bosco asked. "I don't like being used as cover for a drug lord."

"We're going to go back to the loft with it," Nathan decided.

Bosco registered confusion. "Back to the loft? You're the one who's been saying we shouldn't go back at all."

"I know, but the more I think about it, we need to go about it differently. We go back as if we never looked inside the box. After the evening circle, we leave, but not all at once. The girls go first. Don't take anything with you but whatever money you have."

"But then what?" asked Biv.

"We get the hell out of town. We go someplace hip, where no one will be looking over our shoulders. Then we lie about our ages, get jobs, and wait to turn eighteen."

"Sounds good, but I have no money at all," Montana said.

"Me either," added Bosco.

Biv said, "I have like five dollars."

Nathan thought for a minute. "Anyone know any junkies?"

Bosco said, "Hey man, I dealt a little pot, but no way am I messing with the hard stuff. If you get caught, they lock you up and throw away the key."

"We're talking maybe one or two sales today. What are the odds of getting caught our first and only day of dealing?"

"I'd feel guilty selling this stuff," Montana said. "You don't know what it's like."

"It's Econ 101," Nathan remarked. "Basic supply and demand. It's not my fault if someone's a drug addict."

"You have a point," Bosco admitted. "If they don't get it from us, they'll get it someplace else."

"And this stuff looks pure," Biv added. "It's not like we'd be ripping them off."

Montana said, "Oh, like you're the big expert."

"Will you shut up?" Biv said.

"If we're selling, where should we go?" Bosco asked.

"The park, I guess," said Nathan. "And we need plastic bags."

"Good point," Bosco affirmed.

"Don't stores have hidden cameras?" asked Montana. "They'll have us on tape buying baggies. On those true crime TV shows, they always have the murderers on tape, buying rope and duct tape. I always wonder why they need duct tape to kill someone."

"That gives me an idea," said Biv.

"Very funny," Montana commented.

Nathan grew thoughtful. "Wait a second. What if the whole thing's a set-up?"

"Huh?" Montana bellowed.

"Last night Mr. Rogers gives me this talk, and now he thinks I'm not going to peek inside the box? He knew I'd look, and that I'd tell the three of you everything. Forget I ever mentioned selling. He's setting us up to get busted. He knows cops, right?"

"Why would he do that?"

"Think about it, Bosco. His deal with the cops probably includes the occasional sacrificial lamb. I'm high risk because—because of some stuff that happened a while ago. And obviously he doesn't give a crap about the three of you."

A distant—but not distant enough—police siren became louder and louder. Montana panicked, grabbed the two bags of hard drugs, and slipped them through a grating. They fell into an unreachable pile of mud and garbage. In so doing, she tripped over herself, and the plaster bust in her hands fell to the ground in pieces.

"Oops," said Montana.

"You incredibly dumb fuck," Biv said. "Now we're totally screwed."

"Save it for later," Nathan said. "Let's just walk calmly back out."

"I don't think so." A cop appeared before them like a ghost on Halloween. "What are you kids up to?"

"Nothing, officer," Bosco said.

"Yeah, nothing," Biv agreed.

The cop tilted his head and squinted to get a better look. "Say, aren't you Nathan—"

Before the cop could finish speaking, my son shoved Bosco out of the way and started running down the alley. He turned at the corner, the cop not far behind. I had no idea

Nathan could run so fast. In different circumstances, he would've been an asset to the Yale track and field team.

Biv said, "Let's scram."

And so they did. They ran out of the alley in the opposite direction, though Montana almost tripped over herself again. A horn honked as they zigzagged through the flow of people trying to cross the street. An elderly person in a wheelchair slowed down the mob of foot traffic.

"What will we tell Mr. Rogers?" Montana wanted to know.

"How about as little as possible?" Biv replied, looking all around for cops. There didn't appear to be any.

It didn't seem possible, but they walked no more than a block in the thick crowd before Nathan called out to them. They waited for him to catch up.

". . . So the next thing I knew, the cop stopped chasing me," I managed to hear Nathan say as I got within earshot. He panted as he spoke, out of breath from running.

"Why would he stop chasing you?" Bosco asked.

Nathan shrugged. "He must've gotten an APB or something."

"So what do we do next?" Biv wondered aloud.

Nathan shrugged. "So now we beat Mr. Rogers at his own game. We'll say we dropped the bust, and it broke. But that's all we'll say. He'll, of course, want to know about the drugs, and he'll know we're lying, but he won't be able to say anything."

"I don't think that's such a hot idea," Bosco said. "He could, you know. . . like, have you bumped off."

"Or all of us," Montana added.

Biv turned to face her friends and stuck out her arms to make everything come to a halt. "This is nuts. Either we shit or we get off the pot."

"Such unladylike language," Montana chided.

"Oh, go fuck yourself," Biv answered back.

"You know, on second thought Biv's right," Nathan said. "Without the bust it is best we don't go back at all. It's too risky. But we need a way to get someplace else. And do it fast before Mr. Rogers finds us."

Montana said, "You sure do change your mind a lot."

Biv poked her in the ribs.

Everyone grew quiet. Finally, Montana said, "Maybe we can open up the grating and climb down and get the drugs."

Biv said, "That's a possibility. A stupid one, but a possibility."

"I'm not going to sell my body," Montana declared.

"Like anyone would pay for it," commented Biv.

"This is bullshit," Bosco said. "We have nothing to sell, and panhandling takes too long."

"We could set ourselves up in front of a church," Biv said. "We'll say we're collecting money for the homeless. It'd be true, right?"

"Too risky," Nathan decided. "But at least we're thinking on our feet."

"We could come up with some elaborate con," Bosco said. "You know, like those guys who say, 'It's my wife's birthday and I lost my wallet.'"

Nathan brightened. "I got it. It stared me right in the face the whole time. We go back to my hometown. We can walk it in a day through the back roads. No one will see us. Late at night, I break in to my grandmother's flat. She doesn't trust banks so she keeps her cash in a sewing box in her bedroom. I used to steal from it all the time, and she never noticed."

"How much does she have?" Biv asked.

"Enough to get us someplace other than here."

10

The walk took forever. Montana insisted on strolling at leisure, because, she claimed, it upset her to be told to hurry up. With Biv's five dollars, the four of them were able to split a coke and get a couple more candy bars. When they had to follow a wooded trail, Montana kept saying that there better not be any poison ivy. If a cop car drove past them, they kept walking and tried to appear as relaxed as possible.

They arrived at Lizzie's flat at about two in the morning. That marked the first time Nathan came back to his old neighborhood since being adopted by the Rainbows. While it's always haunting to go back to someplace you used to live, that case must've been especially so, given the stark darkness and quiet. I have dreams like this sometimes. I'm alone in the dark on a deserted street. Then I wake up, and I *am* alone in the dark on a deserted street, only it doesn't scare me anymore. Dreams are much worse than life, don't you agree?

The neighborhood looked the same, albeit a few more years dilapidated.

"Man, this is where you grew up?" Bosco said. "I had no idea."

"If you want, we can go by your house, too," Nathan teased. "The town mansion."

Bosco replied, "No way."

"So now what?" Biv wanted to know.

"I get in through the back steps. She keeps a key on top of the doorframe. Everyone just wait here."

Nathan found the key in the place where it used to be kept, and he stepped inside the dumpy flat that had been his home. He allowed himself a few seconds to gaze at Zelda's old bedroom and the alcove he called his bedroom. The rooms were the same mess he remembered them to be. He stood for a moment where Zelda's dead body had been discovered; Lord only knew what he thought. Then he padded like a cat into Lizzie's room. She snored a little. Her long, thin white hair was spread across her pillow. The sewing box remained where she'd always kept it. Nathan opened it. He found a thick wad of one hundred dollar bills. Nathan thought for a moment and decided to take about half of the money.

He put the box back in its place and turned to leave. A hand grabbed his leg.

"Oh my God, it's my grandson," Lizzie said, with mock enthusiasm. "I knew you'd come back to me." She sat up in bed and turned on her bedside lamp. "Now put the goddamn money back."

"Grandma, I'm sorry," Nathan said. "I'm in a jam. I didn't know what else to do."

Lizzie opened her nightstand drawer and took out a handgun. "Your sympathy act never worked with me, not even when you were a baby. Put the damn money back."

Nathan did as his grandmother told him to do. His natural tendency to respect his elders got buried under all the bad publicity.

"So what the hell happened? Did that fancy-shmancy new family throw you out?"

"Not in a literal sense," he replied. "But things didn't work out. When they moved to a different house, I didn't go with them. Didn't they tell you?"

Lizzie looked at him, as if his face could tell her more than his words. "No. As a matter of fact, the last couple of checks I sent Elena were returned to me by the post office. Where did they move to?"

"I don't have the address."

"Why didn't you come to me sooner?"

"I didn't want to burden you, Grandma. But now I have no choice. I have three friends outside. They're homeless, too. We were staying with a bad man. He tried to shoot us up with heroin so that we'd become drug addicts and do whatever he said."

I didn't blame him for giving the story a bit of varnish. Having spared her the gory details of the Rainbows, he needed to express an emotional truth, if not a literal one. Sometimes we balance a lie by telling another lie. And anyway, it's normal for teenagers to fib.

Lizzie said, "I'm glad you had the brains to leave."

It hardly surprised me that she felt no responsibility for what happened to Nathan, nor could she bring herself to say she felt sorry for him.

"I can't stay here," Nathan said. "It would never work."

"So who invited you? You think that at my age I want to deal with some fuck-ass teenager who steals from me?"

"No, I guess not."

"Look, get your friends and bring them in. They can stay here tonight."

Obediently, Nathan brought his three friends into the flat.

"Here they are," he said to his grandmother, a few minutes later.

"What a bunch of losers," Lizzie said, looking them over. Turning to Bosco, she added, "Aren't you the shit who gave my grandson such a bad time?"

"No," Nathan lied. "You're thinking of someone else."

"In my day," Lizzie said, "You did as you were told. It didn't matter if you had a nice little happy family or not. You stuck together."

Nathan must have resisted the impulse to remind her that she kicked him out of the house.

"But Nathan's Grandma," said Montana, "my stepfather used to have sex with me."

"Oh horseshit," Lizzie replied. "I get it all day long on TV. 'They molested me, my boyfriend isn't the father of my triplets,' or whatever the hell it is. Kids anymore—they grow up in trashcans like cockroaches."

"But it's true, I—"

"Look around, and find places to sleep," Lizzie interrupted. "There're blankets in the hall closet and in the other bedroom. Except you, Nathan. We're going to talk."

"Uh, sure, Grandma." He sat at the edge of her bed as his friends scurried about like mice.

"I'm older than sin," Lizzie said. "I could croak at any moment. So I'm glad you came because I want you to know—I think your mother Zelda is better off dead. At the time, those crooked lawyers never gave us five seconds to talk about it. But I ran into this theater hotshot who used to hang around and . . . you know, diddled with her. I realized that I'm relieved more than anything else that she died. Do you understand what I'm saying?"

Nathan grew quiet, and then said, "I don't know what to say."

"Actually, you just told me all I need to know," Lizzie remarked. "Now we never have to talk about it again."

"Who is this theater guy?"

"Nobody. Someone but no one."

"Grandma, I—"

"Shut up, Nathan." She reached to turn off her lamp. "Get some sleep, you have a big day ahead of you. Oh, and by the way—that bullshit about your father being dead. He isn't. He's too crazy to die."

"Grandma, how do you—"

"I know what I know. Go the hell to sleep."

The girls slept in Zelda's old bed, while Nathan and Bosco slept on the floor. Nathan fell asleep fast, while the other three whispered and giggled.

In the morning, Lizzie woke the foursome up. "Get dressed, you little fuckups," she said. "We're going to the bus station."

Montana stretched and yawned. "Can we eat first?"

"Yes, I'm making eggs Benedict with fresh-squeezed orange juice," replied Lizzie. "Of course you can't eat first. Get a doughnut at the station."

The four kids, plus Lizzie, crowded into a local cab. At the bus depot, she looked up at the arrival and departure times and said, "Where do you jokers want to go?"

They turned to Nathan for an answer. He picked a town about four hours away known for being a hip, anything-goes kind of place, where they stood a good chance of blending in.

Lizzie walked them to the ticket counter. "These are my grandchildren," she told the girl at the window. "Make sure they arrive safely." Then she showed the window clerk her ID and paid for four round-trip tickets. I assumed that they were round-trip to arouse less suspicion. When no one looked, Lizzie gave Nathan a chunk of cash.

"This should square us away," she said.

"I appreciate it, Grandma. Really."

"Don't be stupid and spend it on bullshit," she warned him.

Lizzie sat with the four young people until their bus had to leave. Then she gave each one a kiss on the cheek and said, "Be safe, my loved ones. Remember to call me as soon as you arrive."

Then she went up to the bus driver and said, "You keep an eye on my grandchildren. You know how teenagers can be."

He tipped his hat to her and said, "Glad to help, ma'am."

She waved at them as the bus drove off.

It would take me a good week or so to make my way to Nathan's new town and find him. In the meantime, I heard something in the news about a cop in the old city being found dead, but I didn't pay much attention to it.

11

In the new town, business happened pretty much on one main street. This made my search easier. I spotted Biv first. She worked behind the counter of a rarified sandwich shop— the kind of place that sold fancy mustards in fancy jars with ribbons and served sandwiches on croissants.

Something happened there, which I found difficult to abide.

Someone ordered a sandwich that had melted Swiss cheese on top and then on top of that, fresh green lettuce leaves. A major unsolved mystery of my life is why people like lettuce that turns wilted and slimy from heat. I followed behind the girl, who ordered the sandwich to go, and a block or two later, I approached her.

"Your slimy lettuce turns my stomach," I said. She pretended to be startled, but I knew all about her kind of person.

When Biv got off work, I followed her to her new home, if you could call it that.

A garage of a split-level house functioned as living quarters for the four kids. From the vantage point of a side window, I could see the garage door had a padlock, and on the inside someone stuffed insulation into the cracks. The only light came from an industrial bulb that hung overhead. The homier touches included a double-burner hotplate, a makeshift table, and an old refrigerator. A small corner had a shower, sink, and toilet; a room divider covered in rotting fabric gave some illusion of privacy.

They had a homemade bunk bed of sorts, double-sized, so two people could fit on a given mattress. It also functioned as the only place to sit, other than the concrete floor. Bosco and Biv shared the lower bunk, while Nathan and Montana took the upper. Nothing sexual occurred when they'd all bed down for the night, but sometimes when Nathan went out,

Bosco had sex with either or both girls. Nathan never knew about this, or else he didn't care. It crossed my mind that maybe Nathan had the hots for Bosco. As a modern, broad-minded person, I had no problem accepting a gay son. But this didn't seem to be the case, either. For reasons I couldn't begin to fathom, he had zero interest in sex. And not just sex—even the idea of going with someone or for that matter kissing or holding hands.

The sleepy upscale town offered few jobs, but each kid managed to find a gig. Besides Biv working at the sandwich shop, Montana took care of some rich brats during the day, Bosco moved wood at the local lumber yard, and Nathan got paid in what were once again called love offerings at a kind of New Age health spa. There were hot tubs and masseurs and yoga classes, but you could also have your palm or tarot cards interpreted or get a reading from a so-called psychic. Nathan possessed far too much intelligence to believe in any of this shit, but he learned from Elena Rainbow how to BS people with psychic mumbo jumbo. The aging hippie owners told him they'd never seen a pair of hands with so many lines on them, let alone so many mystic crosses. I assumed this meant when the two lines in your palm intersected into an X or a plus sign. I have quite a lot of them on my own hands.

"You see into people," the hippie woman told him. "You know more about them than they know themselves. You live in constant turmoil because you know how to hurt people as much as possible, but you try to stop yourself from doing this."

"Nathan, what am I thinking right now?" asked the hippie guy.

Nathan replied, "You'd like to fuck the girl who's looking at incense."

It didn't take a psychic to know the older guy had the hots for said girl; he eyeballed her like he had never seen a pair of tits before. But the hippie couple doubtless had few brain cells left after decades of drugs, and it didn't take much for Nathan to convince them.

"I had a feeling about you right away," the woman said. "You're so pure and beautiful. There are so many angels surrounding you. Do you ever see them?"

"Sometimes," Nathan said.

So day after day, Nathan sat on a cushion in a small room, with strings of beads in the doorway, and waited for people to come for a psychic reading. Speaking of reading, he enjoyed spending time with books. He had an especial fondness for true crime stories and would devour them for much of his day. But a few people trickled in. Some even became repeat customers. I guessed he averaged about a hundred bucks a week—all tax-free. Nathan's roommates took the whole thing seriously, but he refused to give them readings and insisted he had no psychic abilities, he just found people easy to understand. It is with no small amount of paternal pride that I say he inherited this talent from me. No way did it come from Zelda.

I had a low threshold for this type of crap, so I didn't often watch my son in a session, but I got the general idea one day when a kid about the same age as Nathan came to seek direction for his young life. Nathan sat cross-legged and barefoot on the cushion; a stick of incense burned. He made no effort to move from the cushion or welcome the other kid. He pointed to a cushion on the opposite wall for the kid to sit on.

Neither guy said anything for a minute or so. Then Nathan said, "Well?"

"I. . . I want to know what life means," said the kid. Not what you'd call a small order, yet the dopey kid thought he'd get the answer from some rip-off fellow teen.

"What do you mean, what does life mean?" Nathan replied.

The kid struggled to find the right words. "Everyone but me is interested in life. Nothing means anything. I feel like I'm made of wood. Everyone else gets so excited, but I don't care."

Nathan said, "Aren't you lucky."

"Huh?"

"You understand that nothing means anything except the meaning people give it. Underneath it all, you're the one who's right. Because there really is nothing there. It's a gift to understand that. It means you can make your life anything you want. How old are you?"

"I'm fifteen."

"You're a baby," said seventeen-year-old Nathan. "When you turn sixteen, you'll be happier."

"Will I find a girlfriend?"

"No."

The kid looked crestfallen. "Why not?"

"Because you don't take anyone seriously. You enjoy the chase, but once you nab someone you have no interest in keeping it going."

"How did you know that?" The kid looked flabbergasted.

"I'm psychic."

"Can't I ever change?"

Nathan lit a fresh stick of incense. "No, you'll always be this way. You'll never like anyone much, so no one will like you very much in return."

"You know, it's weird, but I've never been sure if I'm an introvert who pretends to be an extrovert, or if I'm an extrovert who pretends to be an introvert."

"You're an introvert," Nathan answered. "To be an extrovert, you have to enjoy people, which you don't."

"What should I do?"

"Get used to it. Enjoy what you can."

On another day, I watched him counsel some hippie welfare mama. Her bratty kid, maybe five years old, kept sticking out her tongue at her mother.

"I want to know if my boyfriend Christopher is my true love," she beseeched of Nathan.

"No," he replied. "If he were, you wouldn't have to ask."

The woman acted like she experienced an epiphany. "Wow, I never thought of it that way before."

"It isn't about him, it's about you. What do you think is going to change if you find, as you call it, true love?"

The woman tried to ignore her daughter's stuck-out tongue. "Why, I'd be happy. Content."

"Why do you assume that Christopher or anyone else wants responsibility for your happiness? What makes you so great?"

"I—I just figure everyone wants to find love. Isn't that what we're put on this earth to do?"

Nathan scratched his foot. "No, it isn't."

"Oh. I didn't know that."

"You'll keep getting laid a lot, if that's any consolation. You'll have another kid, once this one gets a little older." In so many words, she needed more kids to stay on welfare.

"Will it be a boy or a girl?"

"What difference does it make?"

"Gee, I dunno. Don't they say girls are easier?"

He pointed at her daughter, whose tongue kept wagging back and forth. "Well, what do you think?"

If Nathan said half the things he said as a regular person as opposed to a "psychic," he probably would've gotten punched in the face. But since he was supposed to have special powers, people took him at his word, and left carrying the burden of their foolishness.

The foursome lucked out in finding this spendy yet laid-back town where people rented to minors with no questions asked. Underneath the liberal guise, you found a bunch of rich and snooty people. If you expressed a fondness for Burger King or a dislike for National Public Radio, you'd be as ostracized as a commoner at Buckingham Palace. I could tell Nathan hated phonies, but he tolerated his environment for the time being. He seldom left town, though he did head back home when he heard his grandmother died. As Fate would have it, Mr. Rogers turned up dead at about the same time. Someone banged his head against the wall until his skull cracked open. Police found a baggie of sticky white powder stuffed into the bloodied crack in his head.

Nathan must have felt happy to be back with his roommates. They had a special dinner to celebrate his return. Everyone sat on throw pillows on the concrete floor, using half of an old door on cinder blocks as a table. Bosco got his boss to buy a bottle of inexpensive wine for the occasion, and though Nathan had no interest in drinking, he did participate in the toast.

"Here's to our friendship," Montana said. "May we always be as close as we are now."

"To our friendship," said the others, and their cheap wine glasses clicked.

As they ate the special dinner of take-out meatloaf and mashed potatoes, Biv said, "Why would any of us ever want to be anything but as close as we are now? I never knew I could be so happy."

"Me, either," Bosco said.

Nathan put another slice of meatloaf on his plate. "Well, things do happen to people."

"But not us," Montana said. "Let's take a pledge to always be together."

"Right on," said Bosco, smiling at the others. "I'll take that pledge."

"Me, too," Biv concurred, polishing off her glass of wine.

"What about you, Nathan?" asked Montana.

He swallowed a savory bite of meatloaf. "Sure, why not?"

12

Paradise attracts its share of trouble. Mere days after their heartfelt pledge of eternal devotion to each other, Montana turned out to be pregnant. Oops.

Actually, this is the abbreviated version of the tale. Montana, despite—or maybe because of—having been molested by her stepfather and then put to work by Arnold the Pimp, remained naïve when it came to what were once called the birds and the bees. While aware that sexual intercourse had something to do with how babies got made, she'd never had a formal education on the various nuts and bolts involved. In fact, the matter came up by accident.

On a Sunday afternoon, Montana, Biv, and Bosco were sitting at leisure on the floor in the garage, passing around a joint—or more accurately, one of several joints. Nathan stretched out on the upper bunk, as usual not partaking of the marijuana, and read a true crime book—a sordid tale of a church deacon who made a bloodbath of his wife and six kids. As if their stoner talk followed a logical path, Montana asked, "Have you ever wondered if there's life on like other planets?"

"I don't have to," Biv remarked, which witticism went right past Montana, though Bosco laughed.

Montana continued. "I mean, if you think about how many other planets there are, doesn't it seem like there must be life someplace else? I mean, why here, but not on . . . what do they call it again?"

"Mars?" Bosco offered, taking a hit off the latest joint.

"Right, Mars. No, wait, I mean the moon."

Biv said, "The moon isn't a planet."

"Well, what is it, then?" Montana wanted to know. "It's a round thing in the sky, isn't it?"

"It's a moon," Biv answered.

Montana found this the funniest damned thing she ever heard. "Oh, right. It's a moon called the moon. Like that really makes sense."

"Biv's right." Bosco rolled a fresh joint and lit it. "The moon orbits planet earth. That's why it's a moon."

Montana received the fresh joint with relish. "If it orbits the earth, how come you can't see it in the daytime?"

"Because it's sleeping." Biv inhaled deeply. "The sun is awake during the day, then it goes to sleep at night, which is when the moon awakens."

"You're making this up, right?" Montana determined.

Bosco hogged the joint, but Montana nudged him to hand it to her.

"I'm so sorry, Montana," said Biv. "I should've known I couldn't pull one over on you."

"Anyway," Montana said, "you made me lose my trend of thought."

Biv inhaled the joint. "Oh, please tell me it isn't so."

Bosco laughed some more. "You were talking about life on other planets."

"Gee, thanks, Bosco," Biv said. "I'm forever in your debt."

"I read online about some dude who got abducted by aliens," said Bosco. "They like examined him, and then brought him back to earth."

"Well, then there has to be life on other planets," Montana deduced. "What did the aliens look like?"

"He said they had these weird eyes like Brazil nuts. Green skin or some shit. It's not like I remember everything about it. It happened a long time ago."

"Do you mean a long time ago that you read it, or when the aliens came?" queried Montana.

Biv put her hands to her face. "I can't stand it. Please, someone, make it stop."

"Both," Bosco said. "I read it a long time ago, so that means it happened an even longer time ago."

"Wow, that is so weird," Montana reflected, taking a vigorous hit off the joint. "I never thought about it before. It's like something happens, and then something else happens because the first thing happened. Do you see what I mean? It's like I've been puking every morning for a like a week, but that makes me drink Coke to settle my stomach. And then the guy who put the Coke in the bottle gets paid. Do you see what I mean? Do you get it?"

"Let's rewind the movie," Biv said. "You've been getting sick every morning for a week? When's the last time you had your period?"

Montana shrugged. "I guess it's been a couple of months. Why?"

Biv ignored the joint that came her way. "My God, Montana. Have you taken a pregnancy test?"

"Pregnancy? I don't want to be pregnant. When I fuck, I shut my eyes real tight and think to myself, 'No, no, no.' You know—like no, I'm not getting pregnant. I believe in mind over matter."

Bosco's demeanor became more serious. "You have, though, had sex with other guys recently?" His face wore a poignant look of hope.

Montana thought about it. "I guess so."

"Holy fuck," Bosco said. "What are we going to do?"

"Hold your horses," said Biv. "One thing at a time. I'll go get a pregnancy test. Anyone want to chip in?"

The test proved positive, so Bosco decided to buy a second pregnancy test for Montana. This one showed a positive result, too.

"I never thought I'd get pregnant," Montana reflected.

"Apparently," said Biv. "What are you going to do?"

"You mean, about having a baby?" Montana asked.

"*Yes*," Biv replied. "Are you getting an abortion or what?"

Montana looked wounded. "I'd never get an abortion. I'm going to have this baby."

"And put it up for adoption?" Bosco asked.

"I happen to think I'll make an excellent mother," said Montana. "I'm great with the kids I take care of. Their mother is always telling me how wonderful I am."

"Well, ain't that a motherfucker," Biv said. "Do you have any idea where you'd live with a baby, or how to support it?"

"Yeah," said Bosco, doing his best to seem nothing more than an interested third party. "What about all that stuff?"

Nathan, who throughout all this never budged from the upper bunk, set down the book about the crazy killer deacon. "Ask the woman you work for if you can move in. You said it's a big house, and she's divorced." He went back to reading his book.

Montana brightened. "Nathan, what a great idea. I'll talk to her tomorrow."

Bosco said, "What about . . . like, the father? Do you think it's me or not?"

"Maybe Nathan can use his psychic powers to tell us," Montana said.

Without looking up from his book, Nathan said, "I told you, I'm not psychic. Get a DNA paternity test when the baby is born."

"Doesn't that cost money?" Montana asked.

"Take it to family court. Ask the judge to order a test."

"What about in the meantime?" Bosco asked.

"Wait. What else can you do?"

"Nathan, you always say such helpful things," Biv said.

"Not really. It's easy to figure something out when you step away from it."

I hoped my son would find a more constructive outlet for his intelligence than just sort of hanging around. The Yale side of me didn't want to see him waste his life. Giving the devil his due, Mr. Rogers had a point. Nathan really could do better than these three mixed-up kids.

Case in point: about three weeks after Montana, Biv announced her pregnancy. Even Montana smelled a rat.

"You're pregnant?" Montana said. "Gee, that's original."

Biv shrugged. "What can I say? Shit happens."

"What did you do, put a hole in the rubber?"

Biv's face turned crimson with embarrassment. "I'm not even going to dignify that with a comment."

"Oh yes, little Miss Dignity, spreading her legs for anything with a dick. You're just jealous. I'm moving to a nice house with the lady I work for. I probably-ish have a permanent connection to Bosco. Were you afraid you were going to lose him to me? How pathetic."

A despondent Bosco sat on the floor, looking at no one. "We had a perfectly nice arrangement. What went wrong? It's gotten so complicated."

"What went wrong, as you put it," Biv said, "is that Steve Sperm had the hots for Olga Ovum."

"I used a condom," Bosco protested.

"Maybe it slipped or something," Biv theorized.

"Or maybe you put a hole in it, Biv," Montana reiterated. "Why should anyone trust what you say? Everyone knows you're full of shit."

"Well, it's possible that Bosco isn't the father."

"But you've got your fingers crossed that he is. I know how you operate. You always have to have the last word."

"Look who's talking."

It fascinated me to watch both girls all but tear each other's hair out over Bosco. It's true that he evolved into a kind, easygoing person, quite appealing in his big bear way. I supposed you could call him a good catch if you weren't mature enough to figure in things like what kind of future did he have as a high school dropout with no particular job skill. And PS: No money. Bosco made it known that his father disinherited him. Someone else may have been inspired to make it on his own to prove he didn't need anyone's help. But at this time, anyway, Bosco's psychological balance hinged upon staying poor. In our get-rich-quick world, it's often overlooked that some people are afraid to have money.

Getting ready to sleep under a freeway ramp one night, I asked my Harvard friend Charlie why some people get a chip on their shoulder over money.

"It goes back to how people are raised," Charlie answered. "If parents told their children to hate money, the kids would be determined to make millions. Reverse psychology. Parents don't just provide food and shelter. They provide money. And what normal kid wants to be like his parents?"

As usual, Charlie gave me a lot to chew on. I had trouble falling asleep until I listened to the fast cars overhead, one after the other, and it became like counting sheep.

Anyway, Montana moved in with her single mother boss, but she still came by the garage almost daily to rub Biv's face in it. Biv had plans to move in with her grandmother as her due date approached. Montana considered Biv's relying on a family member to be "cheating," as if they played a game called "No Family Allowed." Biv pointed out that she still didn't speak to her parents, but Montana called her a wimp just the same.

Montana named her baby girl Dakota because the Dakotas were next to Montana. About a month later, Biv had a boy whom she named Leaf. Both kids looked like generic baby blobs. You could make a case that this one or that one looked like Bosco. Montana claimed that Dakota had Bosco's chin, while Biv convinced herself that Leaf had Bosco's ears. But Bosco lay in the eye of the beholder, as it were. Only DNA testing could resolve the matter once and for all. Both young mothers petitioned the court for a test, but no cigar.

"Now what do we do?" Biv asked Nathan.

"Go on one of those talk shows that does DNA testing. They'll pay for it."

"Another great, idea, Nathan," said Montana. "Gosh, I always wanted to be on TV."

13

A few weeks later, Biv, Montana, and Bosco were guests on *The Chip Beverage Show*, in an episode entitled, "Man Up, and be a Father." The producers paid for plane fare, hotel rooms, meals, and childcare. The three kids offered to pitch in so that Nathan could come along, but he barely looked up from the true crime book he read to say thanks, but no thanks.

I made sure I got in front of a TV set when the program aired. I can only assume all four kids did the same, since they didn't own a TV.

A failed actor who hosted a failed game show before finding his niche as a talk show host, Chip Beverage had a shameless greed for fame, which I found obnoxious.

"God had other plans for me," he once told a reporter, when asked if he missed his so-called acting career.

It amazed me, the things that people said were part of God's plan: winning a contest, being on TV, joining an online club. The list went on and on. So God said, "Let there be *The Chip Beverage Show*." Chip, a short guy with dyed blond hair, had a slipperiness about him that would've turned jellyfish green with envy. Especially when he smiled.

"Welcome to the show," he said to the TV camera. "Today we're going to meet several young ladies who want to say to the men in their lives, 'Man up, and be a father.'"

The audience went gaga, clapping and cheering as though this topic spoke to the essence of their beings.

"Now," continued Chip, "first let me introduce to you Bev and Montana. Let's give them a Chip Beverage-style welcome."

The audience applauded as if being presented with Nobel laureates.

Chip continued. "Both Bev and Montana recently had babies." The back screen projected photos of the two clueless infants; the audience uttered a loud, collective "aw."

"On the right," Chip stated, "you have Montana's four-month-old daughter, Dakota. And on the left is Bev's two-and-a-half-month-old son, Leaf."

"Excuse me," said Biv. "My name isn't Bev, it's Biv."

"So sorry," said Chip, looking at the index card in his hand. "Folks, this is Biv, not Bev." But afterward, he went back to calling her Bev.

Biv waved into the camera. "Hi, Grandma."

"Bev and Montana were the best of friends," he continued, "until they found out they both slept with the same man."

The audience could not have been more vocal in its disapproval.

"His name is Bosco, and we'll meet him in a moment. But get this. Both Biv and Montana think Bosco is the father of their babies."

The audience could not have been more flabbergasted.

This led into a short film clip of Biv saying to the camera, "Bosco, you know you're Leaf's father. I want you to man up, and get that"—bleeped out—"whore Montana to leave us alone."

Then came a film clip of Montana. "Biv, you're nothing but a cheap"—bleeped out—"whore who thinks you can take away my man. Bosco, today we're going to send her packing once and for all. I want you to man up."

The audience just sat there, spellbound.

"Before we meet Bosco," Chip said, "let's hear what he had to say."

A brief film clip of Bosco came on. To the disappointment of the audience, he did not partake of the expected stud lingo in these scenarios, for example, "You're both a couple of whores."

"Biv and Montana," he said instead. "I'll man up and be a father to anyone who is my kid. But you both say you had other partners when you got pregnant. And your kids look nothing like me."

Bosco's words were civilized, but the audience booed him anyway.

"Biv," Chip said, "do you think that Leaf looks like Bosco?"

"Yes, I do, Chip. He so looks like Bosco."

"No he doesn't," Montana begged to differ. "Dakota looks like Bosco. When she gets older, people will think they're twins."

Chip decreed, "I think it's time we meet Bosco. Please give him a Chip Beverage welcome."

But the audience would have none of it. They booed again as Bosco made his way to the stage. After shaking hands with Chip, he sat down between the two girls. Big mistake. This inspired Biv and Montana to stand up and shout back and forth a chaotic mess of bleeped out language. The audience responded as though watching the greatest event of all time unfold before its eyes.

Chip got the girls to sit back down, though each moved her seat farther away from the other.

"We gave DNA tests to the babies and to Bosco, and I have the results right here," Chip announced, waving a manila envelope. "But before I announce them, I just want to check with Bosco. On the tape you said you were willing to man up and be a father if either baby is yours. Do you still think that way?"

"I sure do, Chip," Bosco replied. The audience gave him a respectable if somewhat subdued round of applause, with a few lingering boos mixed in.

"Okay, here we go," Chip said. "Bosco, regarding four-month-old Dakota, you are not the father."

The fickle audience cheered as Montana fled the stage in a deluge of humiliation. Bosco buried his face in his hands as Chip Beverage ran after Montana. She looked like the Wicked Witch of the West, melting down to nothing in a puddle of tears.

"We can help you, Montana," offered Chip. "We can test another man. Do you know someone else who might be the father?"

"Y-yes," she demurred through her tears.

"Remember, we're only halfway done," Chip reminded the audience, as he returned to his seat on the stage.

"Montana's always been a whore," Biv interjected.

Bosco lifted up his head; it looked like he'd been crying, too, when Chip said, "Regarding two-month old Leaf, Bosco, you are not the father."

The audience rose to its feet, giving Bosco a standing ovation as he gave Biv a hug. She did not run off the stage but instead chose to stay in her seat as she hurled more bleeped-out language at Montana.

After the show came a newsbrief about possible new leads in the cop killing from a while back. It's funny how something like that can seem less important to people than a couple of girls who got knocked up and hate each other's guts.

In the month between going on the show and the broadcast, Biv and Montana severed all ties to each other and to Bosco. He continued to be roommates with Nathan for the time being. But now they each had to pay half the rent on the sleazy garage, and since neither were minors anymore, they looked to find better living arrangements.

Biv and Montana told Nathan they wanted to stay in touch with him, but he couldn't be bothered with either one. I can't say I blamed him. Their stupid drooling babies made for better company than the mothers themselves. Of course, I wondered, too, if he didn't feel more than a little betrayed. The little makeshift family he had fell apart in nothing flat. But he survived much worse, and he did not dwell on his sense of loss.

Nathan sat on the floor cushions of his psychic room, reading about a serial killer. The woman who co-owned the business came in to tell him that one of his clients hung himself—the kid whom Nathan predicted no one would ever like. He looked up from his book and said, "I'm not surprised." Then he went back to his reading. I found it refreshing that Nathan never felt compelled to display insincere emotions. He didn't pretend to miss people when he didn't. Life's too short to have to prove yourself to other people.

14

Aristotle, I think, compared life to an acorn, and said all that we will be is predetermined. At eighteen, Bosco reminded me of a young tree sprouting its true colors. Released from the purgatory of Biv and Montana, and with his street kid mentality fading into the distance, he thought in earnest about his future. Nathan decided to tag along. They got a book about passing the GED and tutored each other every evening. Nathan had a natural gift for science and math, while Bosco showed talent for writing. They both muddled through social studies as best they could. Upon passing, the two young men enrolled at a local community college. Bosco majored in English, while Nathan majored in criminology. They got campus jobs and student loans as needed to keep a roof over their heads—a no-frills but decent one-bedroom apartment in a student-friendly building. Bosco paid a little extra to have the bedroom, while Nathan economized and slept in the living room. When Bosco brought girls home late at night—a frequent occurrence—Nathan was a heavy sleeper, like his dad. Biv also attended the community college, but when the boys crossed paths with her they kept walking as if they never saw her.

After community college, Nathan and Bosco attended and graduated from the local state college. Bosco got accepted into a graduate program in English at a liberal arts college about a thousand miles away. Nathan chose to stay put at the state college and get a master's in criminology.

They had a little party for themselves their last night in the apartment. Bosco drank quite a lot of wine, but he held his liquor well. Nathan abstained as always, but he could go with the flow of stoned or drunken conversations. He had years of experience at that point.

Having been through so much together, and for so long, it proved a bittersweet occasion.

"I wonder if I'll make friends, and all that stuff," Bosco said. "The people are different there. More conservative."

Nathan shrugged. "Sometimes there's good reason to be conservative. You'll do fine."

"Do you ever think about Mr. Rogers?" Bosco asked.

"Nope."

"They never solved his murder, did they?"

"Not that I know of."

"What about the girls?"

"What happened? Did they get murdered?"

Bosco hit him with a pillow. "Very funny. I mean do you ever think about them?"

"No. I expect they'll both have more babies. With 31 flavors of fathers."

"I feel bad about them. I could've been nicer. I should've been. They went through a lot, and I didn't make it any easier. Shit, man, they were only sixteen or something."

"So were you. And they didn't make it easy for you, either. They both wanted to marry you. And you're not the father of their kids."

"I easily could've been."

"But you weren't. I—" Nathan stopped himself. "Anyway, what happens happens. Is is."

"I guess you're right, dude."

"Of course I am. It's my psychic gift." They both laughed.

"You know," Bosco said, "it's ancient history and all, but I still feel bad for how I treated you when we were kids. Bullying—it's the worst thing I ever did. There's kids who commit suicide from it."

"I never think about it," Nathan assured him. "But in a weird way I got something out of it. It gave me . . . it gave me a kind of voice inside myself. And I've never for a moment thought about taking my life."

"You're the strongest person I've ever known, Nathan."

Nathan made the classic muscleman pose with his arms. "Yeah, I'm Superman. Or at least Batman."

Bosco poured more wine. "I meant strong on the inside, you nimrod. It made me jealous as a kid. Whatever I dished out, you could take it. I wanted to break you, so that I'd feel strong, too. Because I sure didn't."

"Sounds like in a way you really bullied yourself. You still do."

"How do you mean?'

Nathan hit Bosco back with the same pillow. "Look at yourself. Other kids who went through what you did end up in jail or in a nuthouse or dead. And here you are, going to some snooty grad school. You are strong, dude."

"Huh, I never think of myself that way. I read a poem in English class, I can't remember who wrote it. Something about a homeless bum, described as being a gray dot. That's how I feel a lot of the time. Like I'm a gray dot."

This struck me as about the oddest thing I ever heard. I never for a moment in my life saw myself as nothing more than a gray dot. True, I became invisible to most people, but I saw that as everyone else's problem, not mine.

"Everyone's a gray dot," Nathan said. "Life is a gray dot."

Bosco thought for a moment and refilled his glass. "If that's true, don't you think it's depressing?"

Nathan considered. "No. I never get depressed. If I start to feel unhappy, I. . . I do something to feel better."

"What makes you feel better, man?"

Nathan narrowed his eyes. "I dunno. I like to watch people sleep. I know that sounds dumb, but it's true. It's like I'm seeing them for who they really are. I guess you could say the truth makes me feel better."

"But the truth is still a gray dot, right?"

"Yeah, but it's still better."

Bosco laughed. "I get it, I really do. Thanks."

Nathan looked surprised. "You're welcome, but I didn't do anything."

"Speaking of feeling good," Bosco said, "can I ask you something?"

"It's a free country."

"Dude, what's up with you? You're never interested in anyone. If you're like gay or whatever, you know I'm cool with that. But isn't there someone you want to grill your hot dog?"

Nathan chuckled. "That's your specialty. I just don't have those feelings. Now let's talk about something else."

They stayed up past dawn, discussing their futures. Bosco planned to get a Ph.D. and become a college professor. He figured he'd get married and admitted to wanting a bunch of kids. Nathan wished to be a homicide detective and remain single. As the day grew bright, they carried Bosco's suitcases out to the street. They hugged; then they both turned away, Bosco to await his cab ride to the airport, and Nathan to go back inside the apartment. Bosco cried a little. Nathan seemed on the verge of tears but forced them back.

No sooner had Bosco rode off in his cab than Nathan received a visitor.

"Are you Nathan Nightbridge?" asked the unfamiliar man at the door.

"Yes."

"You are under arrest for the murders of Thor, Elena, and Wolf Rainbow. You have the right to remain silent. Anything you say or do can and will be held against you in a court of law. You have the right to an attorney. If you cannot afford an attorney, one will be provided for you. Do you understand these rights I have just read to you?"

"Yes, officer. Thank you."

15

The publicity Nathan got for Zelda's murder proved but an appetizer for the main course of the Rainbow Murders, as they became known in the headlines. I kept picturing these rainbows lying under a sheet at the morgue. It took the cops about six years to build a case against Nathan, which in itself showed bias in the investigation. From Day One, they had it in their heads that Nathan was guilty, and nothing dissuaded them. The fire that burned down the house and rendered the three corpses nothing but bags of charred bones made for a flawed investigation. If they found Nathan's DNA, it proved nothing because he lived there. Ditto if some busybody witness said they saw Nathan hanging around. But the state proceeded, as if the principle of innocent until proven guilty had been deleted from our criminal justice system. How ironic that Nathan sought to work within the very bureaucracy that victimized him not once but twice. This spoke volumes about his character.

The media made this huge stink about the fact that Nathan ran away right after the killings. But any idiot could understand that his actions made perfect sense. When he saw what happened, he took off like a bat out of hell, predicting he'd be charged with the murders. As for never showing any grief, the Rainbows didn't treat him in a way that inspired sentiment. Besides, Zelda's brutal stabbing death prepared him for the inevitable fact that people die, or more to the point that people get murdered. He may have been a virgin in the carnal sense, but he lost his death virginity years earlier.

The vultures from the press waited for Nathan at the police station. He didn't try to hide his face, but walked with cheerful resolution into the building and smiled for his mug shots.

The following morning, he announced his plan to represent himself at trial. "I can't afford a lawyer," Nathan told the court, "and I don't want to waste the valuable time of a public defender on such a specious case."

You'd have thought the judge would make the usual speech about how a lawyer who represents himself has a fool for a client, but he didn't. Nor did he assign a defense attorney to assist my son. Obviously, Nathan entered a plea of not guilty. The DA asked that bail be denied, but Nathan argued that these murders he did not commit happened six years ago, and he did not present a threat to the community. He added that as his own attorney, he needed freedom to build the best possible defense. The judge set bail at a half million dollars.

Since Nathan hardly had 500 G's in his pockets of loose change or for that matter, the $50,000 minimum required, the prosecutor walked away satisfied. But no one could've foreseen what Bosco Sinclair did. He flew back to town and showed up at his family mansion for the first time in years, begging on his knees for his father to post bail for Nathan. This took considerable courage, but it led to a happy reunion for father and son. Crazy Seymour Sinclair apologized for mistreating him and expressed relief at his son's sharp turn to the straight and narrow; Bosco even quit smoking. I only heard about the meeting secondhand, though I imagine there were a lot of hugs and tears and all that crap. But Nathan made bail. I cried tears of joy myself.

For once, Crazy Seymour sought to stay out of the limelight, so Bosco arrived alone to see Nathan be released after only a couple of days in lockup.

"Obviously, I can't thank you enough," Nathan said, as the two young men walked out into the open air of the noisy city. "But you need to get back to school."

Bosco laughed. "You're as bad as my dad." He proceeded to share how happy was the unexpected reunion.

As Bosco finished, he said, "So in a way, I should be thanking you. I can't tell you how great it feels to not have all that hate dragging me down."

Nathan said, "In a month or two years from now, you don't think you'll be pissed off at him again? That you'll regret saying you were sorry, too, since you didn't mean it?"

Bosco looked at Nathan, and then looked at him again. "You're right, I did apologize. How did you know that? In the moment, it felt like the thing to do. You know how it is. Someone says 'I'm sorry,' so you say, 'I'm sorry, too.' I don't think it's that big of a deal."

"I hope you're right."

Only then it dawned on me that Bosco had no mother. Crazy Seymour created such a dominant presence, sucking the air out of every space he entered, that you didn't even notice he had no wife. Divorce? Death? Your guess is as good as mine. Bosco never talked about his mother, or if he did, I never heard it. But maybe that explained the early bullying. Excepting total fuckups like Zelda, mothers provide their children with a moral compass to follow through life.

"Hey, man, I'm fine. You're the one I'm worried about. I shouldn't have gone on so long about my dad. Jesus, three counts of Murder One."

Nathan shrugged. "Shit happens."

"Dumb question—are you scared?"

"I'm glad to be out of jail. I'm claustrophobic. It drives me crazy to be confined."

"But what about the charges? And you're representing yourself?"

They stopped walking at a red light. Nathan pushed the button to get the "walk" sign; then he pushed it again and again. "Well, do you think I did it?"

"Of course not, though after what they did to you, I'd call it justifiable homicide. Man, you have the worst luck."

"Oh, I don't know. I've been through this before, and it turned out okay."

"No thanks to me. I'll never forgive myself for being so mean to you."

"I wish you would. It's history. The main thing is, the truth will win out. And I'm a damn good defense lawyer. I already got the judge to suppress a bunch of stuff for being prejudicial. But I shouldn't be discussing the case."

Though something of a farce, since every day the news media reminded the entire universe about Nathan's earlier court case, Nathan convinced the judge to suppress any mention of it, as well as any mention of his dubious pedigree. When you're on trial for murder, every little bit helps.

Bosco put his hand on Nathan's shoulder. "Is there anything you can't do?"

Nathan laughed. "Stay out of trouble."

Bosco laughed, too. "Oh, did I tell you? I got a postcard from Montana. She's moved to Alaska with her kid. I have no idea why."

"Neither does Montana."

Bosco laughed some more. "I forgot how funny you were, dude."

"By the way, where are we walking to?"

He jabbed Nathan's arm with his elbow. "You'll see."

A few minutes later, they were standing in front of the old building where Mr. Rogers had taken such dubious care of them all. It was almost unrecognizable.

"Can you believe it? Luxury lofts starting at two million five. Talk about depressing."

Nathan shrugged. "It's just a building."

"I wonder if they'll ever find who killed Mr. Rogers."

"I never think about it."

After a minute or two of staring at the building, Nathan said, "We have to get you on the airport shuttle. I just realized I never asked you about grad school."

"It's pretty cool. In fact, I miss it."

"Any hot babes?"

"Nah, they're all nerdy. I'm pretty much into studying. When I get my Ph.D., I'll start worrying about settling down."

They walked over to the bus depot, which likewise had undergone a facelift—fancy cafés, gift shops, and all spanking clean inside.

"Jesus, where do the lowlifes go?" Bosco asked.

"Heaven," Nathan replied.

"No, seriously. They're people, too. They have to live someplace."

"I guess that someplace is anyplace but here."

As the airport shuttle bus pulled over, the two old pals hugged. "Get yourself acquitted," Bosco said. "I've bet money on it."

"Don't worry about me," Nathan assured him. "I have all sorts of aces up my sleeve."

After watching Bosco's bus drive off, Nathan drove back to the small apartment they once shared and got busy on his computer, tracking down those aces.

A few hours later, he said out loud to no one but his shadow, "Let's see them get me now."

16

Each day of the trial, police escorted Nathan into and out of the courtroom through a back door. All the spectator seats were taken, and there were lines of people outside the main entrance. Some of them carried signs that said things like, "Burn in Hell, Nathan," or "Justice for the Rainbows," which made me laugh. But, like the last trial, there were a smaller number of people with signs that read, "We're with You, Nathan," and "Power to the Innocent." These sincere people reminded me of early Christians in imperial Rome. They were their own little cult. The few, the proud, like the saying goes.

This time, the prosecution took the form of a smug, frigid woman. She reminded me of a bank teller who smiles when she tells you no, she won't cash your check without proper ID, even though you haven't eaten in three days and you're begging on your knees as the security guards remove you from the bank. She could've been that hateful girl from the school citizenship club all grown up. When the time came for opening statements, Miss Frigid all but drooled in anticipation as she faced the jury.

"Thor, Elena, and Wolf Rainbow," she began, "were a delightfully unique family who, out of the goodness of their hearts, took in a teenaged boy whose misbehavior had proven too much for his grandmother. They fed him, clothed him, home-schooled him, and most important of all gave him a family's love. That boy is the man you now see seated in this courtroom."

With a scowl on her face that signaled a spirited bought of constipation, she walked over to Nathan and pointed at him.

"Nathan Nightbridge," she said, as if he were Adolf Hitler, "thanked the Rainbows for their many kindnesses by sadistically murdering them. He set them on fire in their charming home. This we shall prove beyond a shadow of a doubt."

Nathan rose to speak in his own defense. He looked so handsome in his dark blue suit.

"Good morning, ladies and gentlemen," he began. "I did not murder or in any way cause the deaths of Thor, Elena, and Wolf Rainbow. I loved them dearly. It is my hope that you find me not guilty of these awful charges as quickly as possible, so that you may return to your jobs and families. The only guilt I harbor is having to waste your time."

Skillfully, he only said he didn't murder the Rainbows. Had he stated that he never murdered anyone, it would've opened the door for the state to bring up the Zelda bit.

The prosecution called the first few witnesses, each of them duller than dishwater. They established that yes, the Rainbows were found dead in their home, blah-blah, which had been reduced to cinders by the fire. Nathan didn't even bother cross-examining them.

Things got livelier when some asshole forensics doctor took the stand. "Were you able to form a professional opinion as to how each victim died?" asked the heartless DA.

The nerdy forensics doctor said, "Yes. Their bodies were used as kindling to start the fire."

"I'm not sure I understand," the bullshitty prosecutor said.

"Given the position and arrangement of the bodies, we determined that the killer tightly bound up each victim with rope, and then placed them in the center of the living room floor. From what little remained of the rope after the fire, we concluded the perpetrator used Boy Scout knots. Then the victims were covered with paper and sticks and pieces of wooden furniture. Next, the killer set each person on fire, and the flames caught the wood and furniture and spread through the cottage."

"Were either gasoline or a propellant used to start the fire?"

"No. The fire spread naturally, so to speak. More slowly."

"And so each victim literally roasted to death? Fully conscious of the fire but helpless to stop it?"

"Yes. They would've been aware that they were being burned to death. And they would've died relatively slowly."

"How slowly?"

"It may have taken upward of an hour for them to lose consciousness."

"So they were conscious for maybe an hour as they burned to death?"

"Yes."

The prosecutor could not help but grin when several people in the courtroom gasped. "The defendant, Nathan Nightbridge, also resided in this home, did he not?"

"Yes."

"Did you find any evidence that links Mr. Nightbridge to these sordid murders?"

"Yes, the small piece of rope that survived the blaze. We didn't find DNA on it, but we did get a partial fingerprint that matches that of Mr. Nightbridge."

After getting the baggie that contained the piece of rope admitted into evidence, the super-bitch prosecutor looked at Nathan and said, "Your witness," as if to say, "Let's see you top that one."

"One moment, please, your honor." Nathan turned away, fighting back tears. The Rainbows treated him horribly, but he pitied them just the same.

"Now then," Nathan began. "How are you this morning, sir?"

"Uh, fine, I guess."

"You said you found a partial fingerprint match. A three-point match, if I recall correctly. That is less certain than a full match, am I right?"

"Well, yes, but—"

"So just to make sure I understand. This partial fingerprint is not one hundred percent reliable evidence?"

The nerd's face flustered. "It's not just some coincidence that the partial matched up to yours. It's—"

"Is it absolutely reliable? Yes or no?"

"No, but—"

"Thank you. Even if the fingerprint is mine, is it possible that I could've touched the rope at some other point in time?"

"Yes, it's possible, but—"

"For example, the Rainbows were marijuana growers and users. Their own son, Wolf, smoked marijuana all his life. I have never tried it. But I had to help with a lot of chores, including care of the—"

"Your honor," interrupted the prosecutor, "is there a question here?"

"Get to the point, Mr. Nightbridge," warned the judge, who looked like a dirty old man.

"Yes, your honor. Sir, is it possible the rope also got used for household purposes, such as gardening?"

"I wouldn't know. I wasn't there."

"No, you weren't, were you? You really don't know for certain who did those. . . those terrible things?"

The forensics fuckup sighed. "No, I suppose not."

"And your theory as to how they died—how one person somehow managed to tightly bind three people and pile objects on top of them with no resistance—it is exactly that, a theory?"

"Yes."

"And when you said it took the poor victims upward of an hour to die, that, too, is speculative, isn't it?"

"Yes."

"You mention Boy Scout knots. Would it surprise you to learn I never joined the Boy Scouts and know nothing about how they tie knots or do anything else?"

"Well, I, uh . . ."

"Never mind. Is there any evidence that these victims were drugged or that the killer had a weapon such as a knife or a gun?"

"No, the bodies were burned too badly. But obviously someone managed to do it."

"Or more than one person? Did you explore that possibility?"

"Yes, but it did not appear to be the case. The bodies were arranged at the exact same angles to each other, and this suggests one perpetrator. Someone methodical and exacting."

"So something did not appear to be the case and something else suggested something. So it is possible that another professional in your field could've reached a different conclusion?"

"Yes." He looked disgusted.

"In fact, were you not the chief forensic examiner in a murder trial four years ago, when—"

"Objection, your honor. Relevance?" The prosecutor tried in vain to hold back a belch; a mild titter passed over the courtroom.

The judge banged the gavel for order. "I'll allow it. Mr. Nightbridge will finish his question, and the witness will answer."

"Thank you, your honor." He turned to the witness. "Four years ago in this very courtroom," Nathan said, "did you not testify against a young woman who has since been exonerated for the alleged murder she committed?"

"I don't recall. I've worked on hundreds of cases."

"Then perhaps this will help you remember." Nathan came forward with a handful of news clippings.

The man read the articles for a moment with a look of disgust on his face. "You're talking about one case in a thirty-year career," he said.

Nathan smiled. "Thirty years? You must be near retirement. Congratulations."

"Your honor." The DA stood up in rage. "I mean, really."

"Jury will disregard. Mr. Nightbridge, I have my eye on you."

The State also called a shrink to the stand. He bore the name—and I kid you not—of Dr. Pepper. More accurately, Dr. Phillip Pepper, but Dr. Pepper nonetheless. We learned that he'd been a witness for the State in some two hundred cases.

"Now then, Dr. Pepper," said the ice-cold prosecutor. "Did you have occasion to examine the defendant?"

"Yes," said Dr. P., who had a strange speaking voice that sounded like a cat getting its tail stepped on. "We met for three hours. I gave him a full range of tests, and we also talked one on one."

"What did you conclude about the defendant's state of mind?"

"In my professional opinion, he suffers from narcissistic personality disorder. NPD."

The DA put a curious finger to her chin. "Hmm . . . narcissistic personality disorder. Would you please explain to us what this means?"

"Someone with an inflated sense of self-importance and who has difficulty caring about or empathizing with the feelings of others. Meaning someone who thinks nothing of using other people to achieve his own goals. He needs constant admiration and will go to considerable lengths to avoid feeling less than special. Rage is a common result when faced with the possibility that he is less than perfect."

"Very interesting," she exaggerated. "And could a person in this state of rage go so far as to commit murder?"

"Absolutely."

"In that case, I'm a little confused. If someone is having a rage attack, is it possible they don't know right from wrong?"

"Not in these cases. NPD patients are much too self-aware to lose sight of reason. They simply think they are above it all. But they know what's right and wrong."

"I see. And what did the defendant say about his life with the Rainbows?"

"He said they were very kind to him. That he felt part of their family."

Nathan did not want to paint an unattractive a picture of life with the Rainbows—that would give him motive to bump them off.

"Why then would he want to see them dead?"

"Two reasons. First, as a narcissist, he is reluctant to admit that he has participated in less than collegial relationships. Second, they must have in some way not bolstered his ego. They may have withheld praise for something he did that he thought praiseworthy. Or perhaps they took the side of their biological son in a dispute."

"That would be enough to commit such heinous crimes?"

"In such an extreme case as Mr. Nightbridge, I would say yes."

"Thank you, Dr. Pepper. Your witness."

"Good afternoon, Dr. Pepper. It's nice to see you again," Nathan said. "This disorder you talk about—do you have any data on what percentage of people diagnosed with it commit homicide?"

"No, I do not."

"Simply stated, is that because not every convicted murderer is diagnosed as having or not having this disorder or for that matter, any disorder?"

"Well, yes, I suppose so." He coughed into his hand.

"But it is true, is it not, that most people with a psychological disorder do not become homicidal?"

"Yes, that's true."

"During the three hours of our acquaintanceship, did I say anything about having violent urges?"

"No."

"Did I in any way lose my temper or even show impatience?"

"You were very polite. Too polite."

"Thank you, doctor. Next time I will make a point of being rude, so that I appear normal." You could hear people giggle for Nathan's sharp wit.

"Objection, your honor."

"Objection sustained. Jury will disregard the last statement. Careful, Mr. Nightbridge."

"Yes, your honor. Now, Dr. Pepper, let's say I really do suffer from PHD—"

"It's NPD."

"Yes, sorry, NPD. And let's say for the sake of argument I did not commit these horrible acts of violence. Might I still have fled the scene, to protect my so-called narcissistic personality?"

He chuckled in a condescending way. "To assume you didn't commit the crimes—that's a bit of a stretch."

"But it is possible?"

"Well, it's possible the moon is made of green cheese."

"No disrespect, but I beg to differ. There is tangible proof of what the moon is made of, and green cheese is not among the components." Some people in the courtroom laughed again.

"Now, Dr. Pepper," Nathan continued. "This diagnosis that you say applies to me—is it something that could be seen in my brain cells? Does it have a physical existence?"

"No, indeed it does not."

"And so it is possible that another doctor might think it did not apply to me?"

"Yes. Anything is possible."

I could sense Dr. P.'s annoyance.

"In the two hundred or more cases the state has paid you to offer your expert testimony, have you ever presented a diagnosis that would have helped the defense?"

"I don't remember."

"Well, according to the records I acquired, the answer is no, you always help the prosecution. No disrespect, sir, but doesn't that sound biased? Over two hundred cases and not a single one that may have inspired at least some sympathy for the defendant?"

"I'm just doing my job. There's a lot of sick, dangerous people out there."

"Yes, there are, aren't there, Dr. Pepper? When your own son committed suicide at age sixteen, had you diagnosed him?"

"Objection," said the pissed-off, pathetic prosecutor.

"Objection sustained," said the judge. "Jury will disregard. Mr. Nightbridge, do you have any other questions for this witness?"

"No, your honor, other than to say I am sorry for his loss."

The stupid woman who, according to Elena, in past lives made quite a name for herself in ancient Egypt and Greece, also testified for the prosecution.

"Mr. Nathan treated the Rainbow family with no respect," she said. "They loved him like their own, and he picked fights and insulted them. He made Elena cry on countless occasions. I worried constantly about what he might do."

"Were you concerned he might get physically violent with them?" the homely prosecutor asked.

"Concerned? I saw it with my own eyes. Nathan attacked his own brother, Wolf."

"Please describe the last time you saw Mr. Nightbridge at the Rainbow home."

She stared at Nathan as if claiming some victory of cosmic proportion over him. "About an hour before the fire started. I saw him outside, gathering sticks."

When it came time to cross-examine the Traveler of Time and Space, Nathan said, "Good afternoon, miss. How are you today?"

"Oh, I'm fine," she said, in a super-defensive way, as if confronting Nathan would give her the cooties.

"Did you ever contact the police or any social service agency about what you called your worry over what I might do to the Rainbows?"

You could catch just a millisecond of surprise in her eyes. "No. I didn't think it my place. People have to work things out on their own."

"Do you still feel that way?"

She leaned forward in the witness box. "It's not my fault you killed them. You can't put this on anyone but yourself."

"Then shouldn't you leave me to work it out on my own?"

"Objection," croaked Miss Frigid. "Badgering the witness."

"Sustained," ruled the creepy judge.

"You cared a great deal about the Rainbows. They were your friends and you wanted them to be happy?"

"Yes, of course. Elena was my closest friend. And my spiritual advisor."

Nathan took out his cell phone. "Your honor, I would like to enter this photograph as defense Exhibit Nine."

The judge looked at the image on the phone screen and ordered the bailiff to pass it on to Aphrodite's priestess whore. She screamed when she saw a picture of herself with Thor, fucking the day away. The picture on the phone got passed around to the members of the jury.

"You little shit!" shrieked the witness. "Thor should've killed you when he hit you on the head."

"Thor never hit me," Nathan replied, staring at her dead-on. "How dare you tarnish his legacy."

"You filthy little liar," she hissed. "They were good people."

"Especially Thor, it would seem. Were you trying to break up their marriage? Did it make you angry that he wouldn't leave his wife for you? Angry enough to commit murder?"

"Objection, your honor. The witness is not on trial."

"Never mind," Nathan said. "I wanted the jury to see if this witness is worth taking seriously. I'm trying to help."

"You are evil."

Exiting the witness box, she ran toward Nathan, though a couple of officers restrained her. "I'll kill him for you, Thor. I know you can hear me," she babbled, as guards carried her out of the courtroom and dumped her in a jail cell for contempt of court.

"Your honor," the prosecutor said, "I request a mistrial."

"She's your witness, counselor," the judge pointed out. "Request denied."

"Your honor," Nathan said. "For six years the State has been building this dubious case against me. But it has not even come close to meeting the burden of proof to sustain these charges. Nothing of substance has been presented to lend credibility to the theory that I tied these poor people up or set the fire."

The judge addressed the prosecutor. "Does the State have any additional evidence that potentially demonstrates that the defendant committed these heinous acts?"

She shuffled through some folders on her desk; one of them fell on the floor. Nathan stepped over to pick it up for her. She grabbed it from his hands in a very unsympathetic way. "Your honor, if we could have just a slight continuance to—"

"Your honor, they've had six years," Nathan reminded the court.

"I agree," the judge said. "I am dismissing the charges against the defendant. Mr. Nightbridge, you are free to go."

This inspired a lot of hubbub in the courtroom; the judge banged his gavel and demanded silence. The prosecutor looked like someone punched her in the stomach. "You can't mean it, your honor."

But he did.

Reporters flocked to the prosecutor and to Nathan like flies to dog shit.

"A gross injustice has occurred," said the fucked up DA. "We are stunned." Then she added, "Stunned," as if everyone didn't hear her the first time.

"Will you attempt to re-file charges against Nathan Nightbridge?"

"I cannot say at this time."

"What will you tell your supervisors when they ask you how a murder suspect acting as his own attorney could beat you so horrendously in this case?"

"I. . . uh, we'll have to see."

When reporters encircled Nathan to get some juicy tidbits about the trial, he said, "No comment," and looked away from them. His supporters—who had grown in number over the course of the trial—chanted, "Nathan rules."

"What are your plans, Nathan?" a reporter asked him.

"No comment."

"Do you want to be a lawyer?"

"No comment."

A man who looked familiar shoved his way into the circle and shot Nathan. My poor beloved son clutched his abdomen and fell down. The blood poured out of him like the tears I spilled over a lifetime.

17

The awful man who shot poor, fragile Nathan proved to be Thor's brother, Stanley Kline. As the cops dragged him away, Stanley the Shit screamed that he did it for his brother, sister-in-law, and nephew. That such lunatics are allowed to roam the streets shows just how far civilization has declined. There followed a bit of a scuffle between the pro- and anti-Nathan folks, but the cops brought it under control. They could've started a riot for all I cared. I only thought about my son. Not running to the ambulance to comfort him ranks among the hardest things I ever did.

Nathan was listed in critical condition. I got so upset and confused, I lost my shopping cart. My good army sleeping bag, my framed baby picture of Nathan, the program from *Cat on a Hot Tin Roof*, from which production Zelda and I conceived Nathan. . . all of it gone forever. I sat on a bench on a park island between two noisy streets. Squirrels were busy living in a tree, oblivious to the traffic all around them. Once someone walked right by me, and I said hello. The guy said, "I don't have any money."

"I just wanted someone to talk to," I said. But the guy walked away from me, as if I were some crazed degenerate. I slept as well as I could on the bench, considering I had nothing to keep me warm. The endless whizzing of the traffic seemed the closest thing I had to comfort.

At the underground station the next morning, some deranged old drunk walked by and said that the serial killer guy who got shot passed away. I wanted to cry but couldn't. My meds wouldn't let me. I wondered if I died, too. Maybe the afterlife consisted of the massive commuter edifice in which I sat, everyone coming and going, as if even after death everyone remained too busy to rest in peace.

Not until later in the day did I see a cheesy newspaper headline and learned that while Nathan almost died, he pulled through, and got taken off the critical list. His will to live, his inner strength—I could only say, "Thank you, God." The headline read, "NATHAN LIVES," as if it were Easter Sunday.

As my son recuperated, he refused all interviews. So much for being a narcissist. Before long, the term "Nathaning" came to mean you represented yourself in court. News headlines would announce things like: "Serial Killer Will Nathan Self," and one such defendant, denied the right to defend herself, yelled at a judge, "I insist on my right to Nathan."

From time to time, I saw people wearing a T-shirt or button with Nathan's face on it. Once I even saw his image on a girl's pantyhose. The general opinion held that in comparison with zit pus, my son was deemed lacking, but to a minority of misfits he became a kind of rock star. Going online at a public library computer—until they told me to leave—I found that Nathan had several online fan clubs, totaling around ten thousand members.

The news media also saw in Nathan a potential focal point for the gun control debate, and both sides lost no time in making him a poster boy for their cause. Liberals lamented about how no one should take the law into their own hands, and Nathan showed what happened without gun control. Conservatives cackled that since the liberal criminal justice system couldn't put scum bags like Nathan behind bars where they belonged, people needed to exercise their Second Amendment rights.

Even my pal Charlie got into the act. A bunch of us guys were hanging around under the freeway, and Charlie said, "As a private citizen, I'd feel safer with more gun control laws. Guns shouldn't be available to the mentally imbalanced."

The constant roar of the cars and trucks overhead made it seem like we guys were going someplace, too.

"Well, if everyone had a gun," said some other man, "no one would shoot anyone because they knew they'd get shot back."

Charlie replied, "I'd like to believe that as a species we've evolved beyond that."

"You mean like that Nathan creep who keeps getting away with murdering people?" said the other guy. "No way would I talk to him without a gun."

"He's never been convicted," I pointed out.

"That's because it's rigged," said the other guy. "Al, look around you. Do you really think our once great nation is still the land of the free? The politicians are in bed with the Russian mob, and they fuck like bunnies. That Nathan son of a bitch obviously has a million mob connections. I'll bet he knows the President and all the Joint Chiefs of Staff."

"Maybe you're right," I said, not wanting to talk too much about Nathan.

"If you ask me," said a fourth guy, "it's a sign of Armageddon. Satan wants us for his own. Nathan. Satan. See how they sound alike? Do you call that a coincidence? I sure as cocksucker don't. Murderers will be rewarded. Good people will be punished. That's what it says in the Bible."

Obviously, this last guy didn't play with a full deck, but I couldn't let someone get away with speaking in such an inaccurate manner, about the Holy Bible or my son. "It doesn't say that at all," I corrected. "The Book of Revelations is about salvation. And 'Nathan' also rhymes with 'Bathan' or 'Dathan.' So what?"

"Yeah, but those aren't words," the crazy guy said.

"The Book of Revelations," Charlie interjected, "discusses both salvation and damnation."

"Function at the junction," said the crazy guy.

"I guess you could say that's true, too," Charlie said, and we all laughed at his dry wit. "Frankly, I don't know what to make of this Nathan character. He's smart, I'll say that much. But they say he's like talking to an iceberg. He stares at you like you're . . . like you're nothing."

"Maybe they'll make a movie about him," said the guy who wanted a gun. "He'd be played by—what's the name of that guy who always plays the weirdos?"

"Or maybe he'll go into politics," Charlie said, which made us laugh some more.

I said, "I think he'd make a good lawyer." I hoped my fatherly pride didn't give me away.

"Yeah," said the gun guy. "He's enough of a shit to be a lawyer. I don't see how anyone could be a lawyer and look at himself in the mirror."

"My family wanted me to be a lawyer," Charlie said. "They sent me to Harvard Law School, but I lucked out."

We passed around a couple of beers and went to sleep. But I couldn't sleep well. I kept worrying about Nathan and wondering what his next move would be.

The next day, I found out. Nathan had agreed to a press conference outside the hospital upon his discharge. But he didn't show up. Good for him. He ran away again.

19

The press milked another week or two of news out of Nathan, salivating as they reported bogus Nathan sightings, each more absurd than the last. According to one so-called news source, Nathan returned to his evil home planet in another galaxy. How ridiculous. Nathan had the misfortune of being an earthling, pure and simple. I can tell when someone is an alien creature like myself.

They didn't run freight trains as much as they used to, so it took me over a week to catch up to Nathan in Bosco's college town. I guessed that my son could count on his old friend to give him shelter and privacy.

Bosco had a ground-floor apartment in a funky old house subdivided into student-friendly units. The apartment consisted of a small living room and bedroom, with a tiny bath and kitchen and a microscopic closet. But a resourceful Bosco arranged the space in an efficient manner. The headboard of the bed doubled as a cabinet, and his dining table also functioned as a storage chest. The living room futon collapsed into a guest bed, where Nathan slept.

Bosco's new live-in girlfriend, Autumn, took up additional space. A fellow graduate student in English, she looked plain by conventional standards, but she had a sensitivity about her that created an aura of beauty. She reminded me a little of Zelda when I first met her. I could tell Autumn had absolute faith in Nathan's integrity because Bosco vouched for him. They had that kind of trust in each other.

"I still can't get over it," Bosco said one evening, sitting next to Autumn on the futon. "All by yourself, without any legal training, you beat that fancy prosecutor."

Seated on a floor cushion, Nathan diminished the compliment. Given today's world of show-offs, I found his omnipresent modesty admirable.

"The lawyer I talked to when they first arrested me—he made it so complicated. To me, it was simple. Common sense."

"You don't scare easily, do you, Nathan?" asked Autumn, clutching Bosco's hand.

Nathan shrugged. "Life dishes it out, and you just have to deal with it."

"Can I see your scar again?" Bosco asked, with no small degree of admiration.

Nathan lifted up his T-shirt. He had a beauty of a scar on his abdomen.

"Wow, it looks like Antarctica." Autumn leaned over to get a better view. "I know this is an awful question, but I've always wanted to ask it. What's it like to get shot?"

Nathan laughed. "Trust me, it's one experience you can skip."

"Did you see your life flashing before you?" asked Bosco.

"No. It just hurt like nothing you can imagine. I passed out."

"I'm sure it at least gave you some sympathy," Autumn offered.

"None that I'm aware of. Not even in the hospital. The doctors and nurses stood as far away as possible when they had to examine me. They treated me like a contagion."

Autumn said, "Poor Nathan. To be fighting for your life and have no one on your side."

"That's rough, man," Bosco agreed. "Have you thought about changing your name?"

"I'd never do that. It would mean they won. That they made me ashamed of who I am." I assumed "they" consisted pretty much of the total population of humanity. Nathan either didn't know about his small but growing following or else lacked the conceit to mention it.

"I hear you, bro. But you may have a hard time finding a job or a place to live with people knowing who you are."

"Then I'll sleep on the street," Nathan said with surprising force. "I'll beg for money."

"If you did change your name, what would you change it to?" Autumn asked, as if the threesome were playing a game.

I found her desire to lighten things up to be genuine. She didn't want Nathan to be unhappy. There's a universe of difference between being nice and pretending to be nice. Possibly it's the longest distance that exists.

Nathan considered the question. "Something that would piss everyone off. Maybe Joe Bob Skunk."

The beaming couple laughed. "I always liked the name Ophelia," Autumn shared. "Although in *Hamlet* she isn't exactly a positive role model."

Bosco ran his fingers through his hair in mock narcissism. "I see myself as a Fabio." This made Autumn laugh some more and kiss him on the cheek.

"It's obvious you're happy together," Nathan observed.

Autumn said, "We met each other in Shakespeare class, and about five seconds later, I thought, 'Oh, okay, here's my life partner.'"

"And after five seconds I thought, 'Oh, okay, here's a piece of ass that'll put out.'" Bosco's joke inspired Autumn to tickle him in the ribs. They both laughed some more, and he amended his remarks.

"No, in all seriousness, I felt the same way about Autumn."

It's always delightful to see young people in love, but I guess I'm old-fashioned. I harbor this strange idea that love should lead to marriage and not just living together.

"What about you, Nathan?" Autumn asked. "You never mention your personal life. Do you have a special someone?"

"No."

"You don't seem like you want to talk about it," Autumn observed. "Did something happen?"

"No, nothing happened."

Bosco said, "Did I tell you, Nathan? Everything's been so crazy. I got my master's. Now all I need is to take my comp exams and write my dissertation. Then I'll be Dr. Bosco Sinclair. Who da thunk it?"

Nathan adjusted his weight on the floor cushion. "What are you writing about?"

"It's hard to explain, but it has to do with the sexualizing of death in e. e. cummings from a critical theory perspective. You know, the poet. The one who didn't put capital letters in his name."

"I think I heard of him," Nathan said, and in that chilling moment I realized that despite his off-the-charts intelligence, Nathan still suffered from gaps in his education.

"Do you write poetry?" Nathan asked.

Bosco's face turned red. "A little. I don't like sharing it because I know it isn't good."

Nathan yawned. "I wouldn't know a good poem from a bad one. I have no feeling for artsy stuff. My mom used to talk about art, but it didn't rub off on me."

Bosco went to the refrigerator, where he got a couple of cans of Coke and tossed one to Nathan and one to Autumn. She caught hers with one hand, like it was no big deal. For some reason, I always found it sexy when a girl acted like one of the guys.

"I'm doing Virginia Woolf," said Autumn. "Depression as feminist discourse."

"Do you get depressed?" Nathan asked, without passing judgment.

"Sure. Doesn't everyone?"

"I would hate to be depressed," Nathan said. "I've had it described to me, and it sounds awful."

Autumn looked a little confused. "So you're always happy?"

Nathan laughed some more. "I wouldn't go that far. I'm just me. I don't know how to explain it."

"Nathan is naturally high, without ever smoking or drinking." Bosco took a hefty swallow of Coke as he walked back to the futon. "Wish I could say the same, though I don't smoke weed anymore. My better half doesn't like it, and it messes with my concentration for school."

"He's such a good little boy," Autumn teased. "But Nathan, I'm afraid you didn't take the hint. When Bosco says he has no talent for poetry, you're supposed to ask him to read some of it out loud."

"Pay no attention to her," Bosco chimed in. "Really, Nathan, it would bore you to death."

"Well, I want to hear you read it," Autumn said. "Nathan, you are free to cover your ears."

Autumn and Bosco went back and forth for a while, but in the end he agreed to read one poem. He cleared his throat about ten million times. "This is called, 'TV Versus the Universe.'"

"Interesting title," Nathan commented, but Autumn put her index finger to her mouth to shush him. Bosco's hands shook as he read:

Okay, TV, you win.
I am trapped in your headlights
and cannot move, as if in a slow liquid dream.
I flail uselessly in your molasses.
My brain is on a morphine drip—

Someone rang the doorbell.

"I like the part about molasses, though I'm not sure I get it," Nathan said, as Autumn went to answer the door.

"Serenity!" she all but shrieked, hugging the visitor. "Nathan, this is my sister, Serenity."

"Wow, two earth-shattering surprises in a row." Bosco's face became a giant grin. "Life is so cool."

In their excitement, it took Autumn and Bosco a moment to notice Serenity's fragile state. She looked well put together in a ladies business suit and of a more conventional prettiness than Autumn. Her eyeglasses gave her an air of power, as if the oblong black frames dared you to treat her as anything but an equal. She had a compact suitcase, and she set it down in the doorway.

"You have to help me." Serenity clasped her sister's shoulders. "He's going to kill me."

I never would've guessed I had my first glimpse of the woman my son would marry.

20

In contrast to her older sister Autumn, Serenity Lamb couldn't care less if Virginia Woolf's depression bore feminist undercurrents. Serenity, though still in her twenties, already made her mark on Wall Street as a power broker. Siblings often divide the world between themselves, and if everything delicate and elusive became Autumn's domain, Serenity lived for everything solid and apparent. Autumn could've been a nymph prancing through the woods; Serenity seemed more like a driver caught in a traffic jam, honking her horn. Autumn and Bosco reminded me of Wendy and Peter Pan, holding hands as they soared through the clouds at night. Nathan and Serenity resembled Jack and Jill forever falling down the hill, never fetching that goddamn pail of water.

Still, at first anyway, it pleased me that Nathan at least and at last found someone. After having Zelda for a mother and then the stoned out disaster of the Rainbows, I could see why Nathan fell for someone driven but uncomplicated, and who knew how to make money. Being rich must have seemed like a phantom birthright he'd yet to claim. He had the money gene, so to speak, which made his lifetime of poverty all the more frustrating.

I found it harder to understand why Serenity would take interest in such an infamous liability as Nathan. But when people are desperate, they are vulnerable. And when people are vulnerable, they do unexpected things.

But I get ahead of myself. That first night, Serenity had other things on her mind. After declining both food and drink, she moved her suitcase out of the way and shared her tale of woe. She could've sat on the floor, but she claimed to prefer standing.

"My boss wants to kill me," Serenity began. "I didn't want to upset Dad, so I figured I'd come here to you guys.

I'm sorry I didn't text first. I just threw some clothes together and drove straight to the airport."

Autumn said, "Please slow down, sis. And tell us what happened from the beginning. Unless of course you don't want—"

Serenity managed to smile at Nathan. "We're all family. I have nothing to hide. And yes, Nathan, I know who you are, and I say bravo. We need more of your rugged individualism. It would make our country a better place. You can call me a fan. A Nathanite."

Nathan looked down in modesty as Bosco said, "I second the motion. Nathan rocks."

"Ditto," said Autumn. "But please. Tell us everything."

Serenity leaned against a windowsill and crossed her arms. The angle of the lamplight exaggerated her shadow, like a wobbly candle flame. "My boss fell in love with me. If you want to call it love. Clay Hinton Jr. of Hinton, Hinton and Moyer. He's married with four kids, but so what? Even when I first interviewed, I thought he looked me over, but I told myself not to be concerned. You know, little boys will be little boys. Or little fuckheads is more like it. And I wanted to be with a brokerage with plenty of opportunities for promotion. Well, it's been absolute hell. I used to be proud of myself, proud of the money I made and how I decorated my apartment and went to champagne galas at art galleries and all these other things that meant nothing anymore. Sometimes that's the hardest part—fighting to live when it seems like there's nothing worth living for. Everything I worked for is gone."

Autumn reached over to touch her sister's hand. "Serenity, I had no idea."

"I didn't want to trouble everyone. You know how Dad gets. Anyway, after working there for a while and minding my own business, Clay asked to take me out to lunch. Since he's a senior partner, I thought he intended to be helpful—you know, a little pep talk, that sort of thing. But instead he . . . God, this is so embarrassing, but he started playing footsie with me. I moved my feet away sort of subtly and hoped he got the message. But he didn't. The next day he asked me out to dinner. I said that would be fine, let's invite a couple of other people, but he made it clear he meant dinner alone with me. For the longest time I declined, but eventually I accepted. I didn't know what else to do. He got drunk. He started telling me these disgusting dirty jokes. I remember one about a woman who got her breasts run over by an army tank. Stuff like that. Then he started reaching for me under the table. He even unzipped his pants and tried to force my hand to—you know, like, touch him. Right there in the restaurant. It made no sense."

As Autumn and Bosco registered expressions of disgust, Nathan, ever the clear-headed student of criminology, said, "He wanted you to beat him off."

Serenity looked confused for a moment before she continued.

"Well, whatever he wanted, I wiggled my way loose and ran out of the restaurant. The next day he called me into his office and said I had to come alone. He said that he hacked into the computer system and would transfer company investments to my personal portfolio. That's a felony offense. He said if I didn't have sex with him, he'd finish the transfer and have me arrested. I offered to resign, but he said that made no difference."

"Couldn't you go to the cops?" Bosco asked.

"Believe me, I tried. But his family owns the cops."

"Don't tell me you had sex with him," said Autumn.

Staring ahead with a blank expression, Serenity seemed almost as though she were hypnotized. "I had no choice. I just lay there in a hotel room while he made me do such bizarre things. It disgusted me. But I met him a second time, and then a third."

Autumn wiped a tear or two from her eyes. "We understand."

"The third time had to be the worst," Serenity continued. "He took out a gun and he—he put one bullet in the cylinder and spun it around. Then he forced the gun. . . you know, inside me. He said if I made any noise at all, he'd pull the trigger."

Autumn put her hands to her face in horror; Bosco hugged her as tears ran down his face. Nathan feigned a need to adjust his floor cushion. I could tell he didn't want to show that Serenity's story got to him. The unfairness of the court system had taken its toll upon his soul.

"I cried and begged him to stop. He laughed some more, and then pulled out the gun so fast it hurt me, and. . . well, he licked it."

She paused as Autumn screamed. Bosco rubbed her arm and kissed her forehead.

"Then," continued Serenity, "he told me, 'Get out of here. Until next time. If you say anything to anyone, if you try to run away, you're dead.' I tried to go to work as if nothing happened. But after a few weeks, I couldn't take it anymore. I couldn't think of what to do besides come here. I hope I did the right thing. What if he's having me followed? What if you guys. . .?"

She put her hand to her face and rubbed her temples. "I am so tired. Can I please go to sleep?"

"You'll take our room," Bosco said. "Autumn and I will take the futon."

"You're sure?"

"Absolutely," said Autumn, holding Bosco's hand.

"Nathan my bro, you're okay roughing it on the floor, right?"

"Of course." He moved out of the way as Autumn, Serenity, and Bosco shared a group hug. Bosco gestured with his head that Nathan should join them, but he declined. He knew a family moment when he saw one, and that it should be kept that way.

After Serenity walked to the bedroom, Autumn said, "She's always been so confident. I wonder if she'll ever be her normal self again. We already worry about her. All she does is work. Now she'll never trust a man."

"Why should she?" Nathan asked.

"You're right," said Autumn. "I guess I'm lucky." She and Bosco kissed.

The next morning, Autumn and Bosco saw Serenity emerge from the bedroom, yawning and stretching like a sleepy cat. Nathan came out right behind her.

Autumn and Bosco burst into applause, while Serenity gave a sheepish look.

"What?" Nathan said, not understanding the fuss.

"Nathan is just what Serenity needs," Autumn said to Bosco, who replied, "It's so nice to know good things still happen amidst the bad."

Serenity said, "I hate it when people talk about me as if I'm not in the room." She burst into a big happy/sad grin, as if determined to put her horrible past behind her.

19

I swear, sometimes I crack myself up. I don't mean to sound conceited, but I am one of the most humorous people I've ever known. Just now, I'm wondering how film critics talk about their dreams. Maybe something like this: "Last night's offering featured muddy black-and-white images and offered little connection between character and action. I give the dream one star." Now you have to admit, that's funny. I love to walk down the street and make myself laugh. Sometimes I pretend I'm on a stage, and the audience is happy from all the funny things I say. We drama majors die a hard death. Once the acting bug bites you, you're hooked for life.

Speaking of good moods, I haven't the words to describe my pleasure in discovering that Nathan had a lil' ol' sex drive after all. Autumn loved that her sister fell for her future husband's best friend, and Bosco told Nathan that now they really were brothers. The thing about Serenity's boss wanting to torture and murder her seemed like a faraway planet in those first days and weeks of Serenity and Nathan being a couple.

It happened in an instant, as true love often does. From the moment the two of them emerged from the bedroom that first morning, they became inseparable. Serenity and Nathan were private people, so they never got physically demonstrative like Autumn and Bosco. But otherwise, they were Bobbsey Twin couples. The funky old house that Autumn and Bosco lived in had an identical apartment available next door, so Serenity and Nathan moved into it. Serenity bought the modest furnishings; Nathan didn't care about things like that.

Serenity made no apologies for being herself. She loved money, and she hated failure. According to Autumn, Serenity had always been that way. One time, all four were outside the house, and Serenity noticed a bumper sticker on a car that read, "Never look down on someone unless you want to help them up." She read it out loud in her crisp voice and then amended it to, "Never look down on someone unless you're eating candy." I thought that should be her epitaph.

But some individuals were less than enthused about Serenity being with Nathan. Her father, who still knew nothing about her psycho ex-boss, held the ironic opinion that Nathan spelled danger, and she should go back to New York. He went so far as to cancel the fancy-shmancy wedding he had planned for Autumn and Bosco unless Serenity broke up with my son. As her father waited for a response to their ultimatum, the four kids decided to go to City Hall for a quickie double wedding. Daddy gave the two young couples nothing. But as often happens with young love, parental disapproval fanned the flames, and in a way, all four of them married each other, given their strong common bond. And Crazy Seymour wrote Bosco a tidy little check that he elected to share with Serenity and Nathan.

Autumn—who, I saw, had a harmless yet neurotic tendency to always think well of people—said her father shouldn't be blamed for how he felt because her mother got shot to death in a grocery store robbery when she and Serenity were still toddlers. I wondered how this tragedy impacted the two sisters, if it made Autumn fragile and Serenity bold. It's weird how the same event affects people in different ways.

The brides, plus Bosco, insisted that the brief ceremonies be held outdoors, on the steps of City Hall. So I snuck a peek. Autumn and Bosco got touchy-feely while exchanging vows, and they both cried a little. Serenity and Nathan seemed much more matter-of-fact about the whole thing, as though a marriage license equaled another business contract. Even their kiss at the end seemed dispassionate. No doubt about it, they had no-frills personalities.

Serenity wanted to keep a low profile so that criminally insane Clay Hinton Jr. did not make good on his threat to kill her. As a financial wiz, she already had a nest egg or two stashed away. So, using her married name, she took a low-paying job as bookkeeper for a local technology consultant firm. Nathan saw no reason why he shouldn't continue with his education in criminology according to his original plan, and enrolled in the master's program of a non-prestigious state school. They didn't want to accept him, but he threatened to sue, and if there's anything every school is scared to death of it's a lawsuit. Hence, Nathan contributed student loans to the household income. He got some dirty looks from his fellow criminology majors, but he'd grown accustomed to being singled out for contempt and got straight A's. He described the goriest murder cases in minutest detail, without batting an eye. When, in a forensics class, the students had to observe an autopsy, only Nathan had the maturity not to leave the room for being grossed out.

I also recall observing him in a required course on the history of law. The professor asked the class, "What is history?"

After a long pause, a student raised her hand and said, "His story—the story of man. Which means women, too."

"Yes," agreed the professor. "But what else?"

Nathan raised his hand. "Violence," he said. "History is one violent thing after another."

The professor's eyes flickered.

"Surely not entirely, Nathan. Birthdays make history as well. And discoveries."

"All the discoveries that make history have violence attached to them. And childbirth is violent, too."

What a creative and original thinker.

For a semester or so, things hummed along and I wondered if my job as a father had become obsolete. As a married man, Nathan didn't need Dad to watch his every move.

However, I guessed wrong.

As far as I know there were no news blurbs about Nathan getting married. But my friend Charlie had a theory that mental illness had something to do with why people were psychic—or was it the other way around? Anyway, somehow, Serenity's old sicko boss found out where she lived and with whom. The false public image of Nathan as a bloodthirsty murderer made Clay Hinton Jr. all the more determined to make Serenity his own. Or maybe he thought he and not Nathan had dibs on killing her. What can I say? Homicidal lunatics have this way of not making sense.

Whatever, it startled me to see the local scandal sheet proclaim a big headline: "Nathan's Done It Again!" Nathan should've sued for libel because, in actuality, both he and Serenity were being held for questioning in the death of Clay Hinton Jr. The fucker got what he deserved. He got hammered inside an oblong crate without food or water, his gun shoved up his ass. A few weeks later, some kids smoking dope in the woods found the crate. A shallow hole next to the crate indicated that someone started digging to bury the crate, but then got bored.

Clay's snooty family took offense not only at their son's demise, but the undignified specifics of it. Late night TV comics wasted no time creating Clay Hinton Jr. death jokes. While it must've been an awful way to die, it made people think that he'd lived a kinky life.

"The death penalty is too good for whoever did this," said a Hinton family spokesperson. Ho-hum.

The feds took over the investigation, since at the mere state level Nathan slipped through the fingers of the justice system not once but twice. The taped FBI interviews with Serenity and Nathan got posted on the web, and they went viral in nothing flat. I went to a public library and listened to them until I could recite them from memory. The interviews took place at the local FBI headquarters closest to where Serenity and Nathan lived. The twosome were separated for questioning. First, here's a dandy excerpt from Serenity:

The corrupt Mafioso FBI agent sat across the table from her, so you could only see the back of his bald head, which shone so brightly you needed ultraviolet protective goggles to look at it.

"You said you filed a police report about Mr. Hinton," said the baldhead. "We've found no record of such a report."

"Then his family had it destroyed," Serenity replied. "They own New York. They probably own you."

"You sound paranoid," said the snarky agent. "Why do you think that is?"

"I'm not paranoid. And by the way, I'm not stupid, either."

"What exactly do you claim Mr. Hinton did to you?"

"What I *claim*? Like I'm making it up? I can't believe this is happening."

"Serenity, there is no evidence—"

"You think I'm going to tell you what happened? I barely can discuss it with anyone."

"Is it safe to assume you wanted him dead?"

"I wanted him in jail, where he couldn't hurt anyone. But sure, dead made a good Plan B."

"So you killed him?"

"No, I'm saying that if he died, I would've been happy. Relieved."

"Are there a lot of people you wish dead?"

"No, just you."

Baldie coughed. "Now then, what exactly happened?"

"In the middle of the night we heard a banging on the door. Then Clay Hinton Jr. started shouting that he came to rescue me."

"Rescue you? What would he be trying to rescue you from?"

"You know perfectly well, dickhead. My husband, Nathan, got falsely accused of. . . of a couple of crimes."

"What do you mean, falsely accused?"

"I mean the courts found him not guilty. What the hell do you think I mean?"

"Yes, well. . . anyway, did anyone else hear him shouting?"

"Obviously, my husband did."

"But no one else can confirm it?"

"My sister and her husband have the other apartment on the floor. But they went camping for the weekend."

"How convenient for you. No one to confirm or deny your story."

"Look, if I'm such a liar, why ask me anything?"

The agent raised his voice. "What happened after you heard him shouting?"

"I very quietly reached for my phone and called 911. He tried to break down the door, but we have three deadbolts on it."

"Then what happened?"

"Everything got quiet. By the time the cops arrived, he'd gone."

"And you're sure that Clay Hinton Jr., your former boss, shouted and banged on the door?"

"Yes."

"How do you explain that a month later we found Mr. Hinton dead inside a crate?"

"I have no idea. Maybe he stalked and tortured other people."

"And these other people just happened to live in your town, miles away from New York?"

"Look, I have no idea, okay? I'm just glad the fucker is dead. And I'm overjoyed he suffered."

"What would you say if I told you we found your fingerprints on the crate?"

"I'd say you were making it up to scare me. If you had that kind of evidence, I'd be under arrest."

After a long pause, the FBI idiot said, "I'll be right back."

"Bring a lawyer with you," Serenity replied. "I've wasted enough time talking to you."

I loved how she stood up to the feds. My son married a woman with cojones.

As for Nathan, he had a lifetime of experience with interrogations, and it showed. He should've given seminars on the topic. They had a woman agent question him, maybe to see if she could flirt a confession out of him. I only saw the back of her head; she had a long ponytail. I bet she had an ugly face. I bet everyone hated her for being such a bitch.

"So, Nathan," the bitch began. "Back again, I see. What a startling coincidence."

Nathan put his elbow on the table and rested his chin in his hand. "I just can't stay away."

"You have the worst luck. Always being falsely accused of murder."

"Oh, really? Are you accusing me of anything?"

"You tell me."

"Nope."

"Your wife claims she experienced violent sexual abuse from Mr. Hinton. What can you tell me about that?"

"Just that whatever my wife said is true. She doesn't lie."

"Describe for me what she said happened."

"Why would I do that? If you're into S and M, I saw a porn shop at the end of the block."

"Sounds like this is a touchy subject for you. It must make you angry to think that someone did those things to your wife."

"Of course."

"Did you want to get back at him? If you did, that's only normal. I understand if in the heat of the moment, you did things you regret."

Nathan leaned over to be more in her face. "The only thing I regret is that when he came knocking at our door, we didn't let him in. I regret that I didn't chop his dick into little pieces and shove them down his throat."

I could tell the FBI lady kind of looked away. "You have quite an imagination, Nathan. You must think an awful lot about ways of killing people, given your past. You've been exposed to murder all your life."

"Would you like to hear how I'd kill you?"

"Uh, let's bring things back to Clay Hinton Jr. What did he say when he pounded on the door?"

"Nothing worth remembering."

"A man who violated your wife comes banging on your door, and you don't remember what he said?"

"Most of what people say is not worth remembering. Sometimes I run into this homeless lunatic who's screaming and kicking street signs. Why should I pay attention to what he says?"

I wondered who this homeless person could be, since I couldn't watch Nathan 24/7. But he had a point. I read a study that said that if we paid attention to everything we heard for just one day we'd all be flipped out.

"And you considered Clay Hinton Jr. a lunatic as well?"

"Don't you?"

"What I think doesn't matter."

"You said it, not me."

The FBI witch sighed. "Do you really expect me to believe that he just happened to turn up dead after he came to your apartment?"

"I have no idea. To hell with what you think."

"You study criminology, am I right?"

"Yes."

"Could you please answer a question for me?"

"I can try." Nathan flashed a sarcastic, toothy smile. He didn't smile often, but when he did, it lit up his entire face.

"Why is it that people commit murder?"

He thought for a moment. "Common sense."

"Um, I see." I could see the back of her head tremble.

Someone unseen called out to the FBI agent. She got up and left the room. Once alone, Nathan yawned and stretched. Then he looked straight into the camera and stuck out his tongue, wiggling his fingers with a thumb in each ear.

"You're free to go, Nathan," said the off-camera voice of the woman agent. "But we'll be in touch, I'm sure."

"I can hardly wait."

21

Serenity's new boss told her not to worry, he would not fire her because of the bad publicity, but she resigned anyway. Once the videos went viral, so did stories about what Clay Hinton Jr. did to her, some even more sordid than the truth. She bore far too much humiliation to go to work and have everyone stare at her or feel sorry for her. Her boss gave her the standard spiel about how as the victim she shouldn't blame herself, but she wouldn't change her mind. Actually, since the job never paid much, I think Serenity realized that she could better spend her time at home on her computer, working on her financial portfolio. So both she and Nathan were almost always in their tiny apartment, as if under house arrest. They shared a compatible vibe that allowed them not to get in each other's way.

One night after the FBI interviewed them, they sat up in bed with their clothes on and devoured an entire devil's food cake smothered in whipped cream, calling it supper. Before she became a drunk, Nathan's mother Zelda had quite a sweet tooth, which they say can lead to alcoholism. But Nathan never drank at all, so I didn't worry that he'd follow in her footsteps.

"What next?" Serenity asked, fixing her pillows to lie down.

"I'm going to study for a while," Nathan replied.

She touched his wrist. "No, my pit bull, I mean what's next with the cops?"

"You mean the feds? Who knows? A bunch of idiots."

Serenity sighed. "I guess all we can do is wait."

"I hate waiting. When I want something, I want it this very instant. When I asked my mom for something, she'd say, 'I have to think about it.' It drove me crazy, and she knew it did. I'd rather be charged with murder than have to wait to find out if I am."

Serenity laughed. "I guess you're kind of used to it."

"Very funny." He hit her with his pillow.

"Ouch, that hurt. Not so rough."

"Gee, sorry."

As I looked, I noticed that their bodies were not touching. Serenity lay under a sheet that Nathan rested on top of. I supposed that as private people, they liked to give each other a lot of space, even with their clothes on.

Serenity sat up, stretching her arms. "I still can't believe that Clay Hinton will never fuck with me again. It's like being told I won the Powerball jackpot. It's like knowing there really is a God."

"No one should have that kind of power over someone else," Nathan replied. "You spend every second hating the person so much, there's nothing else left. You're like this robot of hate."

"I only wanted to do my job. Why couldn't he understand?"

"People are poison. They stop you from living. Sometimes even just walking down the street—I see all the people and it's like I can't breathe."

"Well, I hope you make at least one exception. If not two or three."

Nathan pretended to be deep in thought. "Bosco's cool. And Autumn. That's about it."

"Gee, thanks a lot." She gave his face a playful slap. "Why on earth did I marry you?"

"Because we can't be forced to testify against each other."

"That's nothing to joke about. What if—"

Nathan put his finger to her mouth. "Only dummies get found guilty. A trial is a chess game. You just have to know how to play."

She moved his finger from her mouth and rolled over on the bed, away from him. "Chess—Autumn and I used to play all the time. Either she won right away or the game dragged on forever, and then sometimes I won. It taught me something, though. You take a pawn here, a knight there, and eventually you get what you want. What amazes me is how far you sometimes have to go. So much further than you ever imagined."

Nathan looked down on her. "For me, it's the opposite. I think life is letting everything that's already inside you come out. Nothing I do surprises me. And it pisses me off when someone gets in my way. Like they don't get who I am, and they're so smirky about it."

Serenity rolled over to look up at him. "You've had it hard, I've had it easy. And yet here we are."

For an instant I thought they'd kiss, but instead Nathan told her, "I wouldn't call Clay Hinton Jr. having it easy."

"I mean before that. My dad used to be so much fun. Autumn and I were best friends. Yet now it doesn't make any difference."

"Nothing ever does."

"I'm only learning that, since I. . . you know, since we got together." She giggled. "I should write a book called *Fuck Everything.*"

"At book signings, you can write, 'To Mary, Fuck you.'"

Serenity laughed. "Or maybe 'Fuck off.'"

"That should be for men. 'Fuck off' to all the men, 'Fuck you' to all the women."

"I fucking love you."

"I fucking love you, too."

Someone knocked on the door. "Hey, you lovebirds," Bosco called out. "We're back. Are you decent?"

"No, but come in anyway," Serenity joked.

Weather permitting, Autumn and Bosco went camping on weekends. They had a favorite spot near a lake, where they'd chant Om or do whatever people did when they camped. Upon entering the apartment in their scruffy outdoor clothes and hiking boots, they seemed invigorated and full of fresh country air.

"Anything new?" asked Autumn, their private code for, "Have the two of you been arrested for murder?" They made an unwritten rule never to get more specific than that. Autumn and Bosco had absolute faith that Serenity and Nathan were innocent.

So, for that matter, did I.

"No, nothing new," replied Serenity, as Bosco and her sister sat down on the big throw cushions on the floor.

"That's good," said Bosco.

"Yeah, I guess," said Nathan.

Autumn smiled and put her hand on Bosco's knee. "We have big news. We may have to go easy on camping out for a while, because, you see. . ." She looked at her husband. "You tell them, sweets."

"You're going to have a baby," Nathan said.

Bosco looked a little disappointed. "Dude, how did you know?"

Nathan shrugged. "With a couple, there's only so many things big news can be."

Serenity got off the bed and grabbed Autumn. The two sisters jumped up and down and hugged and screamed.

From the bed, Nathan smiled and waved at Bosco. "Congratulations."

Bosco wore a big grin as he walked over to Nathan and gave him a bear hug. "We've come a long way together, bro."

"Yeah, we sure have," Nathan agreed.

But I could tell my son felt emotionally excluded, which has a way of morphing into anger. Life thus far hadn't done much to convince him that being born paid off. If only we could see into the future, baby announcements would take on a whole different meaning. *Congratulations, you've given birth to a rapist.* I could be wrong, but I think that's closer to Nathan's reaction. However, he had the good manners not to let it show. One time I walked by an electronics showroom, and I heard a voice on TV say, "See her in the role she was born to play." I think that's kind of a stretch, don't you? I mean, when she plopped out of her mother's do-hickey, did the doctor say, "This baby's purpose in life is to star in some bullshit movie?"

Anyway, with the predictability of a drunk puking in the gutter, Serenity asked, "Is it a boy or a girl?"

"We don't know yet," Autumn and Bosco replied in unison.

"This is just what we needed," Serenity decided. "Wonderful news to counter. . . like, the other junk."

"There's even more good news," Autumn said. "We want the two of you to be godparents. Whatever happens."

"Whatever happens," Bosco reiterated.

Serenity got misty-eyed as she hugged them both. "I love you so much."

"I'm not sure that's such a hot idea," Nathan said. "I know nothing about God stuff."

Bosco knitted his eyebrows in sincerity. "You're a good person. That's all that matters."

"You're very close to God, Nathan," Autumn added. "You just don't know it."

I concurred in silence. The problem wasn't Nathan, but the conformist mentality of our society that made people who didn't go to church like every other minute feel as though they didn't have God in their hearts. Except for the beautiful Christmas carols, especially the ones in a minor chord, does anyone like to sing hymns? Or listen to a sermon? Is there anything that makes you feel farther away from God than boredom?

I have always shunned mediocrity. For example, cream cheese frosting. What an awful thing to do to a cake. And you see it everywhere.

22

Nathan got his master's in criminology amidst little fanfare. For his thesis topic, he chose Famous Acid Bath Murders. Nathan being Nathan, he did not attend the commencement, but I'm sure no one minded. Serenity wanted to do something special to celebrate, but Nathan said he didn't want anything, and he had a way of being firm when he wanted to be. In fact, he told Serenity, Autumn, and Bosco that he didn't even want to talk about it.

"I'm shy," he explained. "I don't like drawing attention to myself."

"Whatever you say, dude," Bosco said, on behalf of the three of them.

The job market blowed, but even if it hadn't, it seemed no one who had anything to do with criminology wanted to hire Nathan. In addition to his infamous past, the murky cloud of Clay Hinton Jr. also hung over him. Through her shrewd investments, Serenity brought in enough for them to get by, so one day she told Nathan to stop worrying about a job and instead write a book.

"What about?" he asked, playing Free Cell on his computer pad.

"One of those bizarre murders you like so much." Making a fresh devil's food cake, she licked the batter off her finger. They paid someone to clean the small apartment once a week, but baking relaxed her. Or at least sort of relaxed her. She started getting lines in her face from frowning so much. Unlike Nathan, it made her edgy to be an ongoing person of interest in a horrific homicide case.

"But I can't write," Nathan protested. "I mean, I can *write*, but it's nothing all that great."

"In other words, your writing is nothing to write home about."

"Ha-ha."

"Get Bosco to help you." She poured the batter into cake pans with a spatula.

"Between the baby coming and his doctoral defense, I think he has his hands full."

"So this'll give him something else to think about. You know how he's driving Autumn crazy. He's so nervous about becoming a father. God, I'm glad they're having a girl. If they had a boy, Bosco would be seeing every shrink in town."

Nathan cracked his knuckles, thinking over her suggestion. "There are some very cool acid bath murders. Would anyone buy a book written by me?"

"Actually, they just might. But if push comes to shove you can make up a pen name."

"That might be fun. What name should I use?"

Serenity put the pans in the oven, closing the door. "What about Beauregard Fortescue?"

"That might work. Or maybe Pierpoint Snerd."

She poured herself a large glass of wine. "Of course you could also write an autobiography. That might be worth a couple of sales or so."

"No way. What I do is my business. I'm not going to beg the world for mercy. Besides, it could fuck things up for you, with the stupid Clay Hinton case still open."

"I can't wait until the case goes cold. I'm so tired of feeling like I'm walking on eggshells." Serenity sat next to Nathan on the futon bed, nursing her wine.

"I've never understood that expression. They're eggshells—they're already broken. What's so bad about stepping on eggshells?"

"Dummy, it means stepping on raw eggs still in their shell. You know—like it'll make a big mess if you step too hard."

"I don't think so. If that were true, they'd say, 'Walking on eggs.'"

"No, because walking on *eggs* would mean stepping directly into egg goop. I'm picturing these raw eggs already out of their shells, just kind of sitting there on the floor."

"Then where are the shells?"

"They're gone. I dunno. Someone threw them out."

"Well, why would there be a bunch of raw eggs on the floor? I suppose someone could've dropped them, but otherwise it makes no sense."

"That's why they say, 'Walking on eggshells.'"

A knock at the door cut the conversation short.

"I'll be right there, guys," Serenity called out to her sister and brother-in-law.

However, there were two unfamiliar women at the door—two unsmiling FBI detectives to be exact. It's interesting how the richer you are, the more the feds care what happens to you.

"Serenity Nightbridge, you are under arrest for the murder of Clay Hinton Jr.," one of them said. "You have the right to remain silent."

And cha-cha-cha. The other woman brandished a set of handcuffs. I swear, you could've heard a pin drop.

Nathan stood up, and out of sarcasm or politeness—I couldn't tell which—he put his wrists behind himself in anticipation of getting cuffed.

"You are not under arrest, Mr. Nightbridge," said one of the agents. I don't think I ever saw Nathan look so startled before.

"We know you knew nothing about it," said the other agent. "We believe your wife married you just to set you up. She knew everyone would think you did it."

"And if she got arrested," continued the first agent, "she figured she'd be offered a deal to help us nail you in a coffin. Just like Clay Hinton Jr."

"I really don't appreciate being talked about as if I'm not even here," Serenity said, no doubt too in shock to say anything else.

"She loved Clay Hinton Jr.," said the other agent. "And we have proof. They had an affair, but he wouldn't leave his wife and kids. If she told you anything else she lied. She knew you were living with Autumn and Bosco because Autumn already told her in a text message. That's why she came here."

"A slap across the face to those who really do suffer sexual abuse," editorialized the first woman.

Serenity shook her head. "I can't believe this is happening."

"I know what's going on," Nathan said. "They're using you to get to me."

"We must be going," said the other agent, taking hold of Serenity's arm. "Think carefully, Mr. Nightbridge."

"Nathan, what are we—"

"Don't say anything," he interrupted. "I'm calling a goddamned lawyer."

23

Nathan had a quick, urgent conversation with Autumn and Bosco, then left the house to meet with a lawyer downtown. I couldn't follow him there, but back at the house quite a lot happened. Nathan forgot to turn off the oven, and by the time the firefighters arrived the poor devil's food cake—not to mention the entire small apartment—burned down to nothing. Nathan took it in stride. He never cared much about having possessions, and he knew he could crash next door with Autumn and Bosco (Fortunately, the fire did not spread to their unit.). But the FBI did not chuckle with amusement because it rendered their federal search warrant useless. Presumably they thought Serenity and/or Nathan hid all sorts of wondrous evidence in their home, despite its small size and the fact that they had a house cleaner. Almost the entire front wall fell down into the street. From a distance, the apartment looked like an open garage.

But Nathan couldn't be bothered to look at it as he drove to an outdoor café to meet with Autumn and Bosco. He found them nursing lemonades at a table on the sunlit street; a third glass had already been ordered for him.

"God, that happened fast," Bosco said. "Lucky we got out."

"Fire is like that," said Autumn. "I remember from a movie in grade school. A room can burn up in like two minutes."

She tapped on her enormous watermelon of a belly, as if to reassure her unborn child, or maybe herself. "Thank God we smelled smoke. I called our dad, and he'll be posting bail for Serenity."

Before Nathan could respond, one of the agents who arrested Serenity appeared and helped herself to the empty seat at the table.

"I beg your pardon," Bosco said. "We are having—"

"Nathan, I know everything you do," she interjected, ignoring anything approaching good manners. "Setting a fire—really, how banal. I expect so much more from you. What did you have to destroy? You like to think you're smarter than us, but you know you're not. And what's with the sudden worship of attorneys? Don't you feel up to representing Serenity yourself? Are you afraid of the shit that'll hit the fan?"

Nathan used his straw to stir the ice in his drink. "What's your name again?"

She gave him a quizzical look, as though she couldn't begin to comprehend why Nathan would ask her name. "I am Agent Logan Steiner."

"Well, dumb fuck Agent Logan Steiner, why don't you drop dead?"

The bitch laughed; don't you hate it when bitches laugh? You know the kind I mean—the ones with a giant ice cube where their heart is supposed to be. It's as if you can see the frost in the air when they smile. Zelda excelled at frozen smiles. Heaven save us all from scared little girls in the bodies of grown women.

"You'd like it if I were dead, wouldn't you? In fact, you'd love it. Does your little wee-wee get hard when you kill people? Does murder make you come in your pants? It does for some people, you know. People like you."

"You know nothing about me."

"Oh, I'm sorry. Is it that you can't get it up at all? Are you trying to compensate?"

Nathan had no intention of falling prey to her silliness. "Gee, I'm so intimidated."

Logan the asshole agent got all smarmy.

"Mr. and Mrs. Sinclair, you're a nice young couple. You're about to be parents. How can you possibly associate with Nathan?"

"Relax, guys," Nathan said. "She's trying to bust my balls."

"If you aren't here to arrest anyone, I'll ask you to leave," said Bosco. "You're upsetting my wife."

Indeed, Autumn trembled as she touched Bosco's arm.

"I'll be in touch," Logan promised, as she took her leave. Nathan watched as she walked toward her car; just before she got in, she winked at him. In return, he blew her a kiss.

"Life as soap opera." Autumn looked down at her belly. "Babies, fires, cops. I'm sorry, but it still doesn't seem real to me. Serenity in jail—and for murder?"

"It'll all get straightened out," Nathan assured her. "I got the best defense lawyer in town. He's taking the case pro bono. I knew my reputation would be good for something someday."

"Do you mean Leandro Whatchamacallit?" asked Bosco. "The guy who got that lady who killed her sister set free, even though everyone knew she did it?"

"Yep. Only his last name is Flores. Leandro Flores."

"Leandro Whatchamacallit," teased Autumn, rolling her eyes.

"Maybe it's his middle name," Bosco said with mock seriousness. "But anyway, what did he say?"

"First I asked if I should turn myself in. He said, 'Are you guilty?' Naturally I said no. 'Then don't do it,' he said. 'That's pretty much a no brainer.'"

Bosco laughed. "I'm sorry, I know that's not really funny."

"I did feel foolish," Nathan admitted. "Anyway, he asked me if I thought Serenity did it, and I said no. He had me tell everything I knew about Clay Hinton Jr., and when I finished he got quiet for a minute and then he said, 'I need to find out what proof the cops have of an affair.' Then he told me it's not a question of what people do but why, and he had to meet with Serenity. I think I see where he's going—I mean with the case."

Autumn asked, "What are you saying?"

"Stockholm Syndrome. Serenity thought she loved the man who raped and tortured her, which explains the love notes or phone calls or whatever bullshit the cops have as proof of a so-called affair."

"But that's not true," Autumn complained. "She hated his guts."

Nathan shrugged. "Does the phrase, 'temporary insanity,' ring a bell?"

"How about the phrase, 'not guilty?' My sister didn't do anything."

"Oh, there's that old chestnut, too," Nathan admitted. "But let's let Leandro use his own bag of tricks."

"Remember, sweetness, the burden of proof is on the state," Bosco added.

"Okay, I get it." Autumn sighed as she raised her glass of lemonade. "Here's to reasonable doubt."

24

Serenity's father mortgaged his home to put up the half-million dollar bail required to get his daughter out of prison. He flew in to town and flew back out the same day, refusing to talk to reporters. He looked sort of what I might've looked like if my life remained what other people wanted it to be—a white collar CEO who thought himself charitable when he interacted with other people. Nothing if not consistent, he refused to talk to Serenity or for that matter Autumn, until they both promised never to see Nathan again. As it happened, Autumn's water broke the following morning, so poor ol' Grandpa missed the chance to see his granddaughter at birth.

Checking into the hospital with her married name to avoid publicity—and with Nathan volunteering to stay away from the hospital—Autumn gave birth to her daughter with a minimum of fuss. Bosco helped out as her crazed but ecstatic birth coach. I earlier overheard that they wanted to name the girl Serenity, but Nathan insisted they not do so. In the end, they named the baby Aurora. They also started looking for tenure-track professorships to support their growing family. Take it from one who knows: a couple plus a baby in a one-bedroom apartment is nobody's idea of a good time. Serenity and Nathan stayed at a motel.

Between being on the job market and caring for their baby, Autumn and Bosco somewhat distanced themselves from Serenity and Nathan. If they harbored any doubts about Serenity's innocence, I never heard them voice any. Of course, I didn't watch them 24/7, but it wouldn't surprise me if they never talked about it. The whole thing raised too many disturbing questions—and not only about the case, but about how uncertain life itself could be. Sometimes people shut out anything that threatens their calm demeanor. I do it myself quite often.

Nathan seemed to understand this just fine, but it made Serenity bitter. During her trial, she reacted more to what she considered her sister's betrayal than she did to facing the death needle for being charged with Murder One. I knew this because I spied on Serenity and Nathan in their motel room.

"Would someone please explain," Serenity said one evening after a long day in court, "why I am the only one out of any of you whose life is in the fucking toilet? I made honest money. I knew what I wanted. Unlike my prig sister, who treats me like I'm a pubic hair in the bathtub drain. She's so nice and settled and married, and now she's going to be some boring college professor and probably have more of those creepy babies that drop out of her with such ease." Serenity graduated from wine to bourbon, and she took a generous swallow before refilling her glass. I knew she had a prescription for Valium, never the smartest drug to combine with booze.

"I've been where you are," Nathan said, playing his game on his computer pad. "It'll be over soon."

Serenity yanked the razor-thin pad from his hands. "But I'm already over. Don't you see? What can I possibly do after this fucking trial? Assuming they don't give me the death penalty. That might be better. To die and get it over with."

Nathan sighed. "Not if you use your ka-noodle. You can change your name. Dye your hair. As we both know, you excel at convincing people of whatever it is you want to convince them of, Little Miss Someone-Wants-to-Murder-Me."

"Don't tell me you didn't believe me, either? Gee, this is really turning out to be my day."

"Oh, I believed you. I just wonder what you would've done if I hadn't plopped into your life. Would you still be putting out for your rapist?"

She punched him in the chin with surprising force, causing him to fall backward in his chair. "Well, Nathan, I hope I've convinced you of whatever I wanted to convince you of."

They didn't speak for a couple of days, and then things went back to how they were before.

News cameras recorded the trial, and each day it turned up on the Internet. Nathan came to court every day and looked into the camera whenever it zoomed over to him for a reaction shot. Sometimes he'd wave, with that million-dollar smile of his.

I've thought a great deal about it, and I still don't understand what the FBI thought would happen by charging Serenity but not Nathan for the demise of sadistic rapist Clay Hinton Jr. I knew both of them to be innocent, but if they considered Nathan some weirdo sociopath, then why think he'd confess to get his wife off the hook? Maybe they profiled him to be pathologically jealous, and he wouldn't want Serenity to get all the credit. Yet that didn't jive with the fact that Nathan never wanted to be found guilty of anything. I took a couple of psych classes back at Yale and tried to remember the litany of disorders that people could have in an effort to figure out what in the blazes it all meant. I kept coming back to the notion that the federal prosecutors believed that Serenity did it, and she acted alone. Unless, given Nathan's track record with murder trials, they thought it best not to tempt fate by charging him as well, or at least not until Serenity got convicted first.

The FBI's version of events, which took about a zillion witnesses to map out, went like this: Serenity and Clay had their sleaze-o affair, and guess what, the married man dumped the mistress to go back to his wife and kids. But such affairs often ping-pong back and forth before a super-final decision is reached. So Clay had second thoughts, and when he found out that Serenity had partnered with crazy Nathan Nightbridge, he came to her rescue. According to the FBI, Serenity would've told Clay this herself, to make him jealous, and scared for her. When Clay banged on the door to save her, Nathan, of course, thought Clay must be crazier than a rabid gerbil, but Serenity's phone records showed that she put in a call to Clay later that night. The landlord of the subdivided house testified there used to be a crate in the basement that looked like the one Clay suffocated in, but it disappeared, as did a hammer.

As if all this were not enough, a couple of people who Serenity worked with in New York said that she told them she had an affair with Clay, and his widow testified that her husband told her everything. The coroner said she found a love letter from Serenity in Clay's jacket pocket.

According to the federal prosecution, Serenity's relationship with Nathan existed only to set the trap for Clay, and to have people think Nathan must've done it. This last element in her master scheme failed. But throughout the presentation of its case, the prosecution emphasized that Serenity worked alone.

Stalwart defense attorney Leandro Flores poked holes in the FBI's case with every cross-examination. For years, tenants helped themselves to junk in the basement of the house, and the landlord couldn't say for certain that the disappearance of the crate or hammer had been recent. Serenity may well have called Clay Hinton Jr. in an effort to get him to leave her alone. Former co-workers would say anything the Hinton family told them to say. As for whom Serenity did or did not find attractive, Leandro called Serenity to the witness stand. I have to say she did not look well. Though she'd been out on bail and living with the highly supportive Nathan, she looked more like she'd been locked in solitary confinement.

No member of the Hinton family attended the trial. Probably they thought it beneath them.

"Mrs. Nightbridge," he began, as if to emphasize her respectable station in life. "This love letter that the people entered as evidence. Did you write it?"

"Yes."

"And just to be sure. You wrote it to Clay Hinton Jr.?"

"Yes."

"And did you tell your coworkers you were having an affair with Clay Hinton Jr.?"

"Yes."

"And did Clay Hinton Jr. ever tell you that he told his wife the two of you were having an affair?"

"Yes."

"So, did you have an affair with the late Clay Hinton Jr.?"

"No," she answered, with head held high.

"No? I'm confused. Could you please explain?"

Serenity looked down and away. "He raped me. He tortured me. He played Russian Roulette with a gun . . . a gun inside me."

You could hear a collective gasp in the courtroom. The federal judge banged on his gavel for order.

"Do you need to stop for a few minutes?" Leandro asked.

"No," she answered. "I need to say it once and for all. He hounded me at work to go out with him. He threatened to fire me, to kill me, to set me up for a crime, unless I had sex with him."

"Why didn't you report him to your employer? Or the police?"

"He *was* my employer. The police wouldn't help when I told them his name."

"But I still don't get it. Why would you write him a love letter? Why would you keep seeing him?"

As if on cue, Serenity burst into tears. "I don't know."

Leandro gave her a minute to contain herself. Predictably enough, Nathan's hunch proved right on the money. Leandro veered straight into Stockholm Syndrome and, I imagined, would call an expert witness to back it up. Temporary insanity, here we come.

"And did you kill Clay Hinton Jr.?"

Serenity sat there with a blank expression on her face.

"Did you kill Clay Hinton Jr.?" Leandro repeated.

"I. . . I don't know."

Her lawyer feigned a troubled expression. "You don't know? How can that be?"

"He said he loved me. I hated him. I thought he'd kill me. I—I don't know what I did."

"Your witness."

Two lawyers represented the feds, a man and a woman; the woman rose to question Serenity. I assumed they wanted to create an impression that Serenity's alleged crime had nothing to do with women's lib. The attorney looked like she could've been Serenity's mother.

"Mrs. Nightbridge, I'll try to be as brief as possible."

Serenity dabbed her nose with a Kleenex. "Thank you."

"I'm puzzled. I look over your life up to this point, and I see a very focused and assertive young woman. A budding Wall Street broker, making your own way in New York. And yet when the subject turns to Clay Hinton Jr., you become so demure. So confused. All of a sudden, you have no idea if you nailed a living man into a crate, leaving him to suffocate and dehydrate, with a gun shoved up his rectum. You just can't remember. Golly gee."

Leandro stood up. "Objection, your honor. Is there a question the state wishes to ask my client?"

"Do get to the point, counselor," admonished the judge.

"Mrs. Nightbridge, do you have a problem with anger management?"

"Objection, your honor. Relevance?"

The DA looked irritated. "Goes to state of mind, your honor."

"Overruled. Defendant will answer."

"Again. Mrs. Nightbridge, do you have a problem with anger management?"

"Anger management?" Serenity stood up, pounding the podium. "That fucker got what he deserved. He tortured women, and I'm the one with the problem?"

"But you loved him. You told him so in a letter. You phoned him on weekends."

Serenity appeared to be hyperventilating. "I keep telling you, I don't know." She dissolved into a blob of tears. "I don't know," she kept whimpering.

The judge called for an early recess. "Please have your client in better shape to answer questions tomorrow," he warned Leandro.

Nathan, Serenity, and her lawyer managed to get back to the motel room without being eaten alive by the press.

"Great job, Serenity," Leandro said. "The prosecution played right into it. One of the jurors cried. No way will they convict."

She popped a handful of Valium. "All this weeping. It's exhausting."

"You're in the home stretch," Nathan said. "After you're acquitted, you should take a long vacation. If you'd like, I'll come with you."

"I wouldn't like. I need to be alone for a while."

"Who the hell are you," Leandro joked. "Greta Garbo?"

"Greta who?" asked Serenity.

"You know, from the old movies." Leandro placed the front of his hand on his forehead in mock melodrama. "I vant to be alone."

Serenity and Nathan responded with blank stares.

"No? Oh well, back to the trial. Tomorrow, you should appear as though you've composed yourself. It'll make today's pathos seem more believable. Never lay it on too thick."

'It's a murder trial, not a peanut butter sandwich," Nathan concurred.

25

The next morning, the prosecutor picked up where she left off with Serenity, who acted more her old Wall Street self.

"When someone tortures you," she told the court, "you find yourself doing strange things. I know I called Clay quite a lot, begging him to leave me alone. I made a terrible mistake. It had the opposite effect. Same thing with the letter. I thought I could humor him and make him go away. You know, if I acted serious, it could jeopardize his marriage."

The woman asked, "Then how do you explain coworkers who testified that you had a crush on Mr. Hinton?"

Serenity adjusted her glasses. "I never said I had a crush on him. I had sex with him. Against my will. But I don't blame them for what they said. I know all too well how it feels to be intimidated."

"So if you did not feel affection for Mr. Hinton, is it possible you were using him to get ahead in your career?"

"Objection, your honor."

The judge thought for a moment. "Overruled. Witness will answer."

Serenity stared at the DA with so much hatred it felt palpable in the air around her.

"I got ahead in my career because I worked harder than everyone else. After what he did to me. . . to say I sought it out. . . how can you call yourself a woman?"

"Move to strike," the DA requested, and the judge concurred.

"You certainly do seem calmer today," the DA continued. "In fact, it's hard to believe that you were crying so hard only yesterday."

The judge sustained Leandro's objection. After a few more attempts to get a negative reaction out of Serenity, the DA gave up.

The next defense witness turned out to be that awful FBI detective Logan Steiner, who arrested Serenity and then bullied Nathan at the outdoor café. Agent Steiner coughed a little while being sworn in. She could've coughed up her lungs and died, for all I cared. You could tell she wanted to be there as much as she wanted to be blindfolded in front of a firing squad.

Leandro said, "Detective Steiner, when you arrested Mrs. Nightbridge in her apartment, what did you say to Mr. Nightbridge?"

"I don't remember," she answered in a condescending tone, as if Leandro should've kissed her ass for her being there at all.

"Your honor, I wish to treat this witness as hostile."

"Permission granted."

"Now then, Detective. Did you explain to him why you were not arresting him?"

"I suppose so."

"Did you say that all evidence pointed to Mrs. Nightbridge and none to Mr. Nightbridge?"

"I don't know if I came right out and said this. But obviously, we had no reason to arrest Mr. Nightbridge."

"Because you believe he's innocent."

"Because we do not have any evidence that points to him."

"So you're saying that tomorrow or next week or five years from now, if there is evidence that points to Mr. Nightbridge, the theory the government is presenting here with taxpayer's money will have proven worthless."

"Objection," said the woman prosecutor.

"Overruled, but watch it, counselor."

"Your honor," Leandro replied in his brisk, personable manner, "I have a conversation between Detective Steiner and Mr. Nightbridge that took place in an outdoor café, which Mr. Nightbridge recorded on his cell phone. I enter it as defense exhibit number—"

"Objection, your honor. The people have not been given a chance to listen to this conversation, if in fact it took place."

The two sides had a brief rhubarb in the judge's chamber, and in the end, they emerged with Leandro being permitted to play the recording, though the state would be given time to refute it as needed. So the jury heard how Logan Steiner kept hammering away at Nathan, trying—and failing—to get him to own up to being a bizarre serial killer and by intimation involved in the death of Clay Hinton Jr. More than once, I discerned a collective gasp in the courtroom for the disrespectful language the agent used. Not to mention the way she harped at Nathan—clearly there was more to this case than met the eye.

At the end of the recording, Leandro said, "No more questions for this witness." The prosecution declined to question Logan at all, though both the man and woman shot her a dirty look, as if to say, "Thanks a lot for nothing."

Leandro called a shrink as an expert witness, who explained about Stockholm Syndrome for the benefit of anyone who hadn't heard about it a million times on TV. The shrink also said that after interviewing Serenity for several hours in depth, he concluded she had this condition. The male prosecutor tried to belittle his testimony and asked if he got paid to testify, but the shrink insisted he hadn't been. I thought the defense might throw in a pinch of Post Traumatic Stress Disorder for good luck, but they didn't. Upon reflection, I saw the wisdom of this, since people with PTSD sometimes turned violent, which opened a whole new can of worms. Better to keep it simple.

With that, the defense rested. I found it to be a concise, elegant presentation that would've made the stupidest person in the world vote "not guilty." Finally, each side made its closing remarks, which I had a hard time paying attention to. They both got so technical and talked for so long, my mind wandered. However, the jury deliberated for only one hour before returning with its verdict:

"In the matter of the death of Clay Hinton Jr., the jury finds the defendant, Serenity Nightbridge, guilty of murder in the first degree."

26

I huddled in the crowd outside the courtroom as the verdict blared through the loudspeakers. All these idiotic people burst into applause. Probably they were paid to do so by the DA, or maybe the tacky nouveau riche Hinton family. But off to one side were the Nathanites, fans of my son. They cried and consoled each other. I entered into a state of shock—for Serenity, for Nathan, for all injustices everywhere for all time. I realized how much I missed my friend, Charlie. He would've known how to cheer me up.

In the courtroom, Serenity screamed, "God fucking damn it," as the verdict was read, making it clear she would not go gently into that good night. As the judge banged his gavel and called for silence, Serenity turned to the jurors and said, "Thanks a fucking lot, you motherfucking assholes." (Rebroadcasts would bleep out all the cuss words.)

Leandro put his arm around her in an effort to calm her, but Serenity had none of it. "Why should I be quiet?" she shrieked. "What are you going to do, put me in jail?"

In the end, a couple of guards carried her away as she kicked and yelled and bit, a wild animal obeying its survival instinct.

The next day, the moronic judge sentenced her. They must've really doped up Serenity because she sat there like a zombie. After calling her a brilliant actress and a pathological liar, the judge, in his profound mercy, gave Serenity the death penalty. "The heinousness of this crime deserves nothing less," said the hateful numbskull. Serenity showed no reaction. A quick cut to Nathan showed him staring straight ahead, his eyes seeming to be on fire.

Some people said that Nathan should've stood up and declared that he murdered Clay, to get Serenity off the hook. But this would've made people think they both did it, which solved nothing. Leandro told reporters outside the courtroom that he would be appealing the verdict and would not rest until Serenity was free.

Logan Steiner got fired from the FBI for her unprofessional and uncool conduct. I, for one, would not be surprised to learn she had a long history of disobeying orders. Going into law enforcement requires an integrity that she lacked. Sometimes it seems like all of humankind is becoming less competent and more lazy.

After the horrendous verdict, I'm afraid that Yours Truly suffered a bit of a setback, mentally speaking. I stopped taking the purple capsules and found myself in the psycho ward of the local hospital. I didn't see why they had to straightjacket me, just because I smashed a department store window so I could hump one of the mannequins. No one got hurt, for crying out loud. Later, when they asked me about my meds, I forgot if the capsules were pink or purple, so I said they were pinklepurp. That cracks me up—pinklepurp.

I swear, if you've seen one psycho ward you've seen 'em all. The nurses act so condescending they should wear tiaras, and that includes the male nurses, if you see what I mean. They talk to you like you're a hand puppet. As for the food, I swear if I ever see a plastic cup of green gelatin again I will puke to death. The general populace consisted of your usual garden variety of crackpots. I best remember a woman who spent all day tap dancing without any taps while she belted out, "God Bless America." I got discharged a few months later after all but taking a blood oath to the status quo that I'd take all my meds every day like an obedient slave. The government-military complex breaks the spirit of humanity one soul at a time.

Well, at least I fell off the CIA radar for a while.

Upon release, I went straight to the public library to catch myself up on Serenity and Nathan. Thousands of letters had been sent to the governor calling for Serenity's immediate release. I assumed these came from Nathanites. A TV news reporter got permission to interview her on death row, and she exuded poise. She could've been having tea at one of those fancy department stores on Fifth Avenue. As I thought of it, from time to time some rich celebrity asshole went to prison, and it never humbled the person like everyone in the universe hoped it would. A prison hotshot described Serenity as a model inmate, though I'm not sure you can do much on death row even if you wanted to.

Nathan refused to speak with reporters about Serenity. One time, when a newscaster hurried after him as he got into his car, he blew a kiss into the camera before driving off.

Then I came across an interesting tidbit about former agent Logan Steiner—she turned up dead after Serenity's trial. All the evidence pointed to suicide; she bled out in the bathtub for her slit wrists and left behind a note that matched her handwriting. The message got right to the point. "Fuck everyone," and then her name, "Logan Steiner," underneath.

Now, you'd think that would be the end of it. Nothing possible to quibble about. But FBI lunatics said that Logan never would've told everyone to fuck off, as if someone committing suicide thinks it's important to be polite. They also made a big deal about the fact that Logan signed with both her first and last name. Again, what do people expect from someone who's gone off the deep end? In other words, there were blog postings and the like that all but charged Nathan with Logan Steiner's death.

But the real zinger came after my release from the snake pit. A body popped up in the woods not far from where Clay Hinton Jr.'s corpse had been left, and again in a crate, but sans the gun, so I guess the victim's ass didn't suffer. Police identified the body as none other than Clay Hinton Sr., who according to the press had met with Serenity on death row, presumably to tell her to fuck herself. Like father, like son. Big Daddy Hinton dehydrated and suffocated to death in the crate. But that's not all. They found traces of DNA on Mr. Hinton's necktie, and it belonged to none other than Logan Steiner. Small world, as they say.

Shortly thereafter, an anonymous tip led police to a storage unit in Logan's name that served as a shrine to Clay

Hinton Jr. As an A-list power broker, he'd on occasion be pictured in gossip magazines for having attended charity balls and the like, and Logan scribbled things like, "This should be me," across the face of his wife. Happy as I felt when all this came to light, it disturbed me to think my son had become an all-purpose scapegoat for humanity's sins.

Leandro Flores, Serenity's handsome and stalwart attorney, lost no time in filing a motion to get the conviction overturned. As he told a group of hyperactive reporters, Logan Steiner's DNA on Clay Hinton Sr., and her subsequent suicide along with the storage locker proved beyond a shadow of doubt that she framed Serenity in the murder of Clay Hinton Jr.

Before you could say lethal injection, Serenity got released from prison, a free woman. Upon leaving the imposing, humorless edifice, she turned to give it the finger with both hands, the photo of which act got nominated for the Pulitzer Prize. She checked Nathan and herself into a snazzy hotel, ordered a case of bourbon, and refused all requests for interviews.

But Serenity never had been one to sit around and twiddle her thumbs. The government compensated her months on death row with a cool ten million bucks in restitution. Plus she had a gigantic book deal and sold the film rights to her story. And, as the dollop of sour cream atop the zesty bowl of borscht, the publisher agreed to publish Nathan's book as well—the content of which remained undecided. Add all this to Serenity's investment acumen, and she and Nathan took up lifelong residency on Easy Street.

Life is such a trip. Finally, Nathan had millions. He eradicated the sins of his father or should I say grandfather? His wife got falsely convicted of Murder One, and they lived happily ever after.

Or sort of, if your idea of happiness is living in a war zone.

27

Sometimes innocent people are good sports about getting released from prison after wrongful conviction, grateful to smell the fresh air again. But not Serenity. She resented every day, hour, and minute she spent behind bars and could only explode with fury whenever she remembered that brief period in her life. True, she got ten million for her troubles, but she dismissed it as ten million-shmillion. And she constantly reminded herself of being on death row. Take it from one who knows: pure, full octane anger is addictive. It makes all other emotions—yes, even love, shmove—seem like 3.2 beer in the presence of single malt scotch. In the courtroom, Serenity offered her heart in her hands, and the jury said, "No thanks," which is one of the worst things that can happen to someone. The perpetual sneer on her face made me think the lenses in her glasses would crack out of sheer rage.

For Nathan, I imagine such all-encompassing anger came easy, as if a boa constrictor had long ago wrapped itself around his heart. But he avoided it or kept it under control. Though Serenity always harbored contempt for that which she viewed as beneath her, feeling nothing but hate proved uncharted territory. It wasn't so much that she felt pissed off all the time—on a certain level, everyone does—but that she had no idea how to handle it. Unlike Nathan, she never had cause to develop much inner life and could only take it out on the nearest available target.

Serenity wanted nothing more to do with everyone and everything, so she and Nathan settled in a small woodsy town, the nearest neighbor a good half-mile away. Tall trees and thick shrubs surrounded the house, making it easy to spy on. I blended right in with the leaves and bushes and things. It reminded me of an upscale version of the Rainbows' cottage.

Speaking of déjà vu, as her drinking increased, Serenity took on traits that were reminiscent of Zelda, which irony could not have been lost on one as sensitive and alert as Nathan. Maybe everyone who drinks too much gets this way. I remember something or another from Yale about how alcohol abuse destroys brain cells. It seems to me that up to a point this is a good thing. Everyone has too many brain cells, and if there were fewer of them the world would be a better place. But I guess there can be too much of a good thing. I mean, if everyone got shit-faced drunk all the time, it would be harder for us homeless people.

Anyway, Nathan appeared to be going through some sort of catharsis with Serenity, trying to work through something he couldn't work through with the long-dead Zelda. When Serenity sassed him, he sassed her back. No more scared child who couldn't look Mommy in the eye, scared to death of Mr. Brown.

"You're such a fucking liar," Serenity shouted at him, and Nathan shouted right back.

"You should know. Everything you say is a lie."

"What do you know about having a broken heart?"

"More than you. At least I have a heart."

"You would've liked it if Clay Hinton killed me," she shrieked.

"No, I wouldn't have liked it. But I'd have gotten over it."

"Well, then I'm sure you'd have gotten over being on death row because of the man who raped you."

"Here we go again. You know I did everything I could."

"I'm not so sure. Why were you never found guilty? Why were you never tried in federal court?"

"Look, you're out of prison, aren't you?"

"Yes, in a manner of speaking. Now I'm in the prison of living with you."

Nathan looked exasperated. "I did what I had to do to help you. We have a deal, plain and simple, and you'd be wise to be a woman of your word."

And on and on it would go. It's strange how people's lives turn out. The more unsettled Serenity and Nathan became, the nicey-nicer things got for Autumn and Bosco. Despite the lousy job market, they landed tenure track gigs at the same college and got to live only a couple of hours away from Serenity and Nathan. Autumn became pregnant with their second snot-nosed brat. The threesome-soon-to-be-foursome visited Serenity and Nathan on a bracing, sunny weekend in October. Bosco never looked happier, and being pregnant in a far more settled situation than the last time around gave Autumn a glow of contentment. Their toddler, Aurora, remained oblivious to everything but her pacifier. I have a theory that children of creative people learn at a young age to give their parents privacy. Or maybe they're forming their own private space, who knows?

Nathan greeted the growing family and showed them around the rustic house and the woodsy backyard. Serenity had what Nathan called a headache and rested upstairs with the bedroom door shut. She would have many such headaches from here on out. Nathan and his guests sat in the living room, enjoying a gluten-free carrot cake that Autumn made from scratch, when Serenity descended the staircase like something out of Edger Allen Poe.

"Serenity," Autumn said with a smile. "How wonderful that you're joining us. Aurora, do you see your Aunt—"

"Cut the crap." Serenity put her hands to her head as if to keep it from splitting open.

"I want to chop my head off. Anything is better than such excruciating pain."

She had a lollapalooza of a hangover, which is no fun but not the end of the world. But nothing existed in the universe besides her headache. She had that Zelda way of dissolving everything but herself. If she couldn't be happy, then neither could anyone else.

"Should we take you to the doctor?" Autumn asked.

"Yeah, you'd like that," Serenity hissed. "Get me committed so that you can help yourself to my money.

You're not getting a dime, not even if I croak, so don't bother killing me, either."

"Now wait a fucking minute," Bosco said. "We would never—"

"Ignore it." Nathan munched away on his healthful slice of cake. "Pretend it's a ghost."

Serenity approached him with pure hatred, like Medea casting a spell.

"A ghost? Jesus, everyone wishes me dead. The state sure did, leaving me to rot on death row."

Nathan sighed. "You were there for a few months, and you made out like a bandit. In case you've forgotten, I've been in prison, too."

"For like five minutes," Serenity replied. "I never should've been there at all."

"And what? You're saying I should've?"

He reached for another piece of cake; Serenity knocked it out of his hand. Autumn and Bosco grabbed Aurora and stepped aside. They acted like they wanted nothing to do with the erupting conflict, but they made no effort to leave the room. With their cozy little family, they must've felt light years superior to Serenity and Nathan.

"I'm saying that this money—I could've earned it on my own. At my job. My actual career that I worked so hard to get. Do you think I enjoy being the crazy old witch who lives in the woods?"

Nathan stood over her like a bare tree in a lightning storm. "I have no idea. When have you ever liked anything?"

She glared at him right back. "Look who's talking, Mr. Happiness. You told me it would be a cinch. You said I'd be found not guilty."

"Look, it's over. You'll have to come up with a better excuse to pop pills and drink 24/7."

Serenity stood erect, like royalty. "I certainly have no idea what you're talking about. I have a doctor's prescription for Valium, and I trust my doctor. I enjoy an occasional Wild Turkey. After all I've been through—"

"To hell with all you've been through."

Nathan picked up the dregs of the carrot cake, and smooshed it onto Serenity's glasses. She let out an ear-piercing scream of horror, as if carrot cake contained sulfuric acid.

"Shut the fuck up," Nathan said.

Hurling her glasses across the room, Serenity leapt on Nathan, falling on top of him as she grabbed hold of his throat. Like many drunks, she acquired mysterious physical strength. She squeezed with all her might, and his body went limp. Bosco pulled her off him. Nathan didn't seem to be alive. But then, thank God, he started breathing and coughing, and as he sat up the color returned to his face. There is no greater grief in this world than a parent outliving his child. I don't even like to think about it.

"What is wrong with you?" Autumn asked her sister, putting her hands on Aurora's shoulders.

Serenity swallowed a handful of pills.

"Oh, nothing's wrong with me. The problem is with all of you. You're sorry I'm still alive, aren't you? I'm such a pain in the ass. How much easier it would've been to let me die."

Bosco helped Nathan to stand up. "Are you sure you're all right, man?"

"I'm fine."

Maybe I didn't have a clear view, for there were a great many shadows. But it looked to me like Nathan became aroused and moved his leg about to conceal the evidence. I guess when the body is in panic mode, all sorts of strange things happen. There are those dummies who come like there's no tomorrow when strangled. I forget what they call it.

Serenity wiped her glasses clean, and then sat on the sofa, crying. Autumn took her hand and stroked it in sympathy. I didn't get what Serenity had to bawl about, since she just got done trying to murder her husband. But women are attentive to each other when one of them cries, even if a minute later they're stabbing each other in the back.

Anyway, Bosco womped Nathan on the back and said, "Let's go for a walk, dude."

But they didn't walk far when Bosco sat down on the front porch wall and said, "We need to talk."

We need to talk is never a jolly way to start a conversation, and I felt myself get that sinking feeling inside even though I wasn't the person Bosco addressed. I imagine there are many ways in which father and son experience the same thing at the same time in a conjoined sympathy.

Nathan leaned against a post. "Well, talk."

"It's Autumn. I mean, it's Serenity. Autumn is very worried about Serenity."

Nathan looked puzzled.

"What does that have to do with me?"

Bosco couldn't meet Nathan's gaze.

"Autumn thinks Serenity should live with us. You know, like not live with you anymore if she's going to get better. We're not talking about money. We don't want a dime. But Autumn is worried sick about her sister."

Nathan appeared beyond flabbergasted.

"Oh well, since the great Autumn is worried, I have to do something. You think I don't know a drunk when I see one? That I don't try to help Serenity—"

"We just saw you trying, bud. Cake in the face? C'mon, man, you can't seriously think that's good for her."

"Nothing else works. I tried being nice. Not just with Serenity but with all sorts of people. It never works. All I can do is shock people into their senses."

Bosco shook his head.

"I'm not saying being nice fixes everything. But being cruel—that never works. It makes everything worse."

"Huh."

Nathan looked as though this possibility never occurred to him before. It wasn't surprising, given all the crap he had to take from other people. My friend Charlie used to talk about that—the difference between survival and gain. When someone survives something, they often think they've gained something, even though they haven't. So then they think it's good for other people to go through whatever terrible thing they had to go through.

"Autumn says that what Serenity needs—"

"Autumn can say shit for all I care. What do you say?"

Bosco frowned. "I don't have all the answers, okay? But I don't want to argue with you. You're my oldest friend."

"Yes, that's true. In fact, just a minute ago you rescued me from getting choked to death by poor, helpless Serenity."

Bosco faked a laugh. "You see? It's not working out for you, either. You'll be happier without her."

"You know something, Bosco? You ran away from home and did all this cool stuff, but somehow you ended up exactly the son your father wanted. It's like you have this bullet proof vest that keeps anything nasty from penetrating your life."

"That really hurts, but I'll save it for later. I'm talking about your wife."

Nathan chortled.

"When she surfaces for air, Serenity says you're both fucks. She hates how settled your lives are. She resents it so much that sometimes she smashes things against the wall. You have no idea what you're talking about. It's none of your fucking business."

"Whoa, slow down, Nathan. I'm trying to help."

"By doing whatever Autumn says? She's so worried but she can't tell me herself. And yet she told me how close to God I am. What a fucking bitch."

"You are close to God, which is why you can be so intimidating. She's afraid of you, Nathan. And never call my wife a fucking bitch again."

"Okay, so she's a bitch who doesn't fuck."

Bosco socked Nathan in the jaw; Nathan responded with a punch to Bosco's chin, throwing him off balance. As Bosco fell to the wooden floor of the porch, Nathan said, "I thought you people were my friends. That you knew you had nothing to fear from me."

Bosco rubbed his chin as he stood back up. "I don't mean that stuff. I mean. . . well, people never know what they're going to get when they talk to you. Are you going to say nothing and walk away? Are you going to make fun of them?"

"Bosco, in all the years you've known me, when have I ever done these things?"

"True, you've always been kind to me. But other people—even when what you say is right, there's so much contempt in it. Autumn is a sensitive person. She picks up on these things. She thinks you don't like her, and I have to admit I see what she means. It's hard to explain, but something warm and fuzzy is missing when you talk to her. Even when you say something that's technically nice."

"Wow, Serenity and I must give the two of you an awful lot to talk about. She's crazy, and I'm—I dunno, not nice or some shit. No wonder you're both so perfect, with a perfect kid and another perfect kid in the oven."

"I know you don't mean that, so I'm not going to respond. And I don't believe that Serenity says those terrible things about us. Look for yourself."

He pointed to the living room on the other side of the windows where Serenity cried in Autumn's lap. Autumn stroked her hair.

"See? Being close to her sister, playing with the baby. That's what she needs most. Love to conquer the hate."

A loud bird cawed, perhaps a crow; Nathan turned to find the sound.

"Love only conquers hate when the hate is out in the open. When hate is hidden, hate conquers love."

"What a weird thing to say, man."

"Weird or not, if you want her to get clean and sober, she needs more than touchie-feelies. She needs one of those bullshit recovery programs."

"We know. But first, she has to. . . I dunno, trust people or something like that."

"Okay, fine. Not only am I a total fuckup, but I'm stupid. I'm always wrong about everything and you're always right about everything."

Bosco frowned.

"Hey, Nathan. This wasn't easy to say. You're still my bro. My main man."

He extended his hand. After a moment, Nathan shook it, and they patted each other on the back.

"And when Serenity gets better," Bosco continued, "the two of you—"

"I may well have moved on by then," Nathan interjected. "But we'll see."

"Uh, sure."

But obviously Bosco felt sure of very little.

"And just so you know," he continued, "Autumn and I have our moments just like any couple. Right now we're arguing over handguns."

Nathan looked intrigued.

"Guns? What do you mean?"

Bosco sighed. "With all this Clay Hinton Sr. crap I got to thinking that Autumn and I should have handguns to protect our kids. You never know who might come after us. Autumn is totally against it. She goes on about how horrified she is that I'd even suggest it."

"Do either of you know how to shoot?"

"I used to go hunting with my dad. But Autumn is afraid to even touch a gun. I say she has to get over it. There are too many creeps in this world."

Nathan laughed.

"I have to admit it's hard to imagine Autumn with a gun."

"Well, anyway, let's go back inside." He nudged Nathan's arm. "Trust me, Nathan. In the long run you'll thank us for taking care of Serenity."

Nathan appeared distracted, like his quick mind had already moved on.

"I think you're right. Yes, that's the best thing to do."

"You're a good man, Nathan."

"And you're the only person who thinks so."

Bosco patted him on the back. "That's not true. Surely you know about the Nathanites. There's thousands of them. You're their hero. You beat the system."

"I just did what anyone would do."

"You know, dude, one of these days you're finally going to say something good about yourself."

"Yeah, maybe. Who knows?"

28

As Autumn packed her sister's clothes, Serenity kept saying, "You're not getting my money." Sometimes when she said this she sounded like a bratty five-year-old; at other times, she sounded like Medusa turning people into stone. I half-expected her to say, "I have always depended on the kindness of strangers." At one point, with everyone in the room, she stage whispered in Autumn's ear, "Nathan wants to kill me."

I could see that Autumn, Bosco, and Nathan all suppressed the urge to laugh. Alcohol abuse plants the weirdest ideas in people's heads. By the time Serenity packed her things, Autumn and Nathan were on kiss-on-the-cheek terms, and Serenity kissed Nathan on the mouth. She started to say something, but then changed her mind.

Once everyone left, Nathan stood alone in the big house. For the first time in his life, he had more than one room to call his own. He walked from one end of the house to the other, taking it all in. Then he laughed. Not ha-ha for a second or two, but a deep laugh that went on and on as he rolled over the floor, clutching his belly. Then he lay on his back and looked up at the ceiling, panting to catch his breath. I swear, he had an orgasm of laughter.

He stripped the sheets off the master bed, as if stripping everyone and everything from his soul. He lay on top of the bare mattress and slept for a full twenty-four hours. Then, as people often do when they have an entire house to themselves, he came up with busywork to occupy his time.

The forest surrounded the house on three sides, and the front side featured a huge picture window that had a spectacular panoramic view of mountains and trees. Fearing the presence of gawkers and hecklers, Nathan had the window removed and filled in with wallboard. On the new inside wall, he hung a large Chinese painting of a snake. It was a vivid red snake that stared at the viewer with its blood-dripping fangs showing. Good-bye, mountains and trees. Nathan also put three more deadbolts on the front and back doors. The house became much darker inside with the main window gone, but since I always used one of the wooded sides of the house to look through, I could still see what he did. One night, I tripped over a fallen tree trunk, and Nathan came outside to see what caused the noise. I crouched out of sight, which came as a relief since he brandished a rifle.

Autumn and Bosco had their second baby, another girl whom they named Estelle. They came to visit Nathan with their two baby blobs. Serenity, they told him, had gone to some phony ass recovery center called Paradise Within. The old battle-ax had been sober for two months. Tell me another one.

"She'll be in touch with you after she finishes 120 days," Autumn reported. "She said that you and she need to finish what you started, and that you'd know what that meant."

"Yeah, I know what it means," Nathan said.

"Hey, cheer up, bud." Bosco put his hand on his friend's shoulder. "Everything's going to be great."

But I sensed awkward feelings between Bosco and Nathan after all the crap about Serenity. I felt sad for them and hoped they'd get past it. I'd grown so fond of Bosco over the years. I considered him almost a second son.

Yet the news about Serenity removed Nathan's writer's block, and he typed away like a maniac to produce his book in one short month. When something grabbed his interest, nothing slowed him down. I had no way of knowing its content until it appeared for public consumption some months later. For now, let us say I admired his bravado. While not the world's greatest writer, he had an idiosyncratic style that added to the book's impact.

Serenity bid adieu to Blah-Blah Treatment Center, or whatever the fuck they called it. Reporters crowded around her as she took her first footsteps back into the real world. Autumn stood next to her with a warm, supportive glow.

"Serenity, what are your plans?" shouted one reporter.

"Would you describe yourself as serene?" asked some witty turd.

"What about Nathan?" another asshole wanted to know.

You'd have thought she'd tell them to fuck off or something, but instead she smiled and said, "One day at a time, folks. I'm just glad to be alive."

Something about the phrase, *I'm just glad to be alive*, drove me up the wall. I knew homeless people who said it all the time, so needless to say I heard it quite a lot.

The two sisters walked arm in arm to Autumn's car, cheery as can be. TV station vans followed them as they stopped for gas or to piss or take a dump, and then they stopped again at some roadside sushi bar. Finally, they made it back to Serenity's home. The reporters must have cursed their luck for Nathan's absence. But Serenity and Autumn smiled for a photograph, and the press made do with what they could get. Yet if you look at the picture, you can see Serenity's eyes looking at the filled-in front wall where the picture window should've been, and the corners of her mouth betraying her rage at Nathan.

Serenity all but dragged Autumn back into her car to drive away. The moment Serenity entered the home she ran—not walked—to the master bedroom. She emerged but a moment later with a big bottle of Wild Turkey, presumably hidden somewhere in the room and waiting for her eager lips. Indeed, she turned on the TV and drank until she passed out on the living room floor. I saw several episodes of a *The Brady Bunch* marathon, which included a couple I hadn't seen before, such as the riotous one in which Jan seeks to become the most popular girl in school. That Jan was a card.

At something like midnight, Nathan got back home. He turned off the TV as if tucking it into bed. Spying Serenity on the carpet, he took off his shoes, got down on the floor next to her, hugged her waist, and said, "Welcome home,

Mommy." I couldn't tell if he meant it sarcastically. But when I stared at Serenity as she stirred in her sleep, I could've sworn I saw Zelda.

"I've been a bad boy."

He hugged her tighter and tighter.

"But you're right, let's finish what we started."

Awakened from her stupor, she put her hands through the buttoned front of his shirt.

"I love your bullet scar."

"I thought we should get rid of the front window."

Serenity sat up on her elbow in the jittery manner of one accustomed to hangovers. "The snake is beautiful. The fangs are so cool. Who needs to look at the world?"

"I finished my book."

"I know, my agent called me."

"I hope you like it."

"I'll love it to pieces. Let's never fight again."

"Fighting can be a way of falling more deeply in love. Getting to the truth in the other person."

"I married the most truthful man in the world."

She kissed his cheek.

"And I married the most truthful woman. Even when you lie it's still the truth. There's such a thing as a truth-lie."

Serenity shrugged. "Life is only life."

They fell asleep in each other's arms.

Sometime later, the doorbell rang and rang and rang.

Nathan, the heavy sleeper, did not stir, so it was Serenity who forced herself up, running her fingers through her matted hair.

"Okay, motherfucker, I'm coming."

Even the dim afternoon light made her squint.

"Happy sobriety, Princess!" said the man at the door, a dozen yellow roses in his hand. It took me a moment to recognize him as Serenity's father, Mr. Lamb, and it took Serenity a moment as well.

"Dad, is that you? What did you—"

"I've turned over a new leaf. I lost a hundred and seven pounds. I returned my hair to its original color. The circles under my eyes—gone. The loose skin under my neck—gone. This is the young, new me, and I want you to join me on my journey. It's never too late to start over, Princess."

I never understood how people could know for certain that they lost a hundred and seven pounds, as opposed to just a hundred pounds, or even a hundred and five pounds. How absurd that he said he returned his hair to its original color, as if it involved some wondrous magic spell, rather than say he dyed it.

But in all fairness, Mr. Lamb did a double take of his own at the sight—and I imagine, the smell—of his hungover daughter, who managed a miraculous one-minute of sobriety upon coming back to her home. Then he looked past her and saw the dreaded Nathan lying on the floor.

"What's he doing here?" asked Mr. Lamb. "I thought you knew better by now. Did he get you drunk?"

In his fury, he dropped the yellow bouquet on the porch. But its very existence annoyed Serenity, and she kicked it out of the way.

"Christ, all you have to do is wait for it," she said. "Nothing I do is good enough. For your information, Nathan never touched a drop of alcohol in his life."

"That makes sense," Mr. Lamb replied. "He's too busy bumping people off. I've always known you were innocent, Princess. I always knew that Nathan—"

"That Nathan what?"

My son sat up, and walked over to extend his hand to his father-in-law, who put his hand in his pockets and turned away.

"I will never talk to you, Nathan," said Mr. Lamb, talking to Nathan. "And I certainly would never shake the hand of a mass murderer."

"Oh, cut it out, Dad," Serenity said. "Come in and sit down. Nathan and I have our ups and downs, but he's no more a killer than I am."

"I refuse to step foot inside this house as long as he's in it."

He walked back out to the front porch.

"Fine with me."

Serenity shut the door.

No one stirred for maybe one minute. Then the doorbell rang again and again and again.

"Okay, you win."

Mr. Lamb stepped inside the house. As Serenity closed the door behind him, he extended his hand to Nathan and said, "I'm Chester Lamb."

"Nice to meet you, Chester."

Nathan smiled as they shook hands.

"Do they called you 'Chez' for short?"

Chester Lamb responded with a punch to Nathan's face.

"Do you really think I want to know you? You made my beautiful daughter a drunk. You made her. . . she went to prison because of you."

These groundless accusations offended me as Nathan's father. How could anyone say Nathan made Serenity drink, let alone that it was his fault she put in a guest star appearance on death row?

Always the peacemaker, Nathan raised his hands in surrender.

"I don't want any trouble. You're my wife's father. Can't we all get along?"

Chester Lamb took out a compact pistol and pointed it at Nathan as if he were already dead.

"Sit down," Chester commanded.

Nathan glanced at a couch and chair, each equidistant from where he stood.

"Uh, any preference as to where?"

"Are you fucking with me?"

Chester waved the gun at Nathan's face like a total nut job.

"'Where do I sit?' Jesus, you kids today are so stupid. Sit. . . sit on the couch."

Serenity looked back and forth at the two men with panic. "Dad, I think you should—"

"Shut up, Princess, and sit down next to him."

Nathan quipped, "Don't worry, I don't have cooties."

"Very funny."

She sat down next to her husband.

Chester cleared his throat as he waved his gun.

"Don't think I won't use this."

"Dad, do you even know how?"

"Just never you mind, Princess. Nathan—God, I hate even having to say your name—you are going to tell me everything. You are going to confess all of your crimes right from the beginning. And I'll record it on my phone."

I could see Serenity and Nathan pressing their lips together to keep from laughing.

"This isn't a joke," Chester warned them.

"I'm sorry, Dad, but you look so silly with a gun."

Chester fired the pistol; the shot landed in the wall space between Serenity and Nathan's heads.

"Still think I'm funny?"

Serenity and Nathan looked at each other; she put her hand on top of his.

"Well, Nathan? I'm running out of patience."

"There's only one problem with your plan, Chester. I have nothing to confess."

"He's telling the truth, Dad. Nathan wouldn't hurt anyone."

Chester fired another bullet. It hit the existing bullet hole like a bull's eye, as if to further demonstrate his skill as a shooter.

"I want the whole story, and I want it now. He killed his mother, he killed—I don't know, those other people. And he killed Clay Hinton Jr. as well as Sr. And let us not forget that poor detective Logan Steiner."

Nathan looked back and forth.

"Please, don't shoot Serenity," he shouted.

Chester made a face as if about to puke, and fell face first onto the floor like a chopped down tree. A steady pool of blood spread out from his head.

Autumn stood about ten feet behind where Chester stood before getting shot. The smoldering gun she held made me think of those old black-and-white movies in which everyone smoked. Her free hand covered her mouth, I imagine to keep from screaming.

"Autumn?" Serenity asked of the universe. She could not comprehend that her sweet sister just shot their father to death.

"I—I opened the door and saw his gun, and then I heard Nathan yell," Autumn managed to say. "Who is he?"

"Uh, he's like, you know. . . our dad."

I'd swear on a stack of bibles, the very next words out of Autumn's mouth were, "My God, he lost weight. I wonder how he did it."

Only then did she burst into tears. "Oh my God, I killed my father. Our mom got shot to death. And now I killed our dad."

"It's not like you did it on purpose," Serenity offered.

"Oh my God, am I going to jail? I have two kids in diapers." She looked at the handgun she held as if she never saw it before and dropped it to the floor in horror.

29

Autumn and Serenity cried in each other's arms for what felt like an eternity. Yeah, okay, Daddy died—get used to it. Gradually, though, Autumn shared how Bosco insisted they both carry handguns. Nathan listened and let her tell her story, even though he already knew it.

"The only trouble is, I never really learned how to shoot," Autumn concluded through her sniffles. "I could only bring myself to show up for a couple of lessons. I aimed for his leg."

"Your aim leaves a bit to be desired," Nathan conceded. "But you saved our lives."

In point of fact, she shot her father in the back of the head.

"It happened so fast, But your shouting made me know I had to act."

Nathan said, "I couldn't even tell that it was you, only that someone opened the door, and this was my one chance to save my beautiful wife."

Serenity ignored the compliment, and also did not thank my son for his quick thinking. Instead, she stared at her father's corpse, as if it were unreal.

"Where are the kids?"

"Bosco has them. I came over to see how you were doing."

Serenity made a face of disgust. "You mean, to see if I drank."

"Sis, let's not fight about it. What do I do now? Should I call the cops?"

"Did you actually say, 'Should I call the cops?' I can't believe I'm related to such a ninny. Of course you shouldn't call the cops. Do you want to go to prison? Remember—me, death row? Ring any bells?"

"Even if you're found not guilty," Nathan said, in a saner tone of voice, "think of your kids. Everyone's going to know that their Mommy shot Grandpa. Think of what it will do to your career—and to Bosco's."

"Oh God, Bosco—what should I tell him?"

"The truth," Nathan answered without hesitation. "He's a good person, he can handle it. Besides, we can use an extra pair of hands to dispose of the body."

Autumn looked horrified.

"Dispose of him? I can't even touch him. I killed my own father. I'm a cold-blooded murderer."

She started to cry again.

"Yes and no," said Nathan. "You saved lives by shooting him, including probably your own. Think of your kids without their mother."

"Have you—I mean, disposing of a body. How do you know what to do?"

Nathan winked. "I'm a criminologist, remember? I've studied forensics."

"Call Bosco," Serenity urged. "Tell him to find a sitter for the kids and to come right over."

"Shouldn't I tell him what happened?"

"Obviously, sis. But wait until he gets here."

"He might drive erratically if he already knows," Nathan added.

With considerable trepidation, Autumn took out her cell phone and dialed her husband's number. It seemed odd to me that she didn't have it on speed dial, but academics were quirky people.

"Hi, honey bear," she said, upon Bosco's answering the phone. "Listen, you need to come over to Serenity's house right away—I mean, Serenity and Nathan's house."

"Without the kids," Serenity reminded her.

"Oh, right, without the kids. Myrtle Ann next door will watch them. . . Tell her it's an emergency. . . Well, it's sort of like a surprise, I guess. . . Look, trust me, okay? . . . I know you have a ton of papers to grade, so do I . . . Damn it, will you just come the fuck over? . . . Yeah, I love you, too."

She turned her phone off. "It's like pulling teeth. He gets so stubborn."

"Nathan gets that way, too," Serenity commiserated. "Honestly, sometimes I think about how the world would be if there weren't any men."

"Well, our species would die off, for starters," Nathan said.

Serenity considered his claim. "Not necessarily," she decided. "We could freeze millions of sperm samples before we kill all the men."

Autumn added her approval of the general idea.

"Or maybe science will advance to where there's synthetic sperm. If we can take pictures of Mars, we ought to be able to manufacture sperm. In fact, as I think of it, how like men to care more about outer space than women's bodies."

"What if a male baby is born?" Nathan asked.

"We can engineer the sperm to only make more women," replied Autumn.

"I dig how you talk, girl."

Serenity raised her hand for a high five, which Autumn returned.

Nathan asked, "Is this what you tell your students, Autumn? That there should be no more men?"

"No, but maybe I should. Try explaining *To The Lighthouse* to some prick fraternity fuckhead who wears a T-shirt that says, 'Babe Catcher.'"

"That's so obnoxious," Serenity said. "So like a man."

"Is this your way of saying you want to get loaded?" Nathan asked.

"Oh, go fuck yourself."

If you've ever been around people dealing with someone's death, you already know that they talk all sorts of nonsense to change the subject. But the loopy talk about getting rid of men—it must've meant something on an unconscious level, though since I'm not Sigmund Freud I have no idea what.

"It's still dark out," Nathan said. "I better get us prepped."

"The blood is dripping more in one direction," Serenity observed. "The floors must be slightly slanted. That's unacceptable. I spent a pretty penny on this house."

"As they taught you to say in recovery, one day at a time," Nathan said. "Today is Get-the-Fuck-Rid-of-the-Dead-Body Day. Let the slanted floors be tomorrow's problem."

If one didn't know better, one would've thought Nathan got the fuck rid of dead bodies all the time, he seemed so calm and methodical about it.

"Thank you, chemistry class," he said, kissing a bottle of luminol that he made in college.

I imagined that's also where he acquired a roll of surgical gloves. He then produced a large container of lye, a plastic tarp, and a handsaw. I also saw a box of black heavy-duty garbage bags, a long coil of rope, a box of bleach pads, and about a million rolls of paper towels. He put the sofa cushion with bullet residue in the fireplace and struck a match to get the fire going.

"I guess we'll have to chop up the sofa and burn the whole thing."

"That won't be necessary," Serenity said. "It came with an extra cushion."

"But it will look newer than the other cushions."

"Not necessarily. Remember, the sofa is only about a year old."

Nathan thought about it. "I guess it will be okay."

"Oh, before I forget," said Serenity, "let me get the flowers from the porch."

"That's my girl," Nathan said with a smile.

She read a card attached to her father's yellow bouquet; whatever it said, it compelled Serenity to comment, "What a load of horse shit."

The card got burned with the flowers.

As they straightened up the room, the doorbell rang. Autumn went to the door to welcome Bosco to the murder scene. She lurched to give him a kiss, but he wasn't interested in getting one when he saw the corpse.

"Holy motherfucker," he said. "What happened?"

Autumn whimpered into his chest. "Relax, my love. We have everything under control."

30

Bosco bawled a little as Autumn shared her tale of misery. For quite a while, they held each other in their arms. Finally, though, Nathan got antsy and said, "Hate to break up the lovebirds' annual convention, but we have work to do."

"Nathan, my bro, thank you so much for being here, and for thinking so fast."

Bosco clasped his friend's arm. "I'd die if anything happened to Autumn."

The strain in their friendship officially ended. I felt warm and tingly inside. What a relief.

"One corpse is enough, thanks just the same."

Nathan could be quite witty when the mood struck him. He inherited this quality from me, if I must say so myself. Zelda had about as much wit as a sardine. But I also recognized this as Nathan's way of letting Bosco know he understood all that Bosco meant.

Wearing surgical gloves, Nathan got out Chester Lamb's car keys and wallet from his pants pockets. Nathan then tied a heavy-duty garbage bag around the dead man's head with a triple knot, and then a rope around the knot, to keep it from dripping blood as they carried him out of the house. To be on the safe side, he tied another bag on top of the first one.

"We'll go through the back door," he said, "and carry the body into the woods. I'll grab his head and lead the way."

Serenity said, "Let me get the flashlights."

"Don't forget the shovels," Nathan told her.

"I'll grab his feet," said Bosco.

"No, I should do it," Autumn said. "This is my mess. I should clean it up myself."

"We'll do it together," said Bosco, as if the whole thing were some lovey-dovey interlude, like a couple in a movie romance about to dance.

How fortuitous that the nearest neighbor lived a good half-mile away. They carried the corpse into the thick forest until Nathan said, "This is a good place." Serenity and Bosco helped Nathan dig a hole to accommodate the body. The ground had several inches of steamy, mulchy leaves, and the soil, once they reached it, looked soft. The whole time the others dug, Autumn stood off to the side with her arms crossed, unable to watch. I thought it selfish of her to let the others do the dirty work when she caused the situation. There's an irony to being a good person.

Nathan dug down the farthest; it must've been a good ten feet. Bosco extended an arm to help Nathan get out of the hole. Nathan unfolded the plastic tarp and put the dead body on top of it. He took the clothes off the corpse and put them in another plastic bag. Then he poised a flashlight near the body, took out his saw, and severed the head, hands, and feet. His intense concentration when performing these amputations made me realize he could've been a surgeon, if people like Zelda or the Rainbows hadn't fucked with his mind. For a moment, I sort of squinted my eyes and let myself pretend, *There's my son, the doctor.* The severed body parts went into another plastic bag with a generous helping of lye on top. He then put this bag into another bag, and another bag on top of that, perhaps so the lye wouldn't eat through too quickly. There wasn't as much blood as I would've thought, which I guessed meant the body became ultra-dead, or whatever you called it. Next, he poured more lye into the bottom of the gaping burial hole and shoved the headless, handless and footless corpse on top of it. He poured even more lye on top of the body. Then he stepped back, looked at his work, and whistled the Carpenters' hit song, "Close to You." Everyone else remained quiet. The crickets sounded like a collective heartbeat.

"Anyone want to say a prayer or something?" Nathan asked.

He sounded short of breath, like he just ran a mile in the Olympics.

Serenity nudged her brother-in-law.

"Maybe you could recite one of your poems, Bosco."

"I don't think so," said Bosco.

Autumn sauntered over to the others. "Oh, do recite, Bosco. It would be such a comfort to me now. Do 'Friday Night.' How does it start again? 'Pizza, that infinity—'"

"Not now," Bosco said with unusual force. "Please, give it a rest."

After a moment or two, Nathan took the lack of affirmative response for a no and proceeded to shovel dirt into the hole. Serenity and Bosco followed his example and picked up their shovels to help. As they neared the top, they covered the spot with the same dead leaves that were there before they started. Nathan took extra care to make sure dry leaves covered the very top. For good measure, he asked Serenity and Bosco to help him move a large rock he spotted nearby, to further obfuscate the misbegotten burial ground. The bare, damp ground where the rock had stood for who knows how long got covered with more dry leaves.

"Anything else we can do for you, Your Majesty?" Serenity asked her sister.

Bosco said, "Hey, go easy on her. She's my wife."

They all took off their shoes before reentering the house. Nathan put the shoes in a plastic bag and had each of them tie plastic bags around their feet. "Sorry, guys," he said, "but you're all going to have to buy new shoes." He then carried the bag of body parts to the trunk of Chester Lamb's car. Back in the main room, he patted down a whole bunch of paper towels on the remaining bloodstain on the floor to sop it up. Then he used the bleach pads to wash down the spot. He sprayed the entire room with the luminol he made, checking for the smallest dot of blood. Next, he vacuumed up the ashes from the cushion in the fireplace and emptied out the vacuum into another plastic bag.

After he put all the remaining plastic bags in the trunk of Chester Lamb's car, Nathan climbed in it to drive. Serenity sat beside him. Autumn and Bosco followed behind in one of their cars. I assumed they still had the plastic bags tied to their feet. I don't know where the foursome dumped Chester Lamb's car or the plastic bags, but at daybreak they all returned in one car.

"I think I've earned the right to a drink," Serenity said, as they settled themselves in.

"You mean the right to a bottle," Nathan quipped, which compelled her to stick out her tongue.

Autumn said, "I woke up yesterday morning and fed the kids. A day like any other. What happened?"

Bosco kissed her forehead.

"You did right, lovey. If I hadn't insisted you carry a gun, Serenity and Nathan would be dead now."

"So in other words, you did right by making me get that awful gun. And instead, my father is dead. Is that supposed to make me happy?" Autumn added, "No offense, guys."

"Say, I just remembered," said Nathan. "Didn't your mother also get shot to death?"

The other three people were taken aback by my son's candor. "I already said that," Autumn said, irritated.

"Oh right, I forgot," Nathan said.

"Dad obviously lost his mind," said Serenity. "A crazy person with a gun—something had to happen. How would you feel if he shot people at the mall or like a church or something?"

Autumn wiped a couple of stray tears from her eyes. "When you put it like that, maybe it really did work out for the best."

Nathan said, "When things cool down, you can have him declared legally dead. And you can donate your share of his estate to a worthy cause. Or at least some of it."

Autumn's face brightened. "That's true, I hadn't thought of it that way. I do care a lot about global warming."

"And let's not forget how lucky we were to have a professional criminologist on hand," Bosco said. "Nathan, how can we ever repay you?"

It may have been the overcast morning light, but I could swear I saw Nathan blush. "I did nothing much, guys. I'm sure you'd do the same for me."

31

From bits of conversation over the next few days, I gleaned that no one would be looking for Chester Lamb anytime soon. He'd taken an early retirement, lived alone, had no close friends—gee, I wonder why?—and no other living relatives. All this, not to mention the masterful job Nathan did of concealing the evidence, made me confident that there'd be no nosy cops coming around to harass my son and daughter-in-law. Though I kept my fingers crossed anyway.

You might've thought that Autumn and Bosco would keep a safe distance from Serenity and Nathan. After all, you never knew when someone might pin another murder on either or both of them, and Autumn and Bosco could not afford perceptions of guilt by association. But instead, their visits were constant. It had to be some crazy kind of denial on their part. Autumn always acted like she drank too much coffee—fidgety and walking about the room, unable to sit still for any length of time. Bosco seemed less affected by what happened, save for the tendencies to touch people more than he used to, and to wipe tears from his eyes, which appeared apropos of nothing. But then, he wasn't the one who pulled the trigger. Their two toddlers, Aurora and Estelle, fought most of the time, and Autumn and Bosco paid just enough attention to them to make sure neither killed the other.

If the four grown-ups ever discussed the Mr. Lamb incident, I never heard them do so. Instead, they talked about everything else under the sun. Serenity usually stayed upstairs alone, doing her Lady Macbeth thing. Yet even in the same room as the others, she remained off in her own cloudy stupor. And Nathan always tended to be taciturn, except maybe when alone with Bosco. So it fell to Autumn and Bosco to keep the verbiage coming, sort of like that game you play as a kid when a balloon can never touch the ground.

"Oh, did we tell you? Hamlet's on a diet," Autumn enthused on a breezy and sunny Saturday afternoon, referring to one of her two cats, Ophelia being the other.

"He really is getting gross," Bosco said. "He's like a giant fur ball."

Autumn forced herself to sit down, but then stood back up a second later, as if under a spell more powerful than her self-will.

"The vet gave us this high protein low-fat food for him."

"Naturally, he refuses to eat it," Bosco added. "I swear, I think he does it on purpose. Like he knows what's going on, and he's trying to get back at us."

"Is he starving?" Nathan asked. "Cats will starve to death before eating something they don't like. I heard that someplace. Probably on TV."

"If he's starving, he sure doesn't look it," Bosco assured. "He's probably getting food someplace else."

"Then why bother with the diet?" Nathan wanted to know.

"How are the cats?" Serenity asked, staring into space to emphasize that she didn't care about her own question.

"Hamlet's on a diet," Autumn repeated, with the same bright enthusiasm the first time she said it.

"Stop it," she said to sweet little Aurora, who hit her baby sister on the head with a squeaky plastic duckie. Autumn grabbed the toy from the child and put it on a high shelf.

"That Ophelia," Bosco mused. "She's such a drama queen."

"You mean in the play?" Serenity inquired with a blank look, scratching her ear.

"No, I mean our cat," Bosco replied.

"You've spoiled her to death," said Autumn. "I swear, she hates me. She thinks I'm trying to steal you from her."

"She doesn't hate you," Bosco said. "We've been through this a million times."

"She hisses at me."

"No, she doesn't."

"She only does it when you're not around."

Serenity hissed at her sister. No one paid any attention, so she did it again. This time, Autumn smiled and said, "See? Everyone's out to get me. Sorry, I. . . just kidding."

"Of course you were."

Bosco held back an urge to cry some more.

"Man, that Ophelia."

Nathan said, "Did you hear the latest news? Another random shooting. Four people dead."

"Terrible," said Bosco.

"Inexcusable," Autumn concurred.

"I don't get it," said Nathan. "Why do people murder total strangers?"

Serenity said, "You should know. You're the criminologist."

"Oh, there's all kinds of theories," Nathan replied. "But it doesn't add up."

"I hear you, bro," Bosco said. "It a crazy world, that's for sure."

A pause in the conversation followed, then Autumn and Bosco tried to speak at the same time. But the doorbell interrupted them. A package delivery guy had a box for Nathan.

"I know what this is."

He matter-of-factly tore open the box.

"It's my book."

At long last. *13 Lucky Ways to Bump Off the Jerks in Your Life*, which would be known as *13*, by Nathanial Nightbridge. Any idiot could tell at once that Nathan intended the book to be satiric, his way of giving the finger to all the dopes who thought him a murderer. I read a copy in the public library, and the meticulous details of perfect murders consisted of things like bribing a sushi master to serve a dish with a poisonous worm or slipping someone a downer drug and then convincing the person to commit suicide. I mean, get real, people. And while you're at it, lighten up. To hear the media tell it, people were outraged, and how low could society sink to publish such a book and on and on. Politicians got a great deal of free publicity from it, but so did Nathan. The book rocketed to Number One, even though most every media outlet refused to advertise it. Naturally, Nathan declined to comment on the book to the press. A class act all the way.

But I get ahead of myself. That Saturday afternoon, the gleesome threesome oohed and aahed as he opened the box to reveal stacks of shiny new books. Only Serenity knew the specifics of the opus in advance, so Autumn and Bosco burst out laughing with surprise and delight upon seeing the title. They laughed all the more when they saw that Nathan dedicated the book to himself. "To me," read the inscription, though I think he didn't want anyone close to him to seem guilty by association.

"Man, you are amazing." Bosco offered the high five, to which Nathan responded with a mild grin.

"Can we have an autographed copy?" Autumn asked.

"No," answered Serenity on Nathan's behalf. "It's not a good book for the cops to find in your house, in case of 'you know.'"

As I imagine you've guessed, "you know" evolved into the way they all referred to the shooting death of Chester Lamb. It's always interested me how out-of-it people can have these sudden lucid moments. It's probable Serenity noticed a lot more than she let on.

"Yeah, I guess you're right," said Autumn, pacing the floors. "It's weird, but sometimes I almost forget. About 'you know,' that is."

"I knew what you meant," Serenity snapped.

But if Autumn had a retort, it would have to wait. Two cops entered upon ringing the doorbell and showed their ID. Both of them were women—homely women, I might add. I imagined they became cops because they knew no one would ever want to marry them.

"Is Nathan Nightbridge here?" asked the taller of the two, who reminded me of a duckbill platypus. The shorter one looked more like a porcupine.

"I'm Nathan," declared my son. "Actually, Nathaniel."

"Well then, Nathanial Nightbridge, you are under arrest for the murder of Mr. Boyd Rogers. You have the right to remain silent. . ." As platypus kept talking, porcupine put my son in handcuffs.

When the cop finished her spiel, Bosco said, "Mr. Rogers was a trip." He added, "But Nathan didn't kill him."

Nathan chuckled.

"Thanks for the vote of confidence, dude. It means a lot."

32

The press greeted Nathan's newest trial like a movie star's biggest film ever, the *Star Wars* of murder trials. You'd have thought that Mr. Boyd Rogers walked on water, taking in all those runaway kids to use them in his drug lord racket. But the crack and smack were never mentioned in the media, only his immeasurable humanitarianism. By contrast, evil Nathan couldn't stand do-gooders and had to pound Mr. Rogers' head against the wall until his skull cracked open. Among so many other things, I found it strange that it appeared Nathan murdered people so many different ways. But no matter. It made for good press, which is just a fancy way of saying good gossip. What would people do without someone to gossip about? Sometimes I want to get on my knees and thank the good Lord God—if there is one—for making me a homeless person. I am spared so much human bullshit.

Not everyone fell for the media hype. An ever-growing number of Nathanites competed with the Nathan haters for air time on TV, as both groups crowded outside the courthouse with signs, songs, and chants.

"Nathan Will Nathan Self," read many a headline, which I'm sure came as no surprise to anyone. To the profound annoyance of all the self-righteous pricks out there, Serenity and Nathan managed the million-dollar bail as if it were nothing. I had a passing thought to hit Nathan up for a few bucks, but the thought came and went. No way could I handle it.

Nathan rounded up good ol' Biv and Montana to serve as defense witnesses. Thanks to the Internet, he had no problem finding them. Biv had her act together—sort of—via a website about being a software consultant, whatever the fuck that meant. I figured she got by however she had to, and calling herself a software consultant beat calling herself a welfare whore. Montana, the other welfare whore, now called herself a singer/songwriter—I could imagine what her songs were like, but I'd rather not—and likewise had a web page. I took mild interest in contrasting how their alleged careers dictated different websites. Biv's featured clean modern lines and a bland business photo in which she sported her bland business suit and her bland business smile. Montana, the artiste, had a web page saturated with colors and swirls and flowers. Her long hair fell down over her long hippie dress as she extended her arms before a lake that I assumed to be in a public park. Probably she had to crop off some drunk puking on the grass. You could listen to a free sample of her self-made CD, but I passed, thanks just the same.

Before the trial, Biv and Montana met with Nathan at his house. The gruesome twosome arrived in one car. Even as they walked up the porch to the front door I could tell they hadn't seen each other in years, and neither regretted this fact. I wondered if the two of them—or for that matter, Bosco or Nathan—ever thought about the time they pledged eternal friendship to each other. How human of them all, to say nice things they did not mean.

The two girls shared an argumentative moment as to who should ring the doorbell, though I could not tell if both of them or neither of them wanted to. Biv rang the bell. In her bathrobe and fluffy slippers, Serenity schlepped to the door, as if in imitation of Bette Davis in *Whatever Happened to Baby Jane?*

"Yeah?" she mumbled.

"Uh, we're Montana and Biv. I mean, I'm Montana, and she's Biv. You know, Nathan's old friends. You must be Serenity."

Dead silence. Even I felt uncomfortable watching them standing around, not knowing what to do.

"Okay, come on in."

Serenity opened the door enough for the two gals to enter. No one shook hands or anything.

"Hey, Nathan," she yelled. "Those dumb fucks are here for you."

She looked at Biv and Montana as if studying them.

"If you two dykes want to know where the local dyke bar is, let me know."

"Um, we're straight," Biv said. "But thanks."

Serenity snorted, as if saying, *Yeah, right.*

Montana said, "That is so like you, Biv. You haven't seen me in like a century, yet you assume to know everything about me."

"Well, you are straight, aren't you?"

"That's not the point. The point is that I should be able to speak for myself. Who appointed you my spokesperson? Who made you God?"

Biv sighed. "Montana, give it a rest. Neither of us wants to be here, but Nathan didn't exactly give us a choice. So let's get it over with and forget we ever knew each other, okay?"

"I'm not sure we ever did, as you put it, know each other. Or at least you never knew me. But that's your loss as far as I'm concerned."

"Montana, shut the fuck up."

Nathan entered the living room. "Yeah, Montana, shut the fuck up. You, too, Biv. We have to go over your testimonies."

He got right down to business—with his life at stake, what difference did it make if these two dopes liked him? So he made no effort to greet them or ask them what they'd been doing with their lives. It would've been disingenuous, and that wasn't Nathan's style.

The three sat while Serenity went off to drink some more. Nathan did not offer any refreshments.

"Ah yes, go over our testimonies," said Biv. "Nothing like a little blackmail to brighten one's day."

Nathan frowned.

"Blackmail is an extreme term for what we're doing. You both know I didn't kill Mr. Rogers. If I don't use you, the prosecution will. Why not make sure justice is served?"

"And you just happen to have lots of dirt on us both if we don't lie under oath," Biv said.

"I didn't know either of you went in for such moral grandstanding," said Nathan. "What with you, Montana, popping out babies like Pop-Tarts in a black market baby scam, and you, Biv—"

"Okay, you made your point," said Biv. "That's all you ever did—make you point. You just stood there while everyone else had a life. You watched us like we were something in a petri dish. So what lies do we have to tell?"

Nathan laughed. "I've never heard myself described like that before. I can assure you it hardly seems that way from my end of things. If anything, I'm the one in the petri dish. I'm the microscopic single-celled organism."

I thought it unlike Nathan to get into this touchie-feelie stuff, until I realized he wanted to disarm Biv. But what he revealed about himself touched my heart. My son—always so modest. Modest and honest.

"Gee," Montana enthused, "maybe we're on to something here. Maybe everyone feels like they're a microscopic thingie."

"Yeah, let's write a book about it," said Biv, with a sarcasm that could've cut glass.

Montana leaned forward with interest. "Do you really think we could? I've always wanted to write a book. Do you think it will sell? Maybe I'll be famous."

"I think Biv meant it as a joke," Nathan said.

Biv said, "I think Biv meant to tell everyone to fuck off."

Montana fell into a disgruntled lump on her chair. "All this negative energy. I'm not used to it anymore. I'm into like love and peace and beauty and saving the environment."

"Anyway," Biv said, "tell us what we have to say, Nathan."

"It's simple. You both were with me the entire night that Mr. Rogers got killed. Bosco, too. You probably were, anyway, so it's not a lie. It's just that you remember exactly what we did because it was the night Biv and I announced our engagement. Back in the garage, when we all lived together. We had a party for the four of us and then went to the movies. We saw a revival showing of *E.T.* Then we came back home and talked until dawn."

"Oh, I love *E.T.*," Montana said. "It's so suspenseful but in that really cosmic kind of way."

Biv put her hands to her head in disbelief. "Wait a second. Rewind to the part about us being engaged. As in engaged to be married? You? Me? I thought I heard everything, but this—"

"Look, I already made a statement about it. We broke up a few weeks later because I caught you having a three-way with two other guys."

"What?"

"Look, I said the first thing that popped into my head."

"Yeah, I'll bet. Nathan, you never do anything without thinking it through."

"Have you ever been questioned by the cops for murder? Well, have you?"

Biv rolled her eyes. "No, I haven't."

"In that case, I don't think it's fair to judge me. I didn't kill anybody. I don't want to go to jail."

"So this is how you protect my reputation?"

Nathan shrugged. "The lesser of two evils. We both know about the other things you've done."

"But at least I actually did them. What about Bosco? Did you blackmail him, too?"

"I told you I don't like that word. But no, Bosco is a real friend. He offered to help me."

Montana said, "I always loved Bosco."

"I told you to shut up," said Biv.

33

Nathan's trial got broadcast on TV, just like his others had been. Was the courtroom filled to flowing over? Do drunks piss on the sides of buildings? When newscasters had nothing better to do, they commented on the absence of Serenity from the courthouse. They pretended to analyze why she stayed away, and what this meant for the defense and prosecution, as if no one—including themselves—had said it all before.

The DA this time took the form of a middle-aged guy who to my horror looked quite a lot like me. Or what I would've looked like if I became the Alexander Nightbridge IV my parents wanted me to be. He wore his navy blue suit as if it were his skin, as if even in the uttermost depths of his soul he wanted to be nothing but a dull man in an expensive suit. Everything about him said, *Keep away, peons.* Though Nathan also wore a navy blue suit—there must be some law that says lawyers have to wear one of these—you could see a real human being inside of it. He was a person who, through enduring his own hardships, had developed empathy for others.

The state presented its usual weak, contrived case against Nathan. This time they had a tiny shred of Nathan's skin that turned up in a bag in the cold case files. It came from the floor of Boyd Rogers' room, and had been swept up with dust particles years earlier. The piece of skin measured about one-sixty-fourth of an inch all the way around. Under a microscope, the edges seemed to be jagged, which possibly signaled a struggle. And they found the teeny-tiniest drop of blood that belonged to Boyd Rogers on the skin. Big motherfucking deal.

They also made a huge deal over the fact that Nathan lived at Mr. Rogers' runaway shelter and took off without warning. But of course, so did three other kids. There was also the sudden emergence of some former runaway scumbag who claimed he saw Nathan sneaking out of Mr. Rogers' bedroom window the night of the murder. This dope of a witness came forward, he said, because he needed to clear his conscience. Like such lowlife nitwits have a conscience. What stopped him from coming forward at the time of the murder? Did it take him a decade to get up off the sofa, scratch his butt crack, and finish drinking his beer?

The trial got off to an anticlimactic start with the snooty, full-of-himself DA establishing that Boyd Rogers got his head bashed in, and so on. Then came the DNA expert prick. He told the DA about the flake of skin and tiny drop of blood. Nathan had to destroy this witness. As he stood up and buttoned his jacket like the most professional of lawyers, I got shivers for the pride I felt.

Nathan said, "First let's talk about the bag of white power found in the deceased party's split skull. Were there any fingerprints on that?"

"You mean the bag of flour meant to look like drugs? No, there were no fingerprints."

"And now let's discuss the piece of skin. Were you able to determine the exact date and time that this miniscule piece of skin fell to the floor?" Nathan asked.

"No," harrumphed the DNA asshole.

"And is it possible that while Mr. Brown—I mean, Mr. Rogers got beaten to death, a drop of his blood fell onto this piece of skin?" I found it odd that Nathan should mention Mr. Brown, his old imaginary boogieman that Zelda used to threaten him with. Maybe his nerves couldn't take the strain anymore. After all, a first-degree murder charge isn't a picnic on a Sunday afternoon.

"It may be possible, but a highly unlikely coincidence."

"But yes, it is possible?"

"Yes, okay? Yes, it is possible."

"And since Mr. Brown—pardon me, I don't know why I keep saying that."

Nathan wiped his brow with a Kleenex in his pocket. For a second or two, things looked dicey, but he recovered. "Since Mr. Rogers provided shelter for us runaway kids, is it possible that I talked to him in his bedroom at some point and scratched my hand because it itched?"

The DNA fuckhead sighed. "Yes, that is possible."

"In fact, did you check for skin fragments from other former residents of the runaway shelter?"

"We found yours, nothing else mattered."

"So, in other words, once you found a fragment of my skin you stopped looking for anyone else's?"

"You're twisting my words."

"No, sir, I think that you have been twisting this case."

The courtroom rippled with laughter.

"Objection, your honor," said the DA snob who thought himself better than other people.

"Sustained," pronounced the judge, who reminded me a little of Oprah Winfrey.

"Withdrawn."

Nathan sauntered back to the defense table like a lion that just ate a power lunch.

A witness or two later, the condescending DA called Filbert Nimbleton to the stand, the idiot who claimed to see Nathan climbing out of Boyd Rogers' bedroom the night of the murder.

"Now then, Mr. Nimbleton," said the DA, after the usual routine questions. "Please tell us in your own words what you saw on the night in question."

"Well, it happened about three in the morning," said Nimbletonfuck. "I couldn't sleep so I went outside the shelter for a smoke. Mr. Rogers didn't allow smoking inside. I heard screaming when I got outside. I got scared, so I stood to the side of the doorway, where no one could see me. Then the screaming stopped. I went farther outside and saw someone hurrying down the fire escape. There were blood spatters on his T-shirt and arms."

"And is this person you saw in the courtroom today?"

Boy, was he ever! Nimbleton the Pile of Dog Shit couldn't wait to point at my son and made no effort to suppress his grin.

"Yes. That man."

"Let the record show that you are pointing to the defendant, Nathan Nightbridge."

"Yes, he's the one."

"Your witness." The DA made a point of looking with disdain at Nathan as he walked past the defense table.

Nathan wasted no time. "If you saw this as you say you did, why did you not come forward sooner?"

Nimbleton made a smarmy face.

"I thought you'd come after me."

"Well, I'm standing right in front of you. Are you afraid now?"

His head trembled ever so slightly.

"Of course not. This is a courtroom."

"But what about outside of the courtroom? Why were you suddenly no longer afraid of me?"

The asshole shrugged.

"I dunno. I finally realized I had to do the right thing."

"It doesn't have anything to do with a recent book deal you signed? Maybe some free publicity? I believe the title is going to be *Nathan Nightbridge: I Lived to Tell.*"

The DA all but shouted, "Objection, your honor. Relevance?"

The judge put a finger to her chin in thought.

"Objection overruled. Witness will answer."

"Okay, so I have a book deal. That has nothing to do with the truth. I know what I saw."

He narrowed his eyes in the manner of obnoxious, self-righteous people in the wrong.

"And what exactly did you live to tell about living under the same roof with me?"

"Objection, your honor. This has nothing to do with the matter at hand."

"No, I think it might. I'll allow it."

The stupid ass got all squirmy. "We. . . It's not like we were real good friends, but we did do stuff together. Clean up around the house. The group circle."

"It sounds like you wrote a very short book."

"You were so weird. That's what the book is about. I wasn't surprised at all when you killed Mr. Rogers."

"'Weird.' Is that a professional diagnosis?"

"You know how weird you are. You have to. You kill people."

Nathan sighed with exasperation.

"Your honor, I ask that the witness's last three remarks be stricken."

"So moved. Jury will ignore last three statements made by the witness."

"Thank you, your honor. Now then, Mr. Nimrod—"

"It's Nimbleton, damn it. Stop making fun of me."

"Oh, did I scare you?"

The judge banged her gavel and looked ready to say something, but Nathan spoke first.

"I'm sorry, your honor. It won't happen again."

"It most certainly will not, Mr. Nightbridge. Now, proceed."

"Thank you, your honor. Mr. Nimbleton, does your book make mention of an incident that occurred approximately the same time as Mr. Rogers' murder?"

Nimwit shuffled around in the leather witness box chair, like a dog trying to hide itself.

"I don't know what incident you're referring to."

"Weren't you charged with raping a Miss X who stayed at the shelter?"

Nim-Dim stood up and pounded on the witness box rail, his face as red as cherry licorice.

"Nothing came of that. She lied."

The DA tried to object, but the dumb fuck spoke before he could. You could tell from the DA's sour face that his star witness neglected to mention his happy days as a rapist.

"That liar, as you called her, committed suicide before the case could go to court. I suppose that's one way of getting charges dropped. But you tell the truth, is that what you want us to believe?"

Nathan walked closer to the witness box, until he got right in the shithead's face.

"Someone leaves a room covered in blood. Inside the room someone else is found dead. You do nothing for years, until you have a book coming out. Mr. Brown believed Miss X, didn't he? Wasn't he about to have you arrested?"

"Who the fuck is Mr. Brown?"

The dirt bag leapt up to grab Nathan, who dodged out of the way. A courtroom guard restrained the crazed liar of a witness, who started shouting, "You motherfucker. You can't pin it on me. You won't get away with it," and more of that general type of remark. The judge ordered the witness removed from the courtroom. On his way out, he got served with a libel suit for his forthcoming book on Nathan. "You motherfucker," he hissed.

People sure did have a way of losing control at Nathan's trials.

"No more questions, your honor," Nathan stated.

Again a wave of giggles overtook the crowded room, and the judge banged her gavel to make it cease. After three trials, it dawned on me that even the so-called Nathan-haters didn't hate Nathan—they love-hated him, the way they love-hated mafia kingpins or other people who beat the system. People may have said, "Oh, he's guilty for sure," but they didn't mean it. They wanted him to get away with murder, not that he did anything of the sort.

Now came time for Nathan's tidy defense.

34

Nathan's defense began by calling Bosco to the witness stand. Not a bad way to start, if you ask me. After the swearing in and all that malarkey, Nathan referred to his best friend as Dr. Sinclair and made certain Bosco came across as a respectable college prof, happily married with two beautiful little daughters. Boring, but necessary. I could sense that Nathan and Bosco found this stale small talk as tedious as anyone else.

Finally, Nathan got to the good part. "Dr. Sinclair, please tell us in your own words where you were on the night in question."

Bosco flashed the most wholesome smile he could. "That's easy to remember because you and I were roommates with two girls from the shelter. One of the girls, Biv, announced your engagement to be married to her. We celebrated in the garage we rented, and then went to a movie. Afterward, we came back to the garage and talked all night. It was light outside by the time we went to sleep."

Nathan smiled in fond reminiscence. "Do you remember the movie we saw?"

"Yes. *E.T.*"

"And what did we—excuse me, what did you and your friends talk about after the movie?"

"Oh, you know—the future, our dreams for our lives. Things that young people talk about."

"And you're sure this is what happened on this particular night?"

"Absolutely. Some nights you never forget. I remember sitting on the floor with some throw pillows. Biv and you were holding hands on the upper bunk of the bed, and Montana, our other roommate, sat in a beanbag chair. We kept playing this Harry Chapin CD. We did a group hug to that song about how the cat's in the cradle. A magical, special night."

"Thank you, Dr. Sinclair. Your witness."

The DA cleared his throat. "My goodness, Dr. Sinclair. I imagine you four runaway teens feasted on cookies and milk. Perhaps you read passages from the Bible aloud or stood with your hands over your hearts to recite the Pledge of Allegiance."

"Is there a question?" Nathan wanted to know.

As much as I hated to admit it, Nathan did instruct Bosco to pour the syrup thick. They weren't Harry Chapin types. Bosco and the girls listened to alternative hard rock in those days. Nathan had no feeling for music one way or the other, thanks to Zelda. And why had he chosen the song about the father being too busy to be with his son? It had to have been a joke.

"Yes, I do have a question," the DA said. "Dr. Sinclair, I assume you are an intelligent man. Do you really expect anyone to believe the story you just told?"

"Objection, your honor. Argumentative."

"Objection sustained. Counselor, rephrase or move on."

"Very well. You seem to recall this alleged occasion in considerable detail. Do you always have such a good memory?"

"Not always, no," was Bosco's smooth response. "Only for things that matter."

"Do you remember how long your wife spent in labor with your children?"

"Yes, I do. Eight hours and forty minutes for the first, Aurora, and only a little over two hours for Estelle, our second."

Oops, that didn't work, did it? Mr. Fancy Pants DA. Better try again.

"Would you describe the defendant as your best friend?"

Bosco's face crinkled into a sunshine grin. "Absolutely. For years, and for many years to come."

"A respected college professor. Devoted husband and father. Does it bother you that the defendant has an unsavory reputation?"

The judge banged her gavel in fury. "Approach."

Nathan and the DA had a quick, hushed discussion with the judge. I guessed that it had been declared prejudicial to mention Nathan's previous trials.

After an intense hushed minute or two, the DA continued as if nothing happened.

"Now then, Dr. Sinclair. Your father-in-law, Chester Lamb, has been missing for several years, has he not?"

Nathan could have objected but didn't. Obviously, he expected this to come up.

"Yes, sir," Bosco answered. I liked the way he called him "sir." A nice little touch.

"And Mr. Lamb is or was a wealthy man?"

Bosco paused before answering. "Not poor, certainly. I don't know his net worth."

"But if he turns up dead or is declared legally dead, you and your wife stand to benefit monetarily, do you not?"

"Yes, sir, I suppose we do." Bosco said this with the innocence of an angel.

"And your sister-in-law is married to the defendant, is she not?"

"Yes, sir, she is."

"And she and the defendant also would financially gain from Chester Lamb's estate?"

"I suppose they would, sir."

"Isn't all this a wee bit more than coincidental, Dr. Sinclair?"

Bosco turned to the judge. "Excuse me, but I'm not sure I understand the question. Isn't all of what more than coincidental?"

The judge said, "I share your confusion, Dr. Sinclair. Counselor will rephrase—and be careful how he does so."

"Dr. Sinclair, has it never crossed your mind that the defendant is a murderer?"

"No, it hasn't. I've seen Nathan step out of the way for an ant. I know him as well as I know myself. He isn't capable of hurting anyone."

"And you honestly expect people to believe this?"

Bosco shrugged. "I have no control over what other people believe."

The DA got nowhere, and he knew it. He also knew he risked alienating the jury if he came across as bullying.

"No further questions," he said, with that unconvincing smirk lawyers use to suggest the current witness is a waste of time.

Nathan next called Montana to the stand—or, as she now billed herself, Montana Sky. She wore a T-shirt that advertised herself as a singer/songwriter and a long flowing skirt that featured dozens of images of her self-produced CD. I half-expected her to give out a free CD to everyone gathered in the courtroom, as if she were a guest on a daytime talk show.

"Miss Sky," Nathan managed to say with a straight face, "please tell us the events of the night in question."

Was she ready to talk!

"Oh, what a wonderful night. You and Biv looked so happy, just the cutest couple in the world. I think Bosco sort of took the hint and fell in love with me that same night. I can always tell when someone is in love with me. It's like I look into his eyes and he looks into my eyes and everything gets all fuzzy. Like you're underwater. Anyway—"

"Your honor," said the DA, "could you please instruct the witness to stay on topic?"

"I was just about to," Montana protested to the DA. "Do you like it when people interrupt *you?*"

She looked up at the judge with an assumption of a shared bond. "Prosecutors just don't like people, you know? Why would someone want to put someone else in jail?"

The DA looked exasperated. "Your honor, please."

The judge looked down on Montana as she might look down at a brain-damaged kitten. "Please, Miss Sky," she said.

"Remember you are in court, and conduct yourself accordingly."

Montana winked at the judge. "Yes, ma'am, I'll do that for you."

"And the jury will disregard the witness's remarks about the prosecutor," the judge added.

"Oh, do I talk now?" Montana asked, not waiting for an answer. "Did I say we went to the movies? *E.T.* God, how I cried. But a happy cry, you know what I mean? I mean, if everyone loved everyone else regardless of what planet they came from, we'd have world peace. Or do they call it something else if it's like more than one planet? Then we went back to our garage apartment and talked. Bosco kept giving me the eye."

Nathan asked, "When did we stop talking?"

"I don't know the exact time. I don't pay attention to those things. Like, when I recorded my self-titled CD, I worked any old time I felt like it. But I remember we stayed up until morning. Bosco liked that he could see more of me in the daylight, if you know what I mean."

"Your witness," Nathan said. He knew when to quit.

The DA walked up close to Montana as if to frighten her. "Miss Sky—by the way, is that your real last name?"

"Yes. I picked it out myself. How real can it get?" Laughter filled the courtroom until the judge made it stop.

"Is it possible, Miss Sky, that your memory about the night in question is faulty?"

"No. My best friend got engaged. I could never forget that."

"But she didn't end up marrying the defendant, did she?"

"No. Nathan caught her in bed with two guys at the same time." Despite her somber demeanor, I could tell Montana loved sharing this answer.

"I see." The DA looked excited, like a perverted creep. "And do you also remember when this happened?"

"Yeah—I mean yes. Exactly two weeks after the engagement party."

"Two weeks from the evening, or two weeks from the morning it finally ended?"

"Oh, two weeks from the morning. He found them in bed together."

Nathan thought of everything. I had a passing notion that he would've made an excellent wedding planner.

The DA rubbed his temples. "No more questions for this witness."

Montana smiled. "Your honor, may I please say one last thing?"

"No, Miss Sky. You are excused."

"Shit—I mean, shoot—I wanted to tell everyone about my new CD."

How shrewd of Nathan to save Biv for last. If she had any lingering ideas about blowing the cover story, she wouldn't want to implicate Montana and Bosco on charges of perjury. She still had a thing for Bosco, and despite her bitchy relationship with Montana, she wouldn't want to send her to prison. Women have never made sense to me—they go around hating each other's guts but then act like they're best friends. Once in the nuthouse, I told a nurse what some other nurse said about her, and I ended up getting shot up with something that put me to sleep for days.

Anyway, back to Biv. Nathan asked her to describe the night in question.

"Ah yes, the happiest night of my life," she replied with a scowl, her voice borderline civil as she spat out her words through clenched teeth. "I never felt so in love with anyone as I did with you that night, Nathan. I felt like the luckiest girl in the world to be marrying you. During *E.T.,* when those cute kids on the bicycles went up into the air, I thought to myself, 'This is my love, soaring to the moon.' I don't know why I threw away such an opportunity for happiness. I guess I'm just funny that way."

"Are you feeling all right?" Nathan asked.

"I have a slight headache, but otherwise I'm fine," Biv replied, with a smile so fake it should've been arrested for fraud.

"But you are sure when the night of our short engagement occurred?"

"Yeah, I'm sure. Anything else?"

"No, I think that does it."

The DA remained seated as he said, "You seem agitated. Is there something you'd like to get off your chest?"

"No. I just don't like having to relive my terrible mistake of cheating on Nathan. It pains me to this day."

"You seem more angry than in pain."

"When I'm in pain I get angry. So sue me."

The judge banged her gavel for the millionth time.

"Please, we are in a courtroom. Another remark like that, and I shall have to fine you for contempt of court. Jury will disregard." Biv didn't warm the judge's heart the way Montana had.

"You know," the DA continued, "what you say today in court becomes a permanent record. Are you absolutely sure you want your testimony to remain as you gave it? Is there nothing at all you'd like to change?"

Biv put her hands to her mouth, thinking.

"Yes, there is something I'd like to change."

The DA brightened. "Yes, and what would that be?"

Biv turned to Nathan and stared at him without blinking.

"I never loved you, Nathan. That's why I cheated on you. I knew you'd catch me. It was the only way I could deal with it at the time. And for that, I am so very, very sorry."

Nathan nodded and mouthed the words, *Thank you for your honesty.*

Some flunkie from the DA's office signaled to the lawyer that he had something for him. After some quick, desperate whispering back and forth, the DA said, "Your honor, we have new evidence to enter at this time."

The judge took out her reading glasses.

"All right, bring it forward." She read through some papers with a studied frown.

"Mr. Nightbridge," she said, "I would like to see you and the state's attorney in my chambers."

How exciting—just like what they did on TV. About five minutes later, the three of them came back out and took their places in the courtroom. Nathan looked agitated; he kept fiddling with his fingers.

The DA handed Biv some papers and said, "Will you please read aloud the top line of the first sheet?"

Biv gulped down as she read it to herself. The words shocked her so bad that the papers fell out of her hand.

"No, it can't be. It just isn't possible."

The DA picked up the papers and said, "That's all right. We'll give you a moment. In fact, unless anyone objects I will tell the members of the jury the crucial information these papers contain. We have found at least a partial match to the DNA tests given the children of two young mothers some years back on *The Chip Beverage Show*. The most likely father in both cases is none other than Mr. Nathan Nightbridge. These mothers were the current witness, and the previous witness. This calls into question the testimony of both."

He looked at Biv. "Young lady, would you like to revise your testimony?"

Biv recovered enough to stare at Nathan, nodding her head in utter perplexity. "I. . . I don't know what to say. What is the Fifth Amendment again?"

The judge said, "Mr. Nightbridge, is there anything you wish to tell us at this time?"

"I. . . I guess, your honor, that this actually confirms much of what's been said. I had a close relationship with the witness. So I thank the People for their due diligence."

The DA looked mighty pissed off, because his great new evidence may well have cost him his case, thanks to my son's quick thinking.

Nathan now looked at Biv. "I'm so sorry I never told you about Montana. I had no right to judge you when I'd been unfaithful myself. Can you find it in your heart to forgive me?"

Biv stood up in the witness box and pointed at him. "You are not the father of my child! What did you do, rig the DNA test, too?"

Nathan said, "Your honor, I move to strike."

"Jury will disregard," said the judge. "I think it best that this witness be excused at this time."

"I think the people are satisfied," the DA grumbled.

Biv hissed at Nathan as they filed out of the room, and the judge called for a short recess.

Nathan, I'm sure, thought it some cosmic error made in his favor. I doubted that he ever had sex with Biv or Montana.

And with that, each side made its closing remarks. The DA went on forever, as though he were a congressman enacting a filibuster, and if he talked long enough to the jury it would forget the possibility of a verdict of not guilty. Nathan glanced at his watch at calculated intervals, with just enough body language to communicate to the jury that he shared its impatience.

Finally, Nathan made his eloquent, but brief, closing remarks. "Guilty beyond a reasonable doubt? Of course not. You know it and I know it. Thank you for doing your duty."

And so the jury began its deliberations. It returned with a verdict a half an hour later.

35

". . .We, the jury, find the defendant, Nathan Knightbridge, not guilty of the crime of murder in the first degree. We, the jury, find the defendant, Nathan Knightbridge, not guilty of the crime of murder in the second degree. We, the jury, find the defendant, Nathan Knightbridge, not guilty of the crime of manslaughter in the first degree."

"Thank you, members of the jury," said the judge. "Mr. Knightbridge, you are free to go."

My son glistened with humble gratitude. "Thank you, your honor. And thank you, members of the jury."

Nathan had a bodyguard accompany him to his car. As usual, he avoided all questions from the press.

I have no idea if he assumed any form of responsibility for the two kids, though I suspect that if he offered money Biv would've refused it, while Montana would've taken all he had to offer—and taken it with a smile.

36

Serenity sat on the living room sofa, with Nathan's head in her lap. She stroked his hair with one hand and drank from an icy glass of gin with the other.

"Well, unless you have some surprises up your sleeve, we should be pretty well caught up."

Nathan's laugh got muffled for his face being buried in her thighs. He rolled over and looked up at her. "Who knows what they might try to pin on me next? Your father's still officially missing, in case you hadn't noticed."

She put her fingers to his mouth, in imitation of a key locking a door.

"And may he stay that way, forever and amen."

"I did an okay job disposing of him, if I must say so myself. But I don't doubt for a second they're working to pin it on me."

"So unfair, honey bunny. You didn't even do it." She laughed and took a swallow of her drink. "For some reason that struck me as funny."

"Anything can be funny, I suppose."

He sat up, adjusting his back on the sofa; he tossed aside a throw pillow.

"Well, maybe not everything. War, death camps, plagues—"

"Nathan, I'm impressed. I had no idea you thought about such things."

He directed a quizzical look at her. "I'm human, aren't I?"

"That's debatable."

He hit her with the throw pillow. "Seriously, maybe we should make some sort of charitable donation to something."

"Tax write-offs. Not a bad idea. Though I'm glad we're leaving all our money to Autumn and Bosco and their kids. Those rip-off charities keep all the money for themselves."

Serenity reached over to the bottle of gin, refilled her glass, and tossed in a couple of ice cubes from the ice bucket. She shook the glass as if to make sure the ice cubes were genuine ice.

Nathan said, "I see you really care about making the world a better place."

She almost choked as she took a sip of gin. "Oh, like you do. Please, spare me all that crap. I hate those online petitions and news articles about the corruption and poverty and how the earth is melting. People love to lecture other people on how they're better than you. As if humans can work together without corruption and greed and all that other good stuff."

"I hate those mawkish little sayings people post online about how happy you'll be if you pretend reality doesn't exist."

Serenity nodded in agreement. "I got this dopey e-mail the other day that they said I had to pass along to ten assholes for good luck, whatever that is. It said there were five things you should do to be happy."

"I hate that shit. Do you remember what they were?"

"Let's see. One said to lower your expectations of others."

"Gee, that shouldn't be hard to do. I already expect nothing from anyone."

"Then it said to live in the now—the present moment."

"That's such a stupid thing people say. You're living in the present moment unless you're dead."

"I think they mean not to obsess about the past or the future."

Nathan snorted. "Good luck with that."

"Oh, and start the day with a smile."

"Save the 'fuck-yous' for supper, no doubt."

"Live in your heart, not your head."

"I've done that all my life. So what?"

"And be nice to people even when they aren't nice to you."

"That one's just plain boring."

"Boring and stupid," Serenity concurred. "Being nice when people are mean is so. . . claustrophobic. Like I've locked myself in a coffin and there's no air to breathe."

"There's never enough air to breathe. Not with so many pricks in the world."

"You know, puppy-wuppy, it's funny, but when I die I want everything to end. To finally be at that nothing place. But when other people die, I want something inside them to keep living. I want them to feel the claustrophobia they put me through and feel it for eternity."

"Yeah, I know. My mom used to. . . never mind."

Serenity pinched his nose. "You always do that. You start to talk about Zelda the Monster but then you change the subject."

Nathan leaned his head on her shoulder and closed his eyes. "You're my mommy now."

"Because I drink a lot?"

"I suppose that's part of it."

She slapped his hand. "You don't know why I drink, do you?"

He sat up straight again. "I dunno. Anger?"

"It used to be anger. But now it's fear. I'm just so afraid. Angry, too, but mostly afraid."

"I'm the same way. I used to think anger was like the king of emotions, but now I see that it's fear. You graduate from anger to fear. Being afraid. Making other people afraid. It goes beyond pissed off to a whole other level."

"I guess I'm married to Mr. Fear." She raised her glass in triumph. "Speaking of which, my book is finally coming out next month. *Death Row Survivor*, by Serenity Lamb."

"I wonder who'll play you in the movie version."

She poured another refill. "I think the movie should be done with puppets. In fact, I'll insist on it. Let the little kiddies see what it's like to think every day that you're going to be put to death."

"Some people say our society is afraid of death."

"Of course it is. That's why there's all the health food stuff. Don't eat this, it gives you cancer. Don't eat that, it rots your liver. But you know, in the end you die just the same."

"Life—what a waste."

They were both quiet for a minute.

Then Serenity said, "Oh, speaking of which—I'm going to have a baby."

Nathan reached over to snatch the glass from her hand.

"A baby? How the fuck did that happen?"

37

Supposedly, Serenity stayed on the wagon during her pregnancy, but I doubted it. As for Nathan's question about how she got knocked up in the first place, I assumed they used some form of contraception that failed to do its job.

Autumn and Bosco were ecstatic upon hearing the news, though in a desperate way, I thought. Like it gave them one more thing to deflect their attention away from the dead Chester Lamb. Or maybe if enough nice things happened, the cosmos would erase the killing, like a storm front covered by a puffy white cloud. There were predictable, often-repeated remarks about how the foursome felt closer than ever, welcome to the parenting club, and the like. Yawn.

Serenity bitched about how much she hated being pregnant. Every time she sat down or stood up you'd have thought she got burned alive at the stake. She and Nathan had a screaming match in which he grabbed her by the shoulders and said, "Since when do you like to fuck?"

Still, pregnancy does not last forever, and finally, from the watermelon that became Serenity's belly, there splatted out a baby boy. They named him Chase Nightbridge because, said Nathan, the cops were always chasing the baby's parents.

I vacillated over what to make of being a grandfather. I didn't feel any different. And you know what they say— you're as young as you feel. The baby looked like his mother, and only when I squinted did I kind of see a resemblance to Nathan. But looks change as kids get older, and after a while they don't matter anyway.

Serenity had no intention of breastfeeding her son, which I thought just as well given her less than stellar lifestyle. Besides, Chase had a fulltime nurse named Rosie who did diaper duty and wiped up the puke and all the other things that go along with having a baby. She seldom spoke, and her presence did nothing to change the dynamic of the household. Come to think of it, neither did Chase. Serenity screamed for someone to shut up the baby when he cried, but she screamed a lot anyway. She said all the usual garbage about how motherhood gave her the greatest happiness imaginable, but she spent all of five seconds a day with the kid. The only exception to the rule happened in the middle of the night, when she woke up crying herself. Then she'd wake up the baby and hold it and cry some more, as if trying to protect it in the midst of a nuclear holocaust. As usual, Nathan spent most of his time reading the latest true crime books. But now and then he stared at the baby with a curious expression, as if looking at a creature from another planet.

In fairness to Nathan, it turned out he had legitimate reasons for his hesitancy toward the shitting infant. Nathan always had a good reason for what he did. I found out about the baby when I listened in on a conversation he had outside on the porch with Bosco.

"I wasn't supposed to know this," Nathan told his lifelong best friend. "But my father, Alexander Nightbridge IV, didn't just go missing. He went crazy. Wacko. Nutty as a bowl of granola. Probably he killed himself somewhere along the way."

"I guess your mom wanted to spare you."

Nathan groaned.

"My mom spare me? No way. She made it all about her as always. She got to be more of a martyr depicting my dad as a total scumbag."

I, of course, knew this all along, and experienced enormous relief when Nathan figured it out, too. But then, he had a little something called brains.

Bosco frowned in sympathy. "How did you find out, bro?"

"I dug around and added two and two. But between my dad and my wackadoodle mom, I decided long ago never to have kids. Fate spared me the psycho gene, but I wouldn't risk it on anyone else."

"You mean you got a vasectomy?"

"Hell, no. I wouldn't let someone mess around with my dick. Not even if my life depended on it."

"I have to admit it sounds scary. So you always use protection?"

Nathan's face turned red with anger. "You can't rely on protection. My mom told me about a bajillion times that my dad wore a rubber the night of my conception."

Bosco studied his friend. "So then are you telling me. . ."

"Sex is no big deal. Serenity has her booze, and I have— I have hobbies. I love to read."

"So, then you and Serenity don't. . . I mean, have you ever. . . ?"

"Oh, we've done stuff," Nathan replied vaguely. "But the baby can't be mine. Unless she jerked me off while I slept and put it in a turkey baster." Nathan paused in thought. "You know, I wouldn't put it past her. It's not like guys are standing in line to fuck the bitch."

"Maybe she went to a sperm bank."

"Nah. She has too much pride. Besides, unless she got away with using a phony ID, I doubt that they'd let a former death row inmate use their precious sperm."

"If it really makes a difference to you, bud, get a DNA test."

"Yeah, that's a good idea," said Nathan, in a way that communicated he'd never do it. He looked at Bosco with an earnestness seen seldom in humankind.

"You know, I never told this to anyone before. When my mom died, I felt nothing but relief. Happy to be rid of her. I thought that from now on there'd be nothing to stand in my way. When I met Serenity, something seemed off about her story of her boss trying to kill her. But I pushed it aside. When she started drinking, it didn't throw me for a loop. It's like I knew all along she'd turn into a drunk. It's like I need a drunk woman in my life, or else. . . I don't know. I'd be scared."

Bosco laughed. "It's called being in love. I think you've read too many of those crime books. I'm sure they talk a lot about mother fixation and all that hooey. There's a lot of drunk women out there, but it's Serenity you married. Hey, nobody's perfect."

"But I want to be perfect. I want nothing to affect me ever."

Bosco laughed again. "Good luck with that. Even computers break down. And anyway, wouldn't it be boring to be perfect? To not let in all the emotion? If you were perfect, would we have had all these great talks over the years?"

"You're right, I suppose." Nathan said. "That's the thing about the baby. I. . . well, I think I love the little fucker. You know—he just sits there and makes noises like when you squeak a toy."

Bosco stood up and gave Nathan a bear hug.

"So go be a dad. What's the problem?"

"Because I can't. . ." He looked frustrated, unable to find the words.

"You can't give love you never got yourself?" Bosco replied. "I'm telling you—and I speak from my own experience—you can."

Nathan grew quiet as Bosco smiled at him with understanding. Finally, Nathan said, "Yeah, I guess you're right, dude."

After that, Nathan became a regular fathering fool. He made silly faces that got the baby to laugh. He picked him up and played airplane, zooming him around the room. He took Chase outside and showed him stuff in nature, even though the baby couldn't know the names of things. I remember how Nathan oohed and aahed with the baby over a perfect spider web.

"Isn't that the most beautiful thing you ever saw?" he asked his pre-verbal son. "The natural world is perfect, only humans aren't." Nathan never became one to change diapers and all that other nonsense, but they had Rosie for that sort of thing.

With great tenderness and enthusiasm, he shared his love of criminology with the tot. Nathan got a special set of flash cards made and began showing them to his son, saying the names of each one. From what I understand, this is a teaching method many parents now employ.

"Al Capone," Nathan said, upon showing a picture of Mr. Capone. "The St. Valentine's Day Massacre." "Charles Manson." "Son of Sam." "Aileen Wuornos." And so on. Little Chase always appeared attentive, taking it all in. When Serenity's book came out—and shot up the bestseller lists, just like Nathan's had—he made a flash card of the cover and showed Chase the picture of "Mommy, a death row survivor."

I felt a poetic sense of justice. I couldn't be a father to Nathan, but in the larger scheme of things it all worked out okay after all. So there, Miss High and Mighty Zelda.

However, life being life, my contentment lasted about thirty seconds.

Someone knocked on the front door. Well, what do you know, it was a cop.

38

Nathan said to the dumb-ass cop, "May I help you, officer?"

The cop walked in on a dad playing educational flash cards with his toddler son on the floor. It didn't get much more wholesome than that. The cop looked disappointed.

"Are you Nathan Knightbridge?"

"Yes, officer," my son answered.

The cop sighed. "Mr. Nightbridge, I think you'd better sit down."

Nathan considered how to respond.

"Oh, okay." He scooped up Chase as he sat on the sofa and put the baby on his lap.

"Mr. Nightbridge, were you ever made aware of a Mr. Wyatt Sterling Brown?"

"No." Nathan smiled. Chase clapped his hands so Nathan put his hands on top of his son's, so they could clap together.

"Mr. Nightbridge, this individual just passed away. He appears to have taken his own life."

"How unfortunate."

"Yes. And it turns out that he knew your late mother, Zelda Nightbridge."

"Oh?" He stroked Chase's hair while the toddler made goo-goo-ga-ga sounds.

"Yes. He mentioned her in a note found next to his body. It said, 'Zelda, forgive me.'"

Nathan held Chase in his arms and stood up. I knew him well enough to know when he got upset, but it was obvious he didn't want the sadistic cop to notice.

"Well, my late mother, may she rest in peace, used to kid me about a Mr. Brown. I guess this is the dude." Chase giggled as Nathan tickled him. "Perhaps she wanted to wait until I got older to tell me about him. Assuming she thought it any of my business."

"You seem to have little curiosity. Are you at least interested in knowing how Wyatt Sterling Brown died?"

"By all means tell me, officer."

"He shot himself through the head. Apparently."

"How sad that I didn't get a chance to know him."

"And you have no idea about his connection to your mother?"

"One would hazard a guess that they dated and so forth. Ever since her horrific murder, I frankly try not to think about my mother."

"Well then, perhaps you would like to think about this. The late Mr. Brown worked as a theater angel."

Nathan made cooing sounds at the baby, who smiled with delight. "I'm afraid I don't know what this is."

"Someone who invests in the theater. From what we've been able to piece together, he planned to use his muscle to get your mother cast in a play. On Broadway."

"Wow, isn't that something?"

"Yes, it is something. The city police found an old letter between your mother and Mr. Brown. He got quite upset about her pregnancy. Not only did he stop wanting to cast her, he effectively had her blackballed from the theater."

"He sounds more like a devil than an angel." He tickled Chase's tummy.

"You do not seem particularly upset by this. It does not anger you or make you want to seek revenge?"

"It's a lot of information to take in at once."

"So I see. Mr. Nightbridge, you are hereby ordered not leave town. We will be in touch. Soon, I'm quite sure."

You didn't need to be Albert Einstein to figure out the good-for-nothing cops' intentions. They thought Nathan bumped off Mr. Brown and then staged it to look like a suicide. *Voila*, a brand new murder to pin on my son. While they were at it, why didn't they charge him with every death from traffic accidents or war? They seemed to think him some sort of anti-Christ. Everyone else died for his sins.

Oh Zelda, you were beautiful as "America the Beautiful." What if we hadn't had a quickie that one night? Your whole life could have gone differently. But I couldn't let myself think such things. She would've messed up her chances some other way. And if we hadn't hooked up, there would be no Nathan.

I ran from the house. I felt all jittery and pukey. Downtown, I started shouting nasty words like "cock" and "cunt" and kicking things, so the cops carried me off in a straightjacket. Cops, cops, everywhere you go, there are cops and doctors and secret agents and UFOs.

I wished I could find my friend, Charlie. He always knew how to cheer me up.

39

I did another short stint in the psycho ward. They upped my meds so that I'd be a good boy and not shout bad words and kick things.

Thus far the cop had not made good on his promise. No one came back to arrest Nathan for the murder of Bullshit Brown. Life for Nathan and his family stayed on course, as if another murder arrest didn't hover over them like a long thin shadow. If Nathan told Serenity about the whole thing, they never discussed it in my earshot.

Came the day when Chase took his first footsteps. Rosie held the small body upright, and little Chase hobbled a few steps over to his father. I couldn't even remember the last time I saw Nathan cry. Not that he cried much as a baby. I remember him as well behaved, very quiet. Always looking around.

"Hey, Serenity," he called to his wife upstairs. "You gotta come and see this."

"See what?" she hollered back.

"Chase. He's walking."

"Yeah, yeah, yeah. I'll be right down."

In Serenity time this meant she'd be down in maybe forty-five minutes or so. Rosie went off to do whatever she did while Nathan kept the boy entertained for Mommy's big entrance. Serenity looked older than her years, her bones so brittle they seemed about to smash into a million pieces as she shuffled across the floor.

"So walk," she said, drink in hand.

He placed their son a few feet away from Serenity and let go of him. Nathan kept his hands nearby in case the baby lost his balance.

"There, see?" Nathan enthused. "He walks straight to Mommy. That's cause he loves Mommy so much."

Serenity knelt down to hold the baby around the waist.

"Oh, isn't that just the most adorable thing?" She tried to sound sincere, but given her level of detachment at that point, it seemed more like she commented on someone else's kid.

"Chase says, 'I love you, Mommy.'"

"He's not a ventriloquist's dummy," Serenity complained, setting her son on the carpet; he sat up and stuck his fingers in his mouth. "Howsabout letting the kid have some space? Aren't you the one always complaining that everyone crowds you?"

"He's one year old, for fuck's sake. He doesn't need space. He needs nurturing."

"The implication being that I don't give him any?"

Nathan threw his hands up in surrender.

"Think whatever you want."

"You made me a drunk, in case you didn't know."

"No, I didn't make you anything. And neither did you. Things just happen."

"Oh, listen to this. Since when are you Mr. Pep Boy, all full of *joie de vivre*? Dispose of any corpses lately? And what about every goddamn night since we—"

Nathan wacked her hard across the face. He used an open hand, knocking her on the floor. As Serenity rubbed the side of her face and sat back up, she looked at Nathan and said, "I know what your problem is. Mr. Brown. Every night you see him in the dark, don't you? You're just a scared little boy."

Nathan turned pale, then flustered to crimson. "How the fuck do you know about Mr. Brown?"

"You said his name in the last trial. It had to mean something, so I looked at your old court transcripts. They mentioned him in your Zelda trial. Your mommy used to scare the shit out of you, though admittedly for not very long. Unless of course she still does? Do I scare you, too, Nathan?"

So Nathan, it would appear, never told Serenity about the visit from the cop.

"Go to hell." Nathan scooped up the baby, sat down on the sofa, and turned on the TV in the manner of one communicating to another that he would not pay attention to anything more she said. The channel featured one of those sweaty, hyper evangelical speakers, preaching to a congregation that looked like about a thousand people. It must have been Sunday. Nathan didn't bother changing the channel, though I'm sure he hated fire-and-brimstone preachers. But maybe he wanted it on for that reason. Sometimes what balms our souls is not love but hate.

"You say you want to go to heaven to see your heavenly father," the preacher said. "Do we see heaven as angels shrouded in golden light? With God the Father and God the Son enshrined in their eternal thrones?"

"Yes," came the thunderous answer from the congregation.

"You say yes, but what does the lowly sinner know of our heavenly Father's grand scheme when here on earth we do not honor the heavenly Father? Do we truly embrace the Lord God into our hearts? Malachi 4:6 tells us, 'He will turn the hearts of the fathers to their children, and the hearts of the children to their fathers; or else I will come and strike the land with a curse.' And in Psalm 103:13, we read, 'As a father has compassion on his children, so the Lord has compassion on those who fear him.' Who here remembers these lessons each day? Who knows how to fear and love at the same time?"

No one said a damn thing in response.

Satisfied that he left his audience speechless, he continued. "The Bible even tells us to fear nothing but the Lord God. In Proverbs 3:11-12, we are reminded, 'My son, do not despise the Lord's discipline and do not resent his rebuke, because the Lord disciplines those he loves, as a father the son he delights in.' Then in Proverbs 23:22, we are given the simplest of messages that for some reason we must make difficult. 'Listen to your father, who gave you life, and do not despise your mother when she is old.'"

"Turn that motherfucking bullshit off," Serenity said, walking over to the remote and turning it off herself. "I sent Rosie home for the day."

"Why?" Nathan wanted to know. "Who's going to—"

"Since you're so lovey-dovey with Chase, you can wipe the shit off his ass for a change."

"Like you ever do it yourself."

"I do. You just don't notice. You see what you want to see."

"Yes, you're such a devoted mother."

"Whatever. Chase and I have plenty of time to get to know each other. By the way, the cops should be here any minute."

Nathan tried to remain calm, but even from a distance I could see the panic in his eyes.

"The cops? What the fuck are you talking about?"

Serenity picked up the baby and held him to her breasts.

"Did you think I'd keep you around forever? I can't think of anything else I need you for. The cops offered me a sweet deal a while ago, and I just got off the phone, telling them my answer in the affirmative. Full immunity in exchange for my testimony against you in the murder of my father. You have nothing to hold over me anymore. Autumn and Bosco have full immunity, too, though they don't know anything yet. Oh, and double jeopardy protects me from being tried for Clay Hinton again. After all these years, they're still working on nailing you for that cop killing, and who knows what else." She made kissy sounds at the baby. "You shouldn't have hit me, Nathan."

Nathan stood up, enraged as I'd never seen him.

"I didn't kill your father."

"So what?"

Nathan lunged toward her, then stopped himself; after all, she held the baby. He ran his fingers through his hair in frustration.

"I always knew this would happen when I finally got happy. It's when you're happy that everything falls apart." He looked at his wife. "If I did this to you, I'd feel bad later on. But you won't, will you?"

Serenity more or less ignored his question.

"You wouldn't know how to feel bad if. . . well, if your life depended on it." She laughed. "I know that's not really funny."

The police sirens could be heard in the distance; they grew louder with each second. As Serenity chortled, Nathan ran to his study. He came out a moment later with a handgun. It was long and shiny, just like in the movies. He ran outside to the porch just as the cops got out of their cars. There were a half dozen officers.

For a split instant I thought about what to do. I realized I had to seize the moment, however painful it would be.

I ran toward Nathan, shielding him with my body.

"Get out of the way," yelled one of the cops.

I ignored him and instead glanced sideways at Nathan. What the hell. Still shielding him, I turned around so he could see my face.

"You may not believe me, but I'm your father. I'm Alexander Nightbridge IV."

I thought he might be mad at me or be too dumbstruck to say anything, but he squeezed my shoulder and said, "I always kind of knew you were around. And I knew you'd be like this. I've seen you before, haven't I?"

We both sort of laughed or cried or something.

"Is it okay if I call you Dad?"

"Sure thing, Son."

"You know, Dad, everything I've done my whole life I've done for you. Hoping to reach you."

"Someday we'll all be together in heaven," I assured him. "You, your mom, and me."

"Last warning," screeched the Fascist cop.

"I'm not abandoning you again, Son. If they want you, they have to get me first."

"Thanks, but no thanks." He shoved me out of the way, and I hit my head hard against the porch wall. Staring the cops dead in the eye, and with a gallant smile on his face, Nathan said, "Fuck you." I struggled to get my bearings, but I moved too slowly. Nathan fired a shot straight up into the air, defying the cops to shoot him.

I struggled to my feet as I shouted, "I did it. I killed them all. My son is innocent."

Nathan tried to push me out of the way again, but I punched him in the face with all my might. As he struggled to get his bearings, I punched him again, and knocked him out.

"See, I just assaulted someone so you have to take me in. I stabbed Zelda seventy times. I had a partner. A homeless bum like me. He was. . . I mean, he's dead now. He held her down while I stabbed her. She called out how Mr. Brown was here. Right before she died. The two of us did the Rainbow family. He held them down while I tied them up. I knew the Boy Scout knots. I was an Eagle Scout. We had guns, which was why they did as they were told. I shot and killed that cop. Mr. Rogers—the white powder in the crack of his skull was sticky. They never said it was sticky during the trial, but I know it was. I did the Hintons, Junior and Senior. Logan Steiner. I. . . I did Chester Lamb, too. I did, I shot him. Serenity is lying. She just wants to get away from Nathan."

One of the officers motioned to the others to hold their fire. He ran toward me.

"And who are you?"

"Alexander Nightbridge IV." I did a mock gentleman's bow.

Nathan started to sit up, rubbing his sore jaw. "What the fuck?"

The cop studied me. "Why should we believe you?"

"Take me in. Ask me for any detail about anything. I murdered them all. Nathan is innocent."

Nathan stood up, his entire face one gigantic smile. "And are you by any chance legally insane?"

"As the day is long on June twenty-first. Have been since you were a tot."

"Oh, Dad. I knew, I really did. On some level I can't explain. As a little boy, I'd look up at the stars and wish I could know you. All my life I've been so. . . preoccupied. Like I could imagine you into existence. Or when I saw this cop chasing me and it was like he wasn't there anymore, like you made him go away. But you knew I'd never say anything, didn't you?"

I beamed at him with pride.

"You would've gone to prison for me. Even taken the needle." I turned to the cop. "Arrest me. I demand it."

Nathan hugged me hard.

My son kept chortling as the cop cuffed me and read me my rights. I remembered something my father, Alexander Nightbridge IV—no, I mean Alexander Nightbridge III—said to me when I visited him in jail: "Sooner or later, life is having to stand in the corner."

I could hear Nathan calling out as he ran back into the house.

"Serenity, it didn't work. But it's okay. Everything's fine. I forgive you if you forgive me." I could barely see him as he picked up Chase and swung him around.

"Grandpa will live with us soon," said my son Nathan. "Everything is beautiful."

You know something? When you got right down to it, he spoke the truth. Everything looked beautiful to me. All the murders I confessed to, everything. A good parent does whatever he has to in order for his child to be protected. I saw this old black-and-white movie once called *Stella Dallas*. This mother gives away her daughter so she can have a better life, and in the end she watches from outside as the daughter gets married. I bawled like a baby watching it. But didn't I do the same thing? People can say what they want, but I am no deadbeat dad.

40

I stayed in the slammer long enough for all the various police departments and FBI people to question me. I had a list of things in my head to tell them about, and it made me jumpy to try to remember them all in a cogent manner. A couple of times they told me that something I thought to be confidential information had been made known to the public, but they had enough to believe me.

Nathan arranged for Leandro Flores to be my attorney. It was a no-brainer because of my being legally insane, and a public defender could've handled it, but Nathan wanted nothing but the best for me.

Still, he showed his naiveté when it came to my coming home to join them. I knew I'd be committed for life, and I was. They had me in a padded cell by myself, and they kept me so doped up that I sometimes thought I resided elsewhere. As a youth, I enjoyed our beautiful summer home along the ocean. Sometimes I pretended—or even believed—the humming of the vent in my cell to be the waves of the sea, greeting me at the shoreline of white sands, as if they'd been paid to perform by my stinking rich family.

I think I saw my old pal Charlie one day when they took me out of the cell to give me a shower. But who knows what I saw. Charlie was the partner I said had died. I'm pretty sure that's who I meant.

I never got a chance to tell Nathan about the babies. You see, I did get caught a few times while snooping around. By the Rainbows, for example, just before they got murdered. And also by Biv and Montana. I said to them, "I'm just an old bum," which they thought kind of cool or something. We got drunk together, and I gave them each a purple capsule, and I took a couple of extra ones. I figured we'd all get high from it. They started acting goofy, and so did I. We had a quick three-way—or at least I think we did—and I don't even remember them walking away. But during Nathan's last trial, when the matter of the kids' DNA came up, I got nervous. I saw no reason to be a father to these kids. What could I give them? No, in the real sense I fathered only one child. I loved his mother. That counts for something, doesn't it?

Hearing that Nathan died devastated me. They straightjacketed me first, in case I got so upset I did something, but I couldn't think of anything to do. I guess the crazies who idolized my son thought he was guilty but that he had gotten away with murder all those times. Or at least one of them did. From what I heard, this teenager came up to him with a gun and said something like, "You've lied to us all these years. You're innocent. You're a fraud." You see, it made the news when Nathan no longer had the cops breathing down his neck, even though he tried to keep things quiet. He always hated publicity, and he never once exploited the dummies that worshipped him.

Nathan told the weirdo teen, "No, I killed all those people. I'm guilty. I'm a mass murderer." The kid didn't buy it and shot Nathan six times. Serenity had the body cremated, with no memorial of any kind. But Bosco asked if he could scatter the ashes, and Serenity let him. I asked the hospital people who told me this where the ashes were scattered. They said they didn't know.

I lost track of time, but there came a moment after however long when they got careless, and I escaped. So I'm back to roaming the streets. Or at least I think I am. It gets hard to tell the difference sometimes between being locked up and being free.

But Nathan was innocent. I'm the one who killed all those people. Honest, I did.

ABOUT THE AUTHOR

JP Bloch has a Ph.D. but hopes people won't hold it against him. His last name is pronounced "Block," not "Blotch," but he's gotten used to it. He lives in Connecticut, where he is an indentured servant to his dog. JP writes on his king-size bed with the fan on. His hobbies include eating cashews while watching TV and overdosing on film noir favorites.

JP's novels include *Shadow Language* (a Pegasus book) and *Identity Thief*, as well as pop and scholarly non-fiction. He has appeared on TV and radio numerous times. On his own since age 15, he has many interesting tales of survival on the road to eventually getting a Ph.D.

His turn-offs include Brussels sprouts, bigotry, and people who think life is simple. He enjoys people who have gained wisdom from hardship, and ask questions more than they assume answers. Tumultuous skies are preferred over sunny ones.

A humungous, ginormous thank you to Christopher Moebs of Pegasus, for surviving not one but two projects with me.

OTHER TITLES BY JP BLOCH

SHADOW LANGUAGE
(Suspense thriller, 232 pages paperback, eBook)
A former police chief with a death wish is recruited to solve a string of serial murders, hoping to be the next victim.

order at www.pegasusbooks.net